THE MEND

The Mend

A NOVEL

Scott Lowe

Fly Fish Mend

Contents

To Chrissy, who settles me and helps me keep my focus. You are my north star.

To my kids, who inspire me to always keep my heart (and my eyes) open.

1

The Last Gift

The visitors left; the awkward conversations ended. A tray of sliced lunch meat wraps sat on the kitchen counter. The house was silent. The hollow echo from each of Joe's footsteps down the hallway rattled in his head, almost as loud as the din of the new reality he wished wasn't true. *She is gone.*

In their bedroom, a box on his dresser caught his eye. Joe was usually very observant; he was struck that he had not noticed the box previously. Since Jody passed, Joe was consumed by completing each step that she outlined in her last wishes. He had been on auto-pilot, meticulously carrying out each deed as if their fulfillment would somehow bring her back...and now he was done. *Where did that box come from?*

It was a simple cardboard box, but he can't remember having seen it there before. *Who left this for me?* With all the pain and all the forced smiles, he was tired of surprises and unforeseen moments. Jody would leave him notes, mainly yellow Post-it notes, on the bathroom mirror or in his wallet. In the rare instances she made him lunch, there unfailingly would be a note in the bag. He loved her notes. But not boxes. He hated opening gifts, and she spared him from the discomfort.

The past six days felt like someone else's life. Anytime Joe was faced with pain, he could disconnect. He was already an accomplished compartmentalizer, or so Jody had told him. He chuckled at the thought, realizing that might have been his first authentic smile in months. She could make him laugh even now.

Joe picked up the box and held it for a moment in his hands, appreciating its cube shape fitting between his thumbs and pinky fingers. The edges of the box had weathered, leaving a soft, flaky residue on his thumbs when he grabbed its sides. On its top, four flaps overlapped, with the end of each flap covering half of the adjacent flap. He was thinking he must have left it there but couldn't remember. It had a practical and plain appearance, not like the perfectly wrapped boxes Jody would prepare for presents.

He sat down on the bed. Using his thumbs, he pulled the top and right flaps upwards. The sides of the box strained and shifted as he opened the left and bottom flaps and revealed the box's contents. A sheet of stationary Jody occasionally used for personal notes was folded in half at the top of the box. Water began to fill his eyes for the first time in weeks. Over the past several weeks, they had many tearful moments, but they also shared joyful remembrances. They had time for long, meaningful conversations, and they also had time for heartfelt, reluctant goodbyes. *Was this another goodbye?* His finger followed the lettering.

J - You gave me all of you. You always took such wonderful care of me. I am so grateful for every second I have been able to spend with you. We created so many memories that I hope will keep my love in your heart. I will be gone soon, but you have to keep going. Please take care of yourself for me and find something to throw yourself into. Being on the stream brought you joy with your dad, and maybe it can help you now. Head back to the water and find a way to mend your heart. Go and leave no stone unturned. Love you forever, no matter what. J

He would always tell her that he would love her forever, no matter what. Death wouldn't change that. Tears overtook him, and he cried until exhaustion forced him into a deep sleep.

2

Back to Life

Joe woke up wishing he'd never wake up again. He couldn't move. *What is life supposed to look like now?* Jody gave him purpose, even when the purpose was only not to piss her off. He promised to never let her down. She was all he needed to get through any obstacle, and she was gone. The bedroom felt empty, but he still felt like he was suffocating.

The dreams of their life spent traveling and exploring, all the inside jokes, and memories of sitting together at the cliché café rolled around in his imagination. He wanted those things back. *Why were they taken away? Jody was Joe's whole life.* In their twenty-six-year relationship, he always played the grumpy old man role, not liking crowds, noise, or other people. In general, he fit the role, but the underlying truth was that he really only ever wanted to be with her. If he was with her, he would go anywhere.

They'd find a game to play when they went out in public. Her favorite was picking random people in the crowd and telling the make-believe story of their lives: the acapella-singing dentist, the hip-hop-loving crocheting grandma, and the model-train-making professional wrestler. The bigger the contradiction, the bigger the laugh. No more laughs, no more sunshine. He couldn't even think about that without hearing Bill Withers singing in his head. She always made fun of his constant humming and singing with his never-ending repertoire of songs. He didn't want to sing anymore.

The more his brain worked through missing her, the more he cried. Before Jody got sick, Joe was a crier. Any level of sappiness would open the floodgates, but the tears now were painful, like the source was running dry, like his soul was being pulled from him. Joe never could understand why people tried so hard not to cry at funerals. Jody had tried to convince him that when people are in traumatic emotional pain, they don't want to risk falling apart. Joe would argue that if it's not safe to be sad at a funeral, where is it safe to be sad? Now he realized this level of sadness wasn't about safety; it felt like survival. Each breath, each step, each moment took all he had. Shutting off his brain was the only way to stop the pain. He counted on going first. His family's medical history was bad, and his health felt fragile. Joe closed his eyes, praying his heart would stop.

3

Not Quite

Putting one foot in front of the other is not always as easy as it sounds. Taking a step requires a direction to move in, a willingness to move there, and the ability to generate momentum. As the days and weeks passed, Joe could generate momentum, but in no specific direction and with habit more than will as his driver. Without Jody, he was deteriorating. He thought he could turn off the emotions. Mentally, he had enough capacity to fake it for a while, but physically, his emotional state began to show through the smiles and sport coats.

Joe's interest in architecture started as a creative outlet, matching his analytical, mathematical mind with his love of drawing and order. The ability to create something in your mind and make it real on earth is magical. He had created some beautiful things and felt pride in his accomplishments. His studio within the firm focused on libraries and churches. He particularly enjoyed connecting historical, spiritual, and creative spaces that brought people together in learning and celebration. Jody would joke that for someone who was socially awkward and didn't enjoy crowds, he had an ironic talent.

"Joe creates welcoming, majestic spaces for people to gather away from him." Even with the challenges of combining artistic expression and practical utility, as he gained experience and expertise, he saw his efforts more cynically and suspiciously.

Gaining and managing clients was the key to organizational success, and the more money you brought in, the more money you could make. He made enough money during the 22 years he worked at O'Connell and Wilcock, but he never made it to Partner. Part of that made him happy, like he didn't completely sell out. But a level of jealousy stuck with him and leaked into conversations with his boss and co-workers. He felt he did great work and was a good man, but he seemed to have gotten penalized for not wanting to play the game. The golf trips and business dinners felt forced. He wanted the work to speak for itself. Joe didn't get that people have to generally like you to want to keep working with you and that often that requires more than just the work.

Jody kept him grounded and kept his ego from turning him into an "inauthentic BS'er," as she described the others who advanced into ownership at the firm. She also shielded him from himself and the competitive drive that would induce the 18-hour days and working all weekend. His time with her saved him from his worse impulses. She made Joe safe to be himself without having to prove anything anymore. Joe avoided parties and had a rule against having lunch with more than four people. He prided himself on delivering on his promises, but he didn't want to make friends or serve as a professional mentor. He was kind, but not friendly, and funny, but not social. Joe loved that Jody didn't force him to go to dinner parties or happy hours. But she elevated his social manners tremendously. She could fill the space without pressuring him to contribute. Conversely, Joe could step into stressful or emergency situations without wavering and could back up Jody when confrontations or awkward moments arose. They matched each other's weaknesses with strengths, and it got them through some hard spots in their twenty-three years of marriage.

Without her, the days were meandering. Work didn't deliver excitement or even really stress anymore. He didn't care. Going through the motions can give you cover almost anywhere for a few months, but it was starting to get noticed. The two-hour lunches grew into two-drink lunches. He showed up late and disheveled. Even for someone who never strictly adhered to dress codes, he was becoming noticeably sloppy. Co-workers started questioning his well-being and his performance.

There was a stage of melancholy that Joe would reach after a third drink—even before Jody left—that drained any remaining life from his skin tone and soured his face entirely. He avoided the third drink for years and was better for it. But now, he looked and felt like the subject of *Nobody to Blame* by Chris Stapleton. Having a third drink by 2 p.m. most days became the norm and made him perpetually groggy and distant.

Deadlines were missed, phone calls went unreturned, people avoided him, and work dried up. He left the house dark, but he kept it clean. He didn't want to disappoint her too badly. With Jody, he'd spend his evenings cooking Mediterranean dishes, sitting by the fireplace rubbing Jody's feet and daydreaming about their retirement. Now his evening hours passed by watching television shows he couldn't remember as soon as they were over.

4

A Door Closer

"Hey, Joe. Can you come in here for a second?"

He hated the intercom system through his phone. Jacob had that tone in his voice. Joe had been a part of enough conversations where he had been the one to say those same words. His heart sank, but he also felt a twinge of relief.

Walking down the hall, Joe noticed the feel of the carpet under his feet and the smell of the paper and ink drifting from the print room. He looked at his reflection in the glass panels of the offices as he passed. It sank in. He looked horrible, like a hung-over, burnt-out college professor. Getting fired at fifty-four was embarrassing, and he was glad he wouldn't have to tell Jody. He could hear her voice, "Joe, you need to keep moving. You can't give it away, for me."

He made this walk hundreds of times over the last twenty-two years, as the partners' offices were at the front entrance of the floor. Ownership wanted to show that the leaders were always present and available to interact with clients as soon as possible.

Jacob Miller was tall with thinning, gray hair, and calm, clear, blue eyes. He shook hands with a purpose, confirming he followed through on his commitments. Graduating from West Point, his military training never left him. His discipline and aggressive demeanor served him well in and out of the military. Joe respected Jacob, even if they didn't always agree.

"Joe, have a seat. We need to talk." Joe remained silent; he wasn't going to make excuses or ask for any forgiveness or sympathy, and Jacob knew it. Jacob closed the door and quickly walked to his chair.

"Look, you've been a friend and great contributor to the firm, but you're not performing. I understand the loss of Jody was devastating. We can't keep you here if you continue like this. I know about the drinking and missing the deliverables on the Annapolis Library project. I'm in the place where I should let you go. But you mean a lot to us. So, I'm mandating you take time off. If you need help, reach out to Becky. I'll check in with you in three months, but you can't be here until you're not drinking and you can commit to the work. We will pack up your personal items. Take care of yourself."

Joe remained silent. He nodded. Jacob rose and held out his hand. Numbness fell over Joe. He shook Jacob's hand, smiled a weak smile, and walked out the door. He had stopped bringing a briefcase, so he didn't have much to carry. He grabbed the framed photo of Jody from their wedding day off his desk and headed out.

Every step Joe took tried to lead him into the bar of the nearby Italian restaurant, but he didn't want to risk seeing anyone from the office, so he forced himself into his SUV. Sitting behind the steering wheel, he felt the tears coming back. *What if she saw me now? A drunk, essentially fired from his job.* He wept uncontrollably.

5

The Tumbler

He slid the back door open, walked into the kitchen, and grabbed the heavy glass tumbler. It felt solid in his hand. Pushing the glass against the stainless-steel lever and hearing the ice fall into the glass, he briefly closed his eyes. It brought him back to happy hours with Jody, sipping a cocktail in their chairs on the porch. They would talk or just sit and hold hands, watching the sunset.

The raised rings on the tumbler secured the glass in his hand while the cold condensation sent a chill through his body. Pouring the Irish whiskey over the ice softened the ice and muted the sound of the ice shifting in the glass. He sat at the lonely table for two, staring at the whiskey.

He wanted to dive into the glass. *What am I going to do?* They had built up a reasonable retirement fund, but it was not supposed to happen this way. Joe always thought and said he'd retire before he was sixty. Looking for another job as an architect was not appealing, and he felt that age discrimination would make it nearly impossible to change his position. He lost motivation and just didn't have it in him. Calling Jacob and proving himself again was not a moment he wished to experience.

The whiskey was comforting at first, but now it was undoing him. Joe stared at the glass, afraid to take a sip, thinking he may hear her voice chiding him. The summer evening light began to fade, and he stayed sitting at the table transfixed on the drink.

She'd been gone for ten weeks. He hadn't visited a single friend or family member since the memorial, and he drank away his job. The phone messages, emails, and text messages were all unreturned. *I don't even know the name of the bartenders.* He drank at home, at lunch, and in the SUV on the way home. He had bought pints so they would fit in the cupholders. He remembered the walks around the neighborhood with Jody when she pointed out the discarded beer cans along the path of their walks.

"That's a sure-fire sign of someone hiding a drinking problem. Kids experimenting with beer don't drive around their parents' neighborhood in a specific pattern," she'd said.

Joe didn't have anyone to hide anything from. He was experiencing his greatest fear: being alone. It was eating him alive and would likely kill him. He set the glass down. Losing control and drinking himself to death certainly had some appeal, as his life didn't feel worth living, but he couldn't do that to her. He promised her he wouldn't let her down. He dropped on the couch and turned on the TV. He was out before he even knew what he was watching.

6

The Box

A loud chime entered his dream, like a tiny jackhammer repeatedly striking a bell. Joe tried to hold on to sleep, but the sound shook him free. In each dream, he would try to wish Jody to join him. So far, he was only able to hear her voice. *God, I miss her...and why did I forget to turn off my alarm the day after I was told not to come to work?*

His brain was already moving too much to go back to sleep. He knew it was hopeless to try. Looking past the foot of his bed, he saw something that felt like an old dream. The box. *Leave no stone unturned.* After he saw her note, he was inconsolable. And he hadn't touched the box since. He wondered why she left that note and didn't just tell him directly. She liked riddles. They used to read riddles to each other while sitting at their fire pit during fall evening happy hours. She always got more than he did. And she would giggle when Joe couldn't figure one out that seemed right at the tip of his tongue.

She also was sweetly sentimental for someone who was tough-minded. Her reactions to small, thoughtful moments could be so intense that it felt to Joe that she had a depth of emotion from her life that formed a beautiful, strong, outward armament of a fragile core. He wasn't quite sure he ever saw the core, but the warmth she gave him made him comfortable when he had never been comfortable before. The thought of her sparked a warm sensation through his center.

Joe sat up, walked to the dresser, and grabbed the box. It had more weight than he remembered. The flaps were still overlapping. He always liked the design of boxes, so simple and effective. *Architect's mind.*

Pulling the flaps upwards, he saw the note, and the tears began to well up. He realized he would forever associate the feeling of cardboard with her note. Under the note—he couldn't believe he didn't notice it before—a light brown box with a dark blue label rested at the bottom. He knew that label from his youth, an iconic color associated with the brand Hardy. Jody's last gift to him was a Hardy Bougle Reel. The tears started again.

Joe's favorite memories of his father were the times they spent fly fishing on the river. His father, Liam, was quiet and often impatient. The son of Irish immigrants, Liam Barden was instilled with a strong work ethic, a sharp mind, and a heavy pour. But on the river, he was a teacher and a conservationist. The wild, natural places and everything that lived in them captured his love and curiosity. He never took to hunting, but fishing, he would often say, "is being one with God."

Liam taught Joe how to cast a fly rod and hook a trout, although Joe never mastered the art of fly fishing like his father. Joe remembered catching his first trout at eight years old. He could still feel the rush of the tug of the fish on the rod and the warmth of his father's hand on his shoulder after they put the fish on a stringer. By the time he was ten years old, Joe could mend and read the water and was starting to learn, not just from Liam but from the river, too.

Liam didn't speak much around the house, but his words had weight. With a scowl, he could silence Cindy and Joe immediately. With a smile, it opened the whole family up to be silly. But as he went, the family went. The trips where it was just Joe and his father felt like the only times he completely connected with him. The hand on the shoulder and the patient instruction about flies, casting and, most of all, etiquette on the stream, were rushing back to Joe.

A day before the funeral, Joe had laid out on the living room coffee table all the photo albums Jody had pulled together over the years. After the memorial service, friends and family enjoyed flipping through the pages and reminiscing. Joe couldn't bring himself to look at the albums after the initial effort of finding photos for the slide deck that scrolled on the screen at the funeral home. They still sat sprawled out over the coffee table.

On the bookshelf against the back wall of the living room, the shelf that once held all the albums was bare except for one smaller dark blue album with worn corners leaning against the side. Outlines of the missing albums were evident in the patterns of dust on the shelf. Holding the box containing the reel in his left hand, he picked up the tattered album with his right hand. Memories flooded him as he opened the pages. His mother had put it together for him as a Christmas present after his father had passed.

The first photo was of his father holding Joe as a baby. The time frame of the photos quickly jumped to Joe as a young boy and Cindy, Joe's sister, as a baby. Camping trips, baseball games, and horseshoes in the yard filled the next few pages. Flipping to the fifth page, all the fishing trips they took were memorialized. Several pictures were dedicated to Penns Creek with the scary dark tunnel. Joe remembered counting the steps until he could see sunlight as they walked under the old railroad bridge. Other photos captured the trips to Trout Town, USA, with the great early morning breakfasts at the Roscoe Diner. He loved those trips to Central Pennsylvania and the Catskills. Fishing for trout in Maryland wasn't nearly as much fun as when they traveled and camped. He was smiling through the tears.

Liam passed away the day after Joe's eighteenth birthday, and fishing never was quite the same again. He lost the connection to fishing when his dad passed. Now Jody was telling him to go back to the water. That's what he was going to do.

7

Starting the List

Waking up with a renewed energy and sense of purpose, Joe started making a list. Writing things down helped him to isolate individual thoughts bouncing around his head. He loved whiteboards, scribbling, erasing, and connecting lines between concepts. He was a messy-minded architect, relying on the truly artistic and engineering souls to put the details to paper.

He hadn't been fly fishing in over thirty years, but he was excited to get back to it. Joe needed a mission to get his mind moving, and thanks to Jody, he found it; the new reel and the photo album sparked him. And thanks to Jacob, he had the time. He knew research was required and that he would need many new supplies: waders, a new rod, a new fly line, flies, a wading staff, a vest, etc. *Gear for anglers is part of the hobby*, he thought to himself. Even years ago, he remembers how his neighbor seemed more focused on the gear and the status of new gear, even more than catching the fish. Joe wasn't one to go overboard, and he'd have to be careful not to spend much money now that he was un-employed. He couldn't remember where his old gear was stored, but he imagined it didn't fare well over time and technology had dramatically improved in the last few decades.

He also needed to know where to go. A quick internet search gave him more information than he could imagine on local fly shops, guides for hire, trout streams, and fishing reports. Now he had something to occupy his time and check some things off a list. Jody would be proud of him; he could hear her giggle as he checked things off his list. He was so preoccupied with his new mission that he even forgot to make coffee.

Maybe I could go camping? The thought entered Joe's mind. He and Jody went camping frequently, mainly car camping, but they loved the smell of campfires and snuggling in sleeping bags. Hiking, especially during fall and spring, kept them active, connected, and in nature. He especially loved their hikes along rivers and streams. They would collect stones from each stream and place them as an edge for the planting beds along the front of the house. It had been over two years since they last camped or hiked, since Jody first got sick. They kept saying they would camp across the country once she got better. Another trip they wouldn't take. "Maybe she wants me to take that trip?" he said out loud.

Lifting his head from his list, Joe looked around the kitchen. There were so many memories, he could feel the sadness pulling him down. The house had so many reminders of the pain. Maybe a trip was what he needed. Maybe he needed to be out of the house. Over a twenty-six-year relationship, you accumulate a lot of crap. The sentimental side of Jody kept many things from her parents and grandparents. Although her family had all passed away before their relationship, Joe felt connected to her family through all the photos, certificates, and diplomas she kept from her parents and grandparents.

"They were proud of what they accomplished and enabled me to do, and I can't forget that." she would say. Oddly, she hardly ever spoke of them or shared memories of her life with them.

He had kept the house closed and dark since she passed. Even though it was summer, he felt like he'd been living in a basement. He needed some light and a visitor. At 7:30 a.m. it wasn't polite to randomly call anyone, but he knew Cindy would be up. Joe's younger sister was a morning person her whole life, and she looked it. With an always-beaming smile framed by curly blonde hair, she looked like a kindergarten teacher. Joe always felt she missed her calling. Then again, she always cussed a bit too much for a teacher.

She picked right up.

"Joe, you okay? For God's sake, you scared me half to death. You've never called me before 10 a.m. before."

"Hi, I'm okay. I just...I think I need to take a trip, to get out and be outdoors. I can't get my brain settled, and I haven't really talked to anyone in weeks and...I got fired yesterday."

"Well, shit. You've been through so much. I'll be over in thirty minutes. You got any coffee? Never mind, I'll bring it. See ya soon, J."

He wasn't sure he was ready to deal with her energy, but at least he knew he could tell her to get out of the house at any moment, and their relationship would be no worse for the wear.

8

Let Me In, Bozo

The energetic knock on the door made him smile, but then he immediately wondered what he was getting himself into. Cindy could talk to anyone about anything and for a long time. Growing up, she could occupy the grown-ups with cute stories. That was helpful for him to avoid awkward chit-chat. But as an adult, she could run him over in most conversations.

"Let me in, Bozo!"

The smile came back.

"Hi…"

"Can you turn some lights on? It's like you're living in a basement again."

"Cindy, can you slow it down a bit? I haven't had any coffee."

"Sure thing. A depressed Joe is probably even less of a morning person, right?" She said with a smirk.

"You gotta give me shit all the time, huh?"

"Little sister's right and job. Plus, everyone else is probably giving you the pity party, right? I imagine you've had enough of that…"

She could always get to the point without being too mean about it. But that hurt a little. "Ouch. You're probably right."

"So, I thought you were a rock star at your job. What the hell happened there?"

"Well, I've never been a rock star; that's just how Jody described me." He felt the sadness creeping back after the shock of Cindy actually being there started to wear off. "I couldn't stop drinking...and I didn't care anymore. Jacob had no other choice."

"Can you talk to him?"

He slid the box across the kitchen table. "Leave no stone unturned." Joe could barely muster the words.

Tears welled in Cindy's eyes. "That Jody...she really loved you and knew you so deeply."

"I think she wants me to go fishing, reconnect to my childhood. I'm lost without her, and without something to focus on, my mind will likely implode. The whole *Leave no stone unturned* line...I'm not sure what I'm supposed to be looking to find. I could never figure out those damn riddles."

"I can see why you want to go on a trip. You and Dad, you always connected on the river. You need to connect back to yourself. You need goals. That whole goofy saying you'd always repeat, 'It's good to have goals!'" she said in a sarcastic voice, imitating him. "She's asking you to keep going and to find your goals, to find a new path. How can I help you?"

"I made a list. I need to do some shopping. I'm not sure what to do with the house. Everywhere I look, I see her. Without her, the worst of me comes out."

As a part-time Realtor, Cindy knew the path to take with anything house-related. And the pit bull in her didn't give in to Joe's logical but rerouting paths. They both knew they couldn't step in too far without Joe breaking down.

"Drink your coffee, and let's go shopping."

9

A Drive Around Town

"So, is shopping all online these days?"

"Joe, you are depressed and mourning. But dude, how old are you? You haven't been living under a rock for the last ten years. What research did you do? We're not looking for the best deal here. We're looking to get you equipped for a trip in a short period of time."

"Well, I found this shop in Frederick. I think they have most of what I need, except the camping supplies."

"I can handle that part. Let's head out."

Joe had only been to the funeral home, grocery store, liquor store, and bars in the last two and a half months. Shopping with Cindy was like one of the shopping-spree shows on the Game Show Network. Every salesperson smiled at her; she was funny in her interactions. Joe felt like a third wheel in every store. Jody would let Joe be the impatient male shopper, but he loved being with her and stuck to her side. He never sat in one of the pouting chairs set up for the grumpy guys at most stores. Instead, he'd revert to poking fun at the salespeople or what they were buying. Thinking back on those moments, he started feeling the sadness again.

"Joe, stay on point. We're getting you out on the water and turning over some rocks."

"Gotcha."

"So, we've got the camping stuff covered now. Time to go to the fly shop."

"Okay." He was never a prolific speaker.

Driving past the main street shops of Frederick reminded him how much he loved the small-town feel. Part of what drew Joe to architecture was the feeling he felt as a kid, growing up in Baltimore, where walking through the streets of his neighborhood in Hampden connected people together in a cohesive community. The neighborhood, with its architecture and culture, created a charm, with a flavor sometimes only appreciated by its residents, where family businesses and residents sit on their stoops, giving the streets an energy and fullness. Big box stores and suburbs didn't fit Jody and Joe deep down, but it fit their lives where they were. The main street with its ice cream shop, antique store, coffee shop, gift and trinket stores, and fly shop felt like part of a connected community. Getting out of the car and walking through the town helped Joe breathe.

Opening the door to the fly shop, a dog and a hidden voice greeted Joe.

"Welcome, buddy! I hope you don't mind dogs! Hello there, young lady!" The voice of the shop owner set Joe at ease. "What can I help you with?"

With a slight limp, Tom Murray stepped out from behind a small counter. His left arm extended out to his side and the Chesapeake Bay retriever obediently left Cindy and came to Tom's side.

"My name is Joe." He never offered his name without significant urging. It almost felt like he was about to confess something deep inside him. "I need to go on a fly-fishing trip." That didn't come out how he thought it would. Cindy almost did a spit take of her coffee.

"He needs a new fly rod, some waders, a vest, flies, the whole kit and kaboodle!" Cindy left off where Joe's brain couldn't keep up.

"You're like a lottery ticket that hit the jackpot! My name is Tom, this is my shop, and I'm glad to meet you!" Joe and Cindy scanned the shop. Along the right wall, an angled wooden shelf displayed dozens of fly rods of various lengths and colors. In the center of the shop, a large table was filled with hundreds of small compartments, overflowing with flies, with tufts of feathers and fur of every color Joe could imagine. The front of the store was primarily outdoor apparel, with more flannel, fleece, and "wicking fabrics" than Joe could ever remember seeing. He smiled as he thought that Jody would've definitely had a joke about Joe getting decked out in flannel, probably something with a lumberjack reference.

Tom affably asked questions about what Joe wanted to fish for and what types of rivers and lakes he wanted to visit. Joe gained confidence through talking with Tom, realizing he didn't lose all of the fly-fishing vernacular in his absence from the sport. Tom connected the dots for Joe and revived the knowledge that longer rods are required for fly fishing as the bend of the rod propels a weighted fly line with a nearly weightless fly at the end of a thin leader. A weighted line connected to a thinner, translucent leader helped to roll out the fly without scaring the fish. The leader ended in a thin tippet that could be replaced and extended, to aid in a gentle presentation to the wary trout. Trout are especially sensitive to shadows and movement around them and generally eat miniscule insects, so fly-fishing equipment and strategies have adapted to allow the angler to present a small artificial fly with minimal disturbance to the water.

Once Joe settled on a versatile 9-foot 5-eight rod, which also matched his gifted reel, Tom worked with him to see how he casted. Rods vary in weight from one to twelve. The weighting designation refers to the weight of the fly line the rod is designed to cast. Larger fish species eat larger flies, and higher weights of the fly line allow the angler to cast heavier, larger flies.

Joe and Tom headed out the shop's back door to a narrow strip of grass along the alley. Feeling the rod bend under the weight of the line felt natural to Joe and took him back to hearing his father's voice coaching him, "accelerate, stop, accelerate, stop," as the line looped and moved straight out behind him and then curled and accelerated past him towards the five-gallon bucket Tom set as a target.

"All I've got to say is you're no Brad Pitt!" Cindy chided Joe. "Golfing has *Caddyshack,* and fly fishing has *A River Runs Through It.*"

Tom continued to encourage Joe.

"Easier to compare you to Bill Murray than to Brad Pitt, but you are doing great! You're shaking off the rust in record time! I can tell you were taught well. Are you feeling the rod load?"

"I think so?" Joe turned his head and squinted his eyes.

"What does that mean?" Cindy inquired.

"Well, fly rods are designed to bend under the moving weight of the fly line. When the line is extended behind the rod and the rod is bent, we call it loading the rod. When Joe casts, he's moving forward before the line is fully extended behind him. That will create knots in the line and limit the accuracy and distance of his cast. But he keeps getting better. When you pause and feel the line load, you can use the power in the rod as it bounces back forward to propel the line forward."

"All those years watching my dad and Joe fish, and I never paid attention to the casting."

"You were always playing in the water, scaring all the fish!"

"Just like my kids!" Tom patted Joe on the shoulder and provided a few more minutes of instruction before they headed back into the store.

After a couple hours and a good amount of money, Joe was loaded up with all he needed for his trip. He and Cindy were all smiles, and Tom was wishing him a great trip.

10

Start a New Chapter

Checking off the items from the shopping list was satisfying, but now it was sinking in that he really was going to travel by himself. Being afraid wasn't part of his self-awareness until Jody got sick, and now he felt afraid more and more. The anxiety of dealing with people at work and pretending he was okay only went away after the second drink. But this anxiety wasn't exactly fear; it was knowing that no one there could possibly understand what he was going through. Now, there was a new and different level of anxiety in calling Cindy and preparing for this fishing trip. Facing this trip without Jody…alone…this was fear, and he knew it.

Joe was thinking about a drink. He still wasn't convinced he was an alcoholic, but pressure was building inside of him. With a voice he wouldn't quite describe as harmonious, Cindy sang along with the Indigo Girls to "Least Complicated." It was almost too much to take. He was angry that he let drinking take a hold of him. He had an aversion to dependence of any kind, but he had become so dependent on Jody. He was replacing her with booze.

"The hardest to learn was the least complicated…" Cindy belted out, breaking Joe's rumination.

"Wasn't that fun? What's next?"

"I'm running out of gas, Cindy."

"It's only 12:30. How about we get some lunch? You gotta eat, right?"

Joe wasn't hungry, but he knew how Cindy was when she was hungry. She pitched a legendary fit in the car on a family road trip once when the car snacks their mom packed weren't cutting it. "You're starving me! Staaaarving MEEE!" He winced slightly at the memory. It was no wonder he grew to love the quiet so much.

"Sure. Sushi?"

"Why'd you wince?"

"Because you're staaaarving meee," Joe said in a mocking tone.

"Dick."

"Never gets old," Joe said, allowing himself to chuckle.

Lunch got his mind off drinking, and Cindy's ordering off a menu cracked him up. She always had to change at least one item.

As she started the car to take Joe home, she paused, "I think you should sell the house, Joe."

He couldn't find any words.

"Maybe you can treat this trip like an adventure to start a new chapter."

"Where? My life is here."

"It was. It's not anymore. She's telling you to explore, to find your purpose."

"I'm not sure I'm ready for that."

"Okay. I understand. Just know that when you're ready I can help with all of it. I have a great moving company that can do all the packing. And I can handle the real estate stuff. I haven't been able to do much for you in our lives, but this is what I do, and I think you'll need it. Packing up that house may be more than you can bear."

The tears were back. He knew she was right. Maybe it was time to start the new chapter.

11

Planning a Trip

After Cindy dropped him off and helped him unload all his new gear, Joe sat at the table with everything he bought spread out. Instead of cutting off the packaging and putting everything in one of the fifty pockets in his new fishing vest, Joe was staring into the kitchen blankly. He was trying to picture Jody working in the kitchen. They had so many good conversations over a cutting board. She always asked him to cut the onions, to avoid the tears that messed up her mascara. He missed cutting the onions; she would always rub his shoulders as a thank you. Now there were no onions, no shoulder rubs, and no Jody.

Joe didn't seem to have any trouble recalling all the memories, but he couldn't magically conjure her image. He was alone. Maybe Cindy was right; being here was too hard. He could feel the pull from the bottles behind him.

Joe decided to put his mind toward planning his fishing trip. Deciding to sell the house could wait. It was helpful to have a sister in real estate. He realized how grateful he was to have Cindy with him today. She filled the quiet spaces that otherwise he alone awkwardly occupied.

But those quiet spaces allowed him to think deeply. He ran through the possibilities in his mind. And then he thought of his father. He selected Montana as the ultimate destination. The Yellowstone,

Madison, and Gallatin Rivers and dozens of other rivers in Montana were the subjects of Joe's father's dreams, and he was unfortunately unable to visit them. Roughly 2,100 miles of driving to get there. Joe's analytical mind was in full-on map breakdown mode. He wanted to hit Penns Creek and Spring Creek in Pennsylvania and The Delaware and Willowemoc in New York to recreate the memories of his photo album.

The Catskills of New York were a little out of the way, but they were part of Joe's fondest fly-fishing memories with his father. *I don't have anywhere to be*, Joe said to himself, cementing his loneliness. Back to the trip. He would love to visit the Pierre Marquette River in Michigan, the birthplace of Trout Unlimited. The Driftless Region of Wisconsin could be great, too.

Liam was a member of Trout Unlimited when Joe was younger. Joe remembered attending fish stocking events and fly-tying nights with his dad. The older men would teach Joe about the different insects in the stream and talk about which flies were working best. His dad would say, "Don't believe all the fish stories, Joe! You catch more fish than these guys do!" As an eight- or nine-year-old boy, Joe wasn't interested in tying flies, but he loved exploring the old church where many of the meetings were held.

He suddenly realized that his stops didn't all have to be fishing related. He had a few more states and points of interest to check off the list. He could go to South Dakota and see Mount Rushmore, the Arch in St. Louis, or any of the national parks he hadn't visited yet. Even as an architect, Joe was drawn to natural beauty more than that created by man.

Joe and Jody had also wanted to visit the Rockies in Colorado. Any time it would come up, Joe would sing "Rocky Mountain High" by John Denver. The words of the song were running through his head now. One verse struck him:

> *Now he walks in quiet solitude, the forest and the streams*
> *Seeking grace in every step he takes.*

His sight has turned inside himself to try and understand
The serenity of a clear blue mountain lake

Colorado needed to be on the trip. That was decided. The memories of Jody and their dreams brought back Joe's tears, but he felt like he had a mission, and he wasn't going to let her down.

12

Time to Start Packing

After all the years since he was in school, Joe always took notes in composition books. He loved the marble covers and was always surprised at how the binding somehow kept them together, even with the abuse he put them through. Organization was not his strength, but Jody helped with that. Even as an architect, he was an outlier. Papers were spread over his desk and, while not a complete mess, his workspaces made Jody cringe.

"LEAVE IN A WEEK" was written across the first page of the new composition book. Joe needed deadlines. He worked best under moderate tension; otherwise, the creative part of his brain couldn't be forced to decide. He just wandered through theories and ideas. But when it counted, he would deliver. He learned to build habits that created patterns in his behavior to keep up with "drudgery" like invoicing and budget estimates to keep himself in line at work. But he liked to meander in his intellect.

"PACKING LIST" was on the next line. Thankfully, Cindy had made sure his list was complete—at least as complete as it can be when you only partly know what you're doing. All the items purchased during their shopping trip were still stacked neatly on the kitchen table. Transcribing all the items to a list in his composition book made the whole trip begin to seem real.

"ITINERARY" followed the packing items. He had to look that one up on his phone to make sure he spelled it right. He chuckled thinking about words he could never correctly spell, no matter how many times he wrote them. Poe Paddy State Park would be first on his list. He liked Central Pennsylvania and camping at rustic campgrounds, where just a stream and a campfire provide the perfect place to "walk in quiet solitude."

From there he would head to Hancock, New York, to stay at an angler resort, where he could take a shower and have a good base location for the West and East Branch of the Delaware River and the hallowed streams of the Catskills. Joe didn't want to set too many hard and fast dates from that point forward. He scheduled three days in New York and then he would head west. It was set. He'd reach out to Cindy and have her take care of things at the house while he was gone.

Joe decided he would commit to documenting the trip in his notebook, and maybe something would come from it. He had started reading again and loved the stories about fishing trips and tall tales. There was comfort in the stories of outdoor adventures for Joe. Getting lost in the stories of overcoming challenges and seeing the beauty in nature was a welcomed distraction from sitting in his dark house, watching television, and wallowing. Now it was time for Joe to create some of his own fishing stories.

13

Going On a Drive

The week flew by. Preparing to be out of town for a period took a lot of work. He had to prepare the house and make sure he had what he needed to be on his own. Cindy had helped him set up the yardwork crew, timed light switches, and all the other things he never would have thought about. In the back of his mind, he thought he wasn't coming back.

Joe appreciated Cindy's help packing up the car and helping him with the house. He knew he wouldn't have been able to do it on his own. But he was ready to be by himself again. Conversation was still painful for Joe, but Cindy knew not to force him to talk too much.

"Who knew it would take 50 years for me to appreciate you messing with my stuff."

"Joe, I'm glad I could help. Lord knows you need it." Cindy poked him a bit. "So, where are you headed? What are you going to do with yourself? How am I going to keep tabs on you?"

"I think you've exceeded your allotment of questions for the day. I'm headed to State College, then to the Catskills. I'll stay in touch."

"Your version of staying in touch is less frequent than your church attendance."

"I don't know where I will end up, Cindy. I appreciate your help, and I promise I'll stay in touch."

"Be good to yourself," she said as she got in her car and drove off. She was torn between hope in him finding himself again and feeling like she may never see him again. As he watched her drive off, Joe's mind wondered if he would ever see his sister again.

Joe returned to the house, turned off the lights, locked the doors, and said goodbye. Tears streamed down his face. The SUV looked like a combination of a kid driving to college and the Griswold family vacation, overflowing with camping and fishing supplies. Beside him on the front seat, he had his favorite picture of Jody and his composition book.

A feeling of trepidation shortened his breath as he backed out of the driveway. Not a fan of goodbyes, he hadn't reached out to neighbors or many friends to let them know he'd be leaving. Before his mind got caught up in things he wasn't doing and things he should've done, he turned on some music.

"Traveller" by Chris Stapleton was the first song of the trip. "On the Road Again" or "Life Is a Highway" were too predictable and, frankly, too chipper. Chris Stapleton seemed to perpetually suit his mood. Once he made his way out of the neighborhood, he gave a quick nod and headed for the Beltway. Thankfully, the rush-hour traffic had passed, and although there were still the impatient and stressed-out drivers darting around him, he felt relaxed and content.

It was a warm but not stiflingly hot early August morning in Maryland, and he could roll down the windows, feeling the breeze and singing his way to his fishing adventure.

It suddenly hit him. He hoped he could still cast. Well, he'd have plenty of time to figure that out. He felt 100 pounds lighter and was looking forward to hooking his first trout in decades. Joe knew the rust would come off. It would take some work, but he'd learn.

He envisioned casting a dry fly and having it gently land in a seam, where feeding trout awaited just under the water's surface. He missed fishing. He also missed driving into the rolling hills of farm fields and forests. He wished Jody was with him.

14

Time to Hit the River

The ramp off the highway quickly transitioned from smooth asphalt to gravel road. Every so often, there's a driveway back to a fishing or hunting camp. Many were incredibly charming, with green standing seam metal roofs, small coverage porches, and outbuildings. They would have homemade signs calling out the family name and the date the camp was established. A few looked like they wouldn't last one Pennsylvania winter, but they probably looked that way for forty years. The site of the fishing camps brought him back to his dad. It would've been so much fun to have a fishing cabin with him. Campfires, evening hatches on the water, fish over the grill, and wise words passed from father to son. That wasn't meant to be; it wasn't meant to be for Joe to be a father either. He and Jody tried for years, and it almost ended their relationship. It was something present in their relationship but largely left unspoken.

A bump in the road brought him back to the drive. Looking in the rearview mirror, he was generating a dust cloud as far as he could see. The roads built for fracking and the logging roads spanned the mountain's east side like a spiderweb. *What is called progress always has an ugly side.* Along the hillsides near the Susquehanna River, a series of wind and solar farms speckled the landscape of forest and crop fields.

Joe liked the alien nature of the giant windmills more than the cleared trees and well fields. *If only fossil fuel dependency would end sooner.* Sustainability was always a driver for him in his designs, even when his creations often resulted in more of the built world and less of the natural world.

Cresting the mountain, the old-growth trees began to cover overhead, cutting the summer sun, and it felt like he was about to encounter a trout stream or a black bear around the next bend. Instead, it was just a pickup truck, going a little too fast on the narrow, bumpy road. They each slowed down to pass each other and gave the "country wave" and a smile. Now a small stream paralleled the road with the moss-covered boulders, mountain laurel, and hemlock trees shading the water and forcing the stream's flow to twist and turn across the valley.

A brown painted wooden sign with bright yellow letters announced "POE PADDY STATE PARK" with the proud keystone logo of Pennsylvania over the stacked-stone base. A deep breath. His first stop on his adventure. Joe noticed he was out of cell phone range just over the mountain crest and was looking forward to reading one of the many fly-fishing books he brought and watching the campfire dance.

He found the loop road and made his way to his campsite. This would be home for a few days. He'd spent years designing all sorts of buildings, but he was never so happy to see a simple pavilion, a fire ring, and a picnic table.

He figured the tent out, nearly drawing up new directions in the process. He'd need to get some firewood so he could settle in for the night. *Am I stalling to get to the water?* Joe didn't want to be a flailing nimrod looking like an idiot in front of the typically skilled anglers who made their way to Penns Creek on a weekday. He was hoping to find a secluded length or reach of stream to get the kinks out, maybe catch a fish and maybe see a hatch. It was a little late in the summer for most aquatic insects to emerge from their holding places on the stream bottom into the air as adults, mate, and deposit their eggs back in the water; but the event of a "hatch" was the pinnacle in fly fishing.

As aquatic insects transition in their life stages, the period from nymph to adult presents the most vulnerability for the insects and the highest opportunity to feed for the fish. The main aquatic insects of interest to trout and those who fish for them are mayflies, caddis flies, and stoneflies. For some hatches, especially the mayflies, the bugs can be so thick over the water that flies go beyond obstructing your view and get stuck in your hair, clothing, and unfortunately your mouth. Some hatches become famous for creating trout-feeding frenzies, like the Green Drake hatch on Penns Creek, and attract crowds of anglers to the stream. Joe had checked the hatch chart and was hoping for caddis or terrestrials on dry flies.

Joe walked over to the camp host's site, and it appeared they were out, but he slipped ten dollars into the lockbox and grabbed two twine bundles of firewood for the camp. He probably had about three hours until sunset, so there was no more reason to stall. Time to hit the river.

15

A First Step After a Long Time

Joe had kept the reel in its box except for the trip to the fly shop where his new buddy, Tom, had loaded the reel with 120 yards of backing and a new fly line. Joe had practiced some of the fishing knots in the last week and knew many of them from the strict instructions of his father.

He unzipped the end of the hard, blue, canvas-covered tube. It bent back like a Pez dispenser to reveal a dark blue long narrow canvas bag. The bag was doubled over at the top and secured by a cord tied in a neat bow knot. The bag had four sewn separations lengthwise to hold the four pieces of the rod. Joe remembered the two-piece rods his father owned, in long aluminum tubes that rolled around in the trunk of his father's car. Occasionally the rods would collide and create a dull bell tone behind his seat.

The four-piece rod tubes were shorter and easier to handle when traveling, and the canvas wouldn't create a sound in the SUV. Joe wished the tube had a metallic cover just to have that sound accompany him on his trip. Each piece of the rod is connected to the adjacent piece through the ferrules—metal sleeves and caps that fit inside the sleeve. Small dots helped to align the pieces together to ensure a straight path for the fly line. A small amount of pressure helped to snug the rod into one unit. Joe remembered the care his father took to put together and break down his rods, sliding a small rag over the length of the rod before putting it back in the bag and case. "Never put away a wet rod." His father's words were still with him.

As he removed the reel from the box and connected it to the fly rod, he sat at the picnic table. Feeding the line through the guides, it was like he was teleported back in time and space. The process of rigging up a fly rod came back to him like muscle memory. He connected the leader to the fly line, lifted the rod, and held the loose end of the line, considering which flies to try first.

He had already put on his waders and wading boots. Lacing and tightening the boots had started his transformation that further continued with setting up the rod and reel. Joe started to shake with anticipation as he walked to the river. The crunch of gravel under his feet was hypnotizing, calming his nerves as he looked down at his feet.

Walking to the end of the loop road, he found a trail below the confluence of a small stream with Penns Creek and took a step in the water. The rushing water generated a sound that was both terrifying and soothing, like he was on the verge of being washed downstream but also that his soul would be washed over and cleaned of its debris.

His feet shifted as his weight settled on the slippery cobbles. The force of the water pressed his waders tightly against his legs, causing his knees to bend to brace and balance himself. The feeling of walking into a stream and feeling the power of the flow was a sensation he had forgotten. Flow paths formed in the downstream current, accelerating in short bursts around large boulders and a fallen tree on the other side of the stream. The irregularities of the channel bed created seams in the flow where depths and velocities vary, creating holding spots for the brown trout. His dad would always call them "primary lies." Holding spots for trout could also be an injury for Joe, and he knew it. One wrong step and he could twist an ankle, blow out a knee, or take a spill into the cool water.

A majestic and beautiful creature, brown trout have such camouflage with their surroundings that only the most patient observer staring intently for many minutes can see a flash of movement, the slight adjustment of a white fin or the flick of a tail to give away their position. When trout are feeding near the channel bottom, even in very shallow flow, their presence cannot be assumed. It is not until the emergence of aquatic insects from the cobbles to the surface of the water that trout then show themselves. Insects emerging from the channel substrate through the water column create a piñata effect for the trout, like a toddler birthday party, jumping from their spaces in line to grab a vulnerable insect like a liberated piece of candy.

Rising trout are a sight to behold for the fly angler. Joe knew he had enough skill and knowledge buried in him to be able to catch fish. But regaining the hand-eye coordination, reading the water, and getting good drifts takes continued practice. He had to put some time in on the water. Fooling the fish takes patience, skill, creativity, and some luck.

Casting a line requires a rhythmic motion, accelerating the line in a back cast to a stop, allowing the line to straighten behind you before you accelerate forward, and the line unfurls, presenting the fly as a showman presents the next act. It can be a graceful dance of the fly line over the water, or it can be a mess of catching nearby trees or fellow anglers in tangles.

Joe anticipated the mess, but he wasn't as bad as he imagined. He knew better than to try to catch a fish right away and spent about twenty minutes trying to cast his caddis fly to specific places, practicing. His few minutes of instruction with Tom at the fly shop were invaluable to get his brain thinking through the movements of casting again. He knew he had a lot of rust to shake off, but he felt fourteen again. He was reading the water and rebuilding the muscle memory of handling the line as he moved the rod, mending the line on the water and picking up and aiming his line.

Moving a few steps farther off the bank, Joe eyed a large boulder that created a large wake, or pillow, both in front of and behind the large stone. *There has to be one in there.* He had his target. He would aim for the downstream side of the boulder first, so as not to spook any fish that may be upstream. The first cast was four feet to the left and four feet short. Joe let it drift for ten to fifteen feet and tried again. Slightly closer, he repeated the action three more times until the fly landed just behind the large boulder. He held his breath; a quick flash and the fish struck his fly. It felt like time stood still. The shadow rose, at first slowly and then with a burst, it bolted for the fly. Then time accelerated more than the fish. Joe yanked his arm upwards, pulling the fly from the water and from the hungry fish before it could catch its meal.

Damn.

Joe giggled. He couldn't remember when he last giggled.

"How badass is that!" He startled himself by speaking out loud. His brain focused only on the water and the fish. What a peaceful place to be. For a moment, he was engaged, intent, and even happy. He was ready to cast again.

Dusk was setting in. Joe knew the chance of more risers was likely, but he'd had enough for the day and wanted to get back to camp before dark to start the fire and make some dinner. He looked around at the trees and the stacked elements of nature all around him. He was joyful, and that didn't feel quite right yet.

16

A Dead Drift

Getting skunked on his first time out on the water in decades was expected. The thrill of almost catching a fish still ran through his body. His hands were shaking. Joe was craving a beer and glad he didn't bring any alcohol. He hadn't had a drink since the night after being asked "to take a break" from his job. He was proud of his self-control.

A campfire-side meal was calling him. He loved grilling. The smells, sounds, and tastes were full of remembrance of events central to his life. Camp potatoes were a favorite. They are small, cut potatoes mixed with onions and peppers tossed in olive oil, salt, pepper, and Old Bay, wrapped in foil and thrown on hot coals. Add some grilled bratwurst with spicy mustard and he had a great campfire meal to end a great day.

Watching the flames slide over the logs as they cracked and turned to embers set Joe into a trance. With the backdrop of a star-filled sky framed by hemlock trees, Joe felt calm and settled for the first time in months. All around him, the darkness and quiet were interrupted only by the occasional crackle of a campfire and quiet conversations of his neighboring campers.

Tomorrow he could have a full day on the water, and hopefully he could get a trout to hand. The pressure of life, the pain of terminal illness, and the loss of his love had stained Joe. He already was pessimistic and prone to rumination, but now he was locked in a battle. He had

41

been slipping, and now he felt like he may be finding the ground under his feet. Funny how it takes standing in water to find solid footing.

Joe wanted to get out on the stream early. He found the rhythm of casting and the concentration of watching the fly as calming as meditation. To fool the fish, much of the time the fly needs to have a dead drift, mimicking an insect dislodged from its position and at the mercy of the river's flow. Dragging the fly across the currents is unnatural and alerts the wary trout that what they are seeing is not food. Presenting the fly as naturally as possible takes skill and concentration. Slips of attention may cause an angler to miss the biggest fish of the day, but Joe could remember a few times when he caught a trout just dangling his fly in the water fooling about. His dad would laugh and give him a hard time, "Even a stopped clock is right twice a day, and even a blind squirrel finds a nut once in a while."

He knew that fishing early in the morning was usually productive, especially in the summer. Planning to fish nymphs under the water surface was the way to go and he was prepared. He really wanted to catch a fish. He also didn't want to build up pressure. This was supposed to be fun. Joe liked to be rewarded for this work and didn't want to go too long before he could be successful. "Patience, Joey," he could still hear her voice in his head.

With a full belly and a clear head, Joe put himself to bed, excited for what the next day would bring.

17

Fish On!

Joe was comfortable in his sleeping bag, but with an unfortunate roll to his side, his face touched the damp nylon of the tent. His eyes instantly opened, and he was ready for the day.

Joe quickly dressed and started the small camp stove for some instant coffee. *Not the best, but it does the trick.* A tip from his father on the camping trips they took when they were younger was to bring hard-boiled eggs for breakfast, since they don't break in the cooler, and you don't have to waste time cooking them before you hit the river. So, Joe mixed his coffee and ate his hard-boiled egg.

The sun was rising as he looked at his watch, 5:45 a.m. Joe wanted to fish a little further from camp, so he drove to the end of Tunnel Road and walked upstream, past an old cabin. A long, steep riffle funneled water into a deep run, pushed up against the far bank of the stream. Large boulders formed the toe of the bank with a tall, steep valley wall. Large rocks were exposed sporadically up the hillside, held in place by towering hemlocks.

Peering at the water's surface, Joe could not make out any evidence of rising fish. Joe remembered from his instructions at the Trout Unlimited meetings that trout feed below the surface approximately ninety percent of the time. Joe had a box of assorted flies. Some are wrapped in pheasant tail feathers, others with fur from a rabbit, called hare's ear nymphs. Those were the two most referenced flies on the websites, but there were also nymphs to replicate the immature stages of midges, stoneflies, and other insects present in the water column. Walking into the fly-tying section of the fly shop was arts and crafts on steroids combined with a bit of bird and fur taxidermy. Every color was represented in the myriad of different tinsel, thread, fur, feathers, and more synthetic materials than a plastic surgeon's office.

Joe pulled out his fly boxes, filled with the different shapes and sizes of flies recommended by Tom at the fly shop. Joe rigged up two nymphs, a large chenille-wrapped hook with rubber legs to resemble a stone fly and a pheasant tail, which resembles a mayfly. They would be suspended in the water column by a small float or bobber, which in fly-fishing circles is often referred to as a "strike indicator." He chuckled as he put it on the leader, hearing his dad's voice mocking him: "Fly anglers don't mess with bobbers." His dad only fished dry flies that floated on top of the water, but he encouraged Joe as he was growing up to fish with a bobber and even use bait if need be.

Casting the rig was not as smooth and aesthetic as the dry fly. He laughed at Cindy's wisecrack that he was never going to be mistaken for Brad Pitt in *A River Runs Through It*. After a handful of casts and drifts, he was getting the timing of it. Joe eyed a seam of water flowing inside of some large boulders that had a slightly darker green tint, indicating an area of deeper water. He placed the flies neatly five feet upstream of the boulder and the rig landed with a splat. Joe hoped it didn't scare any fish nearby. The strike indicator floated downstream slightly slower than the bubbles and foam on the surface of the water. As the rig passed the boulder, the indicator paused along its trajectory. Joe held his breath and lifted the rod. He was gathering the line in his left hand and trying not to panic. He felt the tug. And then a head shake. *Fish on!*

The fish darted upstream, and Joe maneuvered the rod to the slide, pulling the head of the fish towards him. It jumped, entirely leaving the water and somersaulting downstream. Joe reeled up the extra line frantically, as the slack was piled up near his feet. After what felt like a long battle, but likely was less than a minute, Joe navigated the fish to immediately upstream of himself and scooped it into his net.

"Woohoo!" He let out a jubilant cheer. His feet shifted on the rocks and he nearly fell in the stream with excitement. He could feel his heart beating in his chest and took a few deep breaths to settle himself.

The fish was approximately twelve inches long with a bright yellow belly, a dark brown line across its back with brown and red circular spots surrounded by yellow halos. The white tips of fins on the bottom of the fish contrasted against the translucent yellow fins along the back of the fish, drawing the eye of Joe. Joe recognized his catch as a wild brown trout. *Such a beautiful creature!*

Joe put his hands in the water, as his father always reminded him to do and gently cradled the fish. It wriggled and slid from his grasp. He took another deep breath and slid his hand under the belly of the fish. With his other hand he grabbed the fly and pulled it from the fish's mouth. *Barbless flies make this so much easier.* Joe lifted the fish from his net and released it back into the water. As it swam away, it disappeared quickly in the water and a feeling came over him. Joy. His heart was racing, and at the same time he was completely calm. All those years had passed since the last time he caught a fish. Now that seemed like quite a shame. He was ignited. Something so simple could bring such joy. And the feeling when the fish is on the line was an amazing rush. Seeing the fish in his net brought him back to his childhood and all the joy of exploring the unknown and seeing how his actions can be rewarded with the connection to a magical, beautiful creature.

Making his way to the bank, Joe sat to watch the water. Looking down at the rocks near his feet, he reached and picked one up. Turning it over, dozens of small mayflies scampered to escape the sunlight. He closed his eyes. *Thank you, Jody.*

18

Loosening the Knots

Joe sat on the rock daydreaming of times spent on the water past and future. *I should journal today!* The thought popped into his head. His father imparted a great deal of knowledge that was now just stuck in Joe's brain. Jody's note was like a key unlocking that hidden trunk of fishing knowledge and memories. He had no one to pass anything along to now, but writing it down may give it a life past his own, at least keep it fresh in his mind.

A mink scampered down the far bank, diverting Joe's gaze. The sleek black hunter slipped into the water along the stream bank and disappeared. Joe searched the glassy surface with his polarized sunglasses and saw nothing. The mink was underwater for minutes and then quietly emerged from the water with a brown trout in its mouth. Joe laughed to himself that the mink was a much better angler than he would ever be.

Competing with the mink motivated Joe to get out of his head and get back to the water. He spent most of the day casting and catching a few fish and many tree branches, underwater logs, and boulders. Joe forgot how many knots you must tie and tie and then tie again. His fingers and his patience were tested throughout the day. He was proud that he never cussed or threw his rod in anger. "They cost too much money to be a reckless child with," Joe thought in his father's voice whenever he felt close to the edge of his temper.

For being a moderate to below-average athlete with below-average motivation and a recent drinking problem, he stayed in reasonably good shape. He was still able to wear pants from ten to fifteen years ago and generally wasn't disgusted by looking in the mirror after a shower. But after seven hours on the water, he was exhausted. Wading in a current, no matter how strong, wears on you. He was not ready for the stamina he needed to be stable in a stream. So, he decided to call it a day.

His boots felt much heavier walking back to the car than they did in the morning, but occasionally dragging his feet didn't drag down his smile. Even when his leader and tippet were tangled up in knots, the knots of emotion inside of him were loosening.

A long fly rod with a fragile tip is in peril around car doors and trunk latches. Joe had read that more fly rods are broken by car doors than by the biggest of trout. Another indication is that the fish is often smarter than the fisherman.

Joe carefully put his rod over the seats, and the tip rested on the dashboard. He sat on the tailgate to unlace the wet laces of his boots and slide them off. Taking off the waders, he felt like a victorious soldier returning from battle. He was by himself and overcame some fear of stepping into the stream, stepping into the world again to reclaim part of himself that had been abandoned years ago.

Once he got back to camp, he hung his waders to dry and set out his boots where some sunlight pushed through the canopy of hemlocks. He grabbed his composition book and started to write. He got as far as the date and his location, and he nodded off in the chair.

Joe woke up before darkness took over, still feeling tired but with enough energy to grill up a cheeseburger and heat some baked beans. Another glorious night watching a campfire and jotting down some notes in his composition book. He crawled back into the sleeping bag and prayed to dream of catching a giant brown trout.

19

A Time Warp

The morning came swiftly, with a few more aches and pains than the previous day. There were lessons learned from those aches. Reminders to look over both shoulders before you cast to avoid trees and how to keep your weight balanced when stepping into a strong current. It wouldn't be long until he could maneuver through a stream with confidence and without recklessness, but he would have to get his legs under him again.

Joe decided not to rush to the stream this morning. He would be leaving for New York this afternoon and wanted to have his site cleared out before he headed to the stream. He thought the instructions for assembling the tent could've been better, but rolling it up and packing it into small bags was even more frustrating. As an architect, Joe excelled at the creative and complicated aspects of the designs, but in the minute details of the plans, his mind would wander. Following directions was a running joke with Jody. She would always question him. "How did you even get through architecture school when you can't follow directions?" His quick response was always, "Charm, caffeine, and memorization," followed by a quick, cheesy grin.

He laid out the collection of fly boxes. All the flies in boxes he bought at a fly shop. He thought back to all the flies his father tied. During winter, almost every night after night, he would sit at his desk, turn the bright lamp on and place it into position over his vice. He tied only a handful of different flies, but he would load a box of dry flies and a box of wet flies for each of them by the springtime. The odd smell of the slowly decaying feathers and wool, and the sound of the thread spooling through the bobbin were nostalgic to Joe. He decided he would start tying flies once he found where he was headed.

Joe packed up all his gear into the SUV and walked down to the stream. He decided to cross the bridge and navigate his way through a tunnel. One of the most charming attributes of the park, and one of Joe's fondest memories of the park as a child, is the Poe Paddy Tunnel. The abandoned railroad tunnel was used by the Penn Central Railroad until 1970. Walking over 250 feet through a dark tunnel under West Paddy Mountain provides at least several seconds of complete darkness before a flashlight-sized guiding light presents itself. Holding his dad's hand was necessary to traverse the tunnel until he turned ten years old, when Joe decided that double digits meant you had to be brave. He smiled a crooked little smile; he still wasn't sure he was brave, but he knew what was on the other side of the tunnel. It was always the not knowing that scared him.

Emerging through the tunnel always felt like crossing through a time warp, even though it was only a shortcut to the downstream end of a long, doubling-back bend. Maybe it *was* a time warp; he could almost feel his dad's hand. Joe closed his eyes at the end of the tunnel and slowly opened them, allowing them to adjust to the light and letting his memories linger. The river was in front of him, with a gravel trail extending to the right and left as far as he could see. A small green, tin-roofed cabin with a wooden porch was nestled down the hill to the right. He walked straight to the water, as the white-water pockets and deep green buckets of water called him.

The water dove and splashed around the large boulders in the stream bed. Small bathtub areas of flat calm water below each large boulder interrupted the ruckus created by the water upstream and alongside the enormous stones. *Soft water next to fast water.* Joe fixated on each of the dark depressions and connected the dots between each of the pockets to determine how he could wade and try his hand at snatching a brown trout from each of them. It looked nearly identical to his memories; the only things missing were his dad leading the way in his old, patched-up waders, and now his perspective was from about two feet higher.

Joe was on his own now. Careful, slow movements helped him get into a good casting position for the first pocket. The first goal of wading is not to fall in, and the second goal is not to disturb the fish you are trying to catch while getting in position to catch them. Once he was settled and got his feet on relatively stable footing, he prepared to cast. He wanted to use a dry dropper rig, which uses a large, dry fly that floats well to suspend a smaller nymph that would quickly drop towards the bottom of the water column. He looked up toward the mountain and took a deep breath. His lungs filled with the cool mist off the river and the smell of pine in the air.

Clear, cold water is required for trout to live in a stream. Many say that trout live in some of the most beautiful, untouched places on earth, and this was one of them. Hemlocks and mountain laurel lined the rocky banks, and large boulders broke the water into dozens of plunging jets that created waves, wakes, and white water. Eagles, ospreys, herons, and kingfishers fly overhead each day. Minks, snakes, foxes, and the occasional bear wander the stream corridor.

Trout have sharp vision and can avoid overhead predators, such as herons and osprey through camouflage and the instinct to bolt into hiding spaces under rocks and other obstructions at the first sign of movement or shadows. To catch them, an angler must be mindful of their movements and shadows. Flat, clear pools can't be disturbed, or the fish will scatter to their hiding places. One benefit of steeper, broken water where turbulence creates white water is that it obstructs vision, protecting the fish from predators but allowing crafty anglers to approach the fish without being discovered. Joe could cast the tandem flies in small windows if he was within twenty to thirty feet and the broken surface of the tumbling water hid his intrusion from the trout. Many of the lessons of his father were returning.

His first few casts always went left of his intended target, and he shook his head and bit his lip. After a few minutes, he had his metronomic rhythm in motion, and he managed to put the combination of flies softly into a fishy-looking pocket. A quick flash and the dry fly plummeted. *Fish on.*

The fish bolted for the faster water, aiding its strength with a boost from the stream flow. Energy is injected into the line and rod, nearly pulling the rod from Joe's hand. The sudden movement stunned Joe, but he quickly turned his footing to bend the rod sideways to pull the trout out of the current and into the calm. His heartbeat increased and pressure built within his mind to make sure he landed the fish. *Don't stress out!* Another deep breath, and he felt the fish's energy subside and he guided it into the net. He let out a happy sigh. *Why do I want to sit and admire every fish when I catch it?* Joe contemplated. It was a thrill, but also a relief, like he was still connected to that brave ten-year-old.

Following his imaginary path between his cherry-picked pockets in the cascading water, Joe was able to catch a half dozen additional fish. Each seemed brighter in color and stronger in spirit than the previous. He broke off a fish, lost a handful more as they threw the hook, and had his fair share of snags and tangles. A full day of fishing, with all the victories and insults he would expect. A good day.

Around 4 p.m., he realized he had stayed longer than he intended and decided he would head to New York before it got too late. A tired body and a three-and-a-half-hour drive wasn't a relaxing way to end the day, but he was in real need of a bed and a shower. Bumping along the gravel road, he turned up the music and replayed in his mind his fishing adventures from the past several days.

20

A Flash of Brown

Joe never took a road trip, for fun or for utility. He was taught to be efficient with his time. Hour after hour sitting in a car when you could fly in a fraction of the time just didn't make sense a few weeks ago. Now, feeling the steering wheel in his hands, hearing the blues on his stereo, and looking out at the mountain and farmland views was liberating. He wasn't enamored with driving, and he wasn't drawn to fast cars or motorcycles, because they lacked practicality and he enjoyed the peaceful pace of a pedestrian. But this trip was changing his affinity for the open road already.

Once Joe drove off the mountain and connected to a strong enough cell signal, he plotted his course. He had decided he wanted to minimize time on interstates and maximize time along rivers. He headed towards New York along the West Branch of the Susquehanna River and did not rush himself. About 30 minutes outside of the angler's resort, he decided he'd check in with Cindy.

"Hey!"

"Joe!"

He didn't think he'd be making a call, let alone be excited to hear his sister's voice.

"How's it going so far?"

"It's great. Caught some fish and I loved sitting by the campfires. Made me think of Dad."

"Hopefully lots of good memories!"

"Yeah, it looks just as I remembered. Being there reminded me that progress hasn't ruined everything."

"Always the optimist!" she poked. "Well, that's great, Joe. And everything is good with the house, plants are watered, and the lights are coming on at the right times."

"Thanks, Cindy. I really appreciate everything. I can't..."

"I know, Joe. Just have fun and check in every once in a while."

"Thanks. Talk to you soon."

"Right back at you, bro."

She always talked like a teenager, even though she was about to turn fifty. Joe wished he had Cindy's energy. A smile crept across his face.

A flash of brown from his right interrupted his thoughts. A buck collided with the hood and windshield right in front of the steering wheel. Instinct took over and he turned away from the impact. His head led his hands, and he jerked the steering wheel, losing control. The Tahoe spun off the road, colliding with a tree on the passenger's side

The impact of his head against the side window was the last thing he remembered before the voice of the police officer startled him.

"Medical assistance is on the way. Can you hear me?" Feeling the officer's hand on his shoulder, Joe's mind began to clear. Blood flowed from his left ear and the seat belt was so tight against him that he struggled to breathe. The smell of burnt rubber, oil, and antifreeze filled his nose, causing him to choke and further struggle against the seatbelt to clean his lungs. His camping supplies were thrown across the inside of the car; a red-and-white checkerboard tablecloth and a package of batteries ended up on the dashboard to his right.

"Sir, I am Officer Baker. You've been in an accident. Can you hear me?"

"Yes, I didn't see the buck...I...need to get out of the car."

"Stay still, please. You're not in danger in the car. It's most important that you are okay. What is your name?

"Joe."

"Joe, are you feeling any pain?"

"My head is killing me. I need to get out of the car..."

"Medical assistance is on the way. We will help you out once they arrive."

Joe noticed his hands were tightly holding the steering wheel, he never let it go. He allowed his head to drop and rest on the top of the steering wheel. Joe started to inventory his body and at first glance nothing appeared to be out of place. His cheeks felt burnt and the expelled airbag remnants around him likely were to blame for that pain. He closed his eyes and slowly reopened them; he realized he had no idea where his phone was and then suddenly something caught his eye that caused his breath to stop. The burgundy top of a green bottle was exposed between his feet. "Shit."

Joe hadn't had a drink in almost two weeks, but with all the trip preparation and binging of fly-fishing YouTube videos, he forgot to throw away his stashed bottle of Jameson. His head began to hurt even more.

21

Settle, Settle, Settle

A panic set over Joe. He knew he had to settle himself, but his mind went over the worst-case scenarios. He could be assumed to be drunk, but a breathalyzer or blood test would prove he was sober. Or did he drink? His head injury was making all the stories run together. Was he drinking? The pace of his breathing accelerated; he could hear his breath getting louder.

"Joe, are you okay?"

"Yes, yes, yes." Joe tried to assure the officer. He dared not take his hands from the steering wheel. He clumsily tried to push the bottle back under the seat.

"Medical assistance has arrived. The paramedic will be right here."

"Okay...okay..." Joe's voice moved inside his head. *Why am I repeating myself? Was I drinking?* His confusion was taking him over allowing the panic to run his thoughts. *Settle...settle...settle.*

When the doctor told him and Jody about stage four breast cancer, Joe shut himself off by repeating. "Settle...settle...settle." Then he needed to be there for her and his purpose was clear. That nearly broke him. Now he wasn't sure he was recovering at all. Was I drinking? He couldn't find the truth. Whatever the paramedic says, he decided he had to deny he was drinking.

Joe heard the paramedics and police officer talking, but he couldn't make out the words. The panic intensified. *Do they know? Do they know I was drinking? Was I drinking?* His thoughts were spilling over so fast that he was beginning to lose track of if he was speaking out loud or if the thoughts were only in his head.

"Joe, my name is Amanda. I am an EMT, I am here to help you. Can I help you?"

"I...need to get out of the car."

"Okay, we will get you out. I'm going to open the door. Were you the only person in the vehicle?"

"Yes, I'm alone. I don't know what happened. I didn't see the buck."

"I'm going to open the door and help you." She looked back at Officer Baker. "Do you know if all the airbags deployed?"

"Yes. It looks like all of the driver's side airbags deployed," he replied.

"Joe, are you having any difficulty breathing?"

"What? ... Oh...the seat belt is very tight. It's so tight."

"Okay. Can you unclip the seat belt or do you need assistance?"

"I can do it." Joe's fingers felt embedded in the steering wheel. He was afraid to make eye contact with the EMT. He felt like he wasn't in control of his words or movements. Spreading his fingers on his right hand took all his mental focus. After a couple pulses of his fingers, he reached down and pushed on the release to the seat belt. It wouldn't budge. He pushed harder and shook the buckle, and the latch sprang from its position.

Joe felt a relief of pressure from his abdomen and chest.

"Nice, Joe. Are you still having difficulty breathing?"

"I ...just don't know what happened."

"Okay, Joe. We can figure that out later. Besides the cut on your forehead, do you feel any other pain?"

"My face hurts, on my cheeks and over my eye, and my back..."

"Okay. Can you move your legs? I'm going to start checking you and pushing on you a little, okay?"

"Yes, I can move my head. Okay."

Amanda checked Joe's head and then inside Joe's mouth and then inspected his neck and pupils. Then she pushed along his chest and abdomen. "Joe, let me help you get out of the car."

Joe was now afraid to leave the car. He would have to face whatever happened.

Settle...settle...settle. He slowly swung his feet down, and Amanda and a firefighter helped him out of the car. Joe now noticed half a dozen emergency vehicles with flashing lights, illuminating the car, road, gravel, and debris all around him. Tree branches and glass crunched under his feet.

They helped him to lay on the gurney. He could see the damage to his Tahoe. He was glad he had a bigger vehicle now; he felt lucky to be alive. He took what felt like his first deep breath in hours.

Officer Baker approached and handed Joe his cell phone. "Joe, have you been drinking tonight?"

Joe froze.

22

Fluorescent Lights

Joe's brain was trying to compose the best possible answer to Officer Baker. His dad's voice came into his thoughts. "Lies follow you until the truth is discovered." Joe's mouth didn't give his mind a chance to come up with a perfect answer, "I don't know. I don't think so, but I'm not sure. I don't know what to tell you."

"How do you not know if you were drinking?"

"I'm not sure. My wife died and I started drinking. She wasn't a drinker, but... Anyway, I've stopped drinking for about a week...I don't know...Maybe longer...But my head, I'm not sure, my head hurts..."

Amanda, busy preparing the ambulance for transport, was now within earshot. "Listen, Chuck. Joe may have a head injury. I can't smell alcohol on him, but we need to get him to the hospital, and they will test his blood."

"Okay, I'll take care of the scene and head over to the hospital in a little while," Officer Baker replied.

Amanda and her partner, Phillip, moved Joe into the ambulance and headed from the accident to the hospital.

"Who's Chuck?" Joe was trying to clear his confusion.

"Oh, Officer Baker. His name is Charles Baker. He and I went to high school together. I've known him a long time."

"Gotcha. Where am I?"

"We are headed to Bracken General Hospital near Remburg, New York. Pretty much you are halfway between Binghamton and Hancock."

"That sounds familiar. I'm not sure why. What time is it?"

"7:45 p.m."

"Okay. Thanks." A rush of thoughts and feelings ran over Joe. His mind was beginning to process information again.

"It's kind of crazy, but my wife grew up in Remburg. I think that's right. But I've never been there, or here, I guess. Her parents died in a bad car accident when she was in high school; and she said it was too painful to come back."

"Really? It's a small world Joe; that is pretty weird. We're pulling into the hospital now. Let's get you inside and get you checked out." Amanda's voice and tone calmed Joe, and his breathing was getting back to normal.

"There may not be a brighter place in the world." thought Joe as they rolled into the hospital and banks of fluorescent lights made the white walls almost glow.

"What have we got here, Amanda?" They were met by David, the triage nurse, a few feet into the lobby. David was barrel-chested, with a thick beard, a welcoming nature, and looked like he may have been a lumberjack in a former life.

"David, this is Joe. An eight point interrupted his drive over to fish the Delaware."

"Well damn, Joe, that is some bullshit," David interjected. "Let's see if we can get you back on the water shortly."

"That would be good." Joe quietly responded, slightly overwhelmed by the loud voice and bright overhead lights. "I have a bad headache."

"Looks like that buck kicked your ass a bit," David replied, dialing down his voice a few notches. "Probably the car, too, right?"

"A tree helped with that," Amanda chimed in.

"Ouch." David rolled Joe into the room and helped him over to the bed. "You will need to put this on." David pointed to a gown. "Will you need any help?"

"Not without dinner first." Joe's sense of humor reemerged.

23

Scan

"Hey, Joe. I'm going to leave you in David's capable hands. Officer Baker will likely stop by in the next hour or so to check in with you. Let you know where your car is. Stuff like that."

"Thank you, Amanda. Thank you for helping me so much."

"It was nice to meet you. Take care of yourself."

"Alright, Joe. I need to clean you up a bit, get an IV in you, check your vitals, and the doctor will be in shortly. You are likely going to have some additional tests. Can I ask you a few questions?"

"Sure."

"I know that Amanda went through your pain levels in the ambulance, so I'll save that for later. Did you lose consciousness after the accident?"

"Yes, I hit my head against the window and was out until the officer woke me up."

"Did you have any bleeding?"

"Some from my ear, a little, and these scratches on my face."

"Is the light bothering you? Are you sensitive to light and sound?"

"Well, I'm always sensitive to light and sound, but it is super bright in here."

"Have you been dizzy or confused?"

"I may still be confused. I am feeling disoriented."

"Is your vision blurry?"

"No."

"Did you drink any alcohol or take any drugs today?"

"I don't think so. When Officer Baker asked me, I didn't know what to say. I was drinking a lot after my wife died, but then I stopped and I don't remember if I started again. But that's how I got confused. I...just don't know."

"I'm sorry to hear about your wife. When did she pass?"

"May 12th."

"That's so hard. My condolences."

"She had breast cancer. It was aggressive. She was sick for seven months and then she was gone. This wasn't part of the plan. She was my purpose. I'm feeling a little lost." Sadness was clawing its way back over him.

The doctor quickly knocked and stuck her head inside the door. "Mr. Barden, my name is Dr. Alvarez. You can call me Maria." Dr. Alvarez appeared older than Joe, with dark hair and some gray peeking through.

"Hello, Doctor Alvarez."

"You met David. Isn't he the best?" David lowered his eyes slightly, with a smile.

Joe's eyes moved from David back to the doctor. She appeared very small next to David, but he appeared to shrink in stature next to her. "Yes, he got me all hooked up to the IV on the first attempt, so that wasn't so bad. He's asking lots of questions, trying to keep me on track."

"That's good. You know I'll need to ask you all the same questions all over again, but I want to get you a CT scan and run all your blood work. When you hit your head as hard as you did and you have blood flowing from your ear, there is a chance you have a skull fracture. We need to look at that as soon as we can, and then we can start to decide what we can do to help you feel better. So, David will run you to the lab and I'll catch up with you in a little bit. Sound good?"

"Sure thing." Joe tried to concentrate on all of her words, but got a little stuck once he heard, "skull fracture."

David connected the IV to the hospital bed and started to wheel Joe to the lab. Officer Baker was walking down the hallway with a purpose.

"Hey David, I need to chat with Mr. Barden. Where are you headed?"

"Hey, Chuck. Joe needs to get a CT scan." Joe sensed a playful, mocking tone in David's voice. "We will be back here in about fifteen minutes."

Joe stared up at Officer Baker, trying to tell how much trouble he may be in, but there was nothing to read. Officer Baker's eyes narrowed and he nodded his head at David. He turned his back and walked towards Dr. Alvarez.

"Let's go check that noggin of yours, Joe."

Joe's heart accelerated and his brain raced, hoping this CT scan would last forever.

24

Seeing What's Inside

"Alright, Joe. You are going to get a CT scan. This is Edward. He is going to help you with the imaging. Do you have to use the restroom?"

"I guess I should." Joe was trying to delay the whole process.

David helped Joe in and out of the bathroom; it felt good to walk around a little. David passed Joe off to Edward. "I'll be back in a few to bring you back to your room."

"Thanks, David."

"Hi, Joe. I'm Edward. We're going to get you scanned here quickly and back to your room. I know it's very cold in here. Let me know if you need a blanket."

"I'm good. I'm hot-blooded."

"Nice. You look rugged!"

"Do they hire based on a comedy routine here?"

"Ha! If so, are you looking for a job?"

"Right about now, I'm just looking not to go to jail."

"It's good to have goals."

Joe couldn't restrain his laughter but then his mind ran off. He was worried about the look on Officer Baker's face. Edward's voice interrupted his worry.

"Okay, Joe. I'm going to move you to the platform. You will lay down with your head facing the tube and then your head and shoulders will slide inside the halo. The x-ray elements spin around and we will get a complete 3-D picture of your head. Then we can make cross sections of your brain like we're cutting a loaf of bread. I'm going to head back to the room over there and push some buttons and you'll be all done in about five minutes."

"Thanks, Edward. Take your time. This makes me want a donut."

"Never heard that one before! The halo does look like a donut. You will need to hold very still. I don't want you stuck in there longer than necessary."

The whirling machine reminded him of the sounds of an airplane as the vent fans kick on and the engine starts to back the plane away from the jetway. Looking around at the white, bare walls, Joe wished he was fishing the Delaware River. A red light crossed over his chest and crossed his neck, moving towards his face. Joe closed his eyes. He wanted to see Jody's face, but instead he saw the face of Officer Baker. His eyes immediately opened again. The background sound of the scanner couldn't drown out all of his runaway thoughts. *Was I drinking? I couldn't have been. What happens if I get arrested?*

"Joe, we are all done. Let's get you back to your room."

Joe let out a deep breath. Edward helped Joe back to the gurney and David was at the door. "Alright, Joe. Dr. Alvarez will get the results quickly."

The wheels of the hospital bed echoed in the clean hallway. "Joe, you're going to be okay."

As they approached the room, Dr. Alvarez stepped out of the room, leaving Officer Baker in the doorway.

25

A Few Weeks

David wheeled the bed into the room, as Officer Baker closed the curtain that served as a door with one hand, while the other hand held tightly to a clipboard with several official looking forms pinned down by the metal clip. Joe's breaths shortened and quickened. *What am I going to do?*

David circled the bed and pushed his foot down on the breaks of the wheels by Joe's feet. The dead, dull thud of each brake being secured added to Joe's apprehension of being locked up. "Alright, Joe. Chuck needs to talk to you real quick, and then shortly after, Dr. Alvarez and I will be back to go through your tests."

Joe nodded.

"Mr. Barden, I requested and received a warrant for a blood sample to test your blood alcohol concentration. As a licensed driver, you have already given consent to having your blood tested when you received your driver's license, if the officer has probable cause to believe you were under the influence. When I found the opened bottle of whiskey under your seat, I had probable cause. One of the blood samples taken from you was used for this test. Do you have any questions?"

Joe looked down and shook his head no. Time felt like it was slowing down.

"I received the results of your test from Dr. Alvarez. Your blood alcohol percentage was well below any legal limit. Well, it was zero."

Joe's lips pulled together and he exhaled forcefully.

"But you had an open container under the driver's seat. It is illegal in the state of New York to possess an open container of alcohol in a vehicle. I will be issuing you a ticket under VTL 1227-1 for violating this law."

"What are the penalties?"

"You are facing a maximum fine of $150 plus fees and up to 15 days in jail. You will be given a date to appear before the county judge who will hear your case and determine the verdict and sentence. Typically, no jail time is assigned. Our court system isn't too busy these days, so you should be able to get a court date in a few weeks."

"A few weeks? I'm supposed to be headed out west."

"About that, your SUV was towed to Stewart's Garage. The garage is located at the corner of Sullivan Avenue and Mill Alley. The Stewart family has owned and operated the garage for three generations here in Remberg. You are in good hands there. I talked to Seth Stewart, who runs the garage, and he thought if you wanted them to repair it, you're going to be here for a few weeks. The good news is at first glance it doesn't look like any of your camping or fishing gear was damaged. My grandpa was a fly fisherman and my father is a fly fisherman. I know you have to take care of your equipment. I packed it up as carefully as I could. With it being towed and all, I didn't want all your stuff to get spread all over the highway."

"That's very kind of you. Thank you."

"Well, Amanda asked me to take care of your stuff. We go way back. Thank her."

"Will do."

"There is a nearby campground if you decide to stay to wait for your car and a couple local hotel/motels that are fine to stay at, if you need a roof over your head. Here is the ticket. Stay away from the whiskey, Joe."

"Thank you, Officer Baker."

"Take care of yourself, Mr. Barden."

David and Dr. Alvarez appeared at the door as Officer Baker was leaving.

"Joe, you lucky son of a gun!" David could produce a smile in the most intense of moments. "Well, crap, I got ahead of myself. Dr. Alvarez has some news to share with you."

Dr. Alvarez allowed a thin smile as she glanced at David. "Well, Mr. Barden, I do have good news. There doesn't appear to be any bleeding or swelling in your brain. And there is no evidence of a skull fracture. But it is very likely you have a concussion. You were very lucky. Your chest and abdomen look to be in good shape as well. I want to keep you here overnight for observation. You were shaken up pretty bad and it's getting late. Is that okay with you?"

"Yes, I don't have anywhere to go. I just need to cancel my reservation at the lodge."

David chimed in, "Oh. Amanda said you mentioned you were expected there. I took the liberty to call over there and let them know you were in an accident."

"Where am I?"

"Remberg, New York."

"I was joking. I know where I am. You all are way too nice."

26

Headlights

Joe held the steering wheel with his left hand and reached out with his right hand to brush Jody's hair from her face. She turned and smiled at him. That smile turned him from a grumpy, pessimistic, and arrogant ass to a more empathetic but still grumpy citizen. Her eyes suddenly widened and her smile transformed into a gasp of absolute fear. Joe saw the flash of brown and lost control of the steering wheel. The windshield exploded as the SUV spun and he reached out for Jody. Joe's body shook him awake in a panic.

His eyes darted around the room. Joe realized he was dreaming and he wasn't sure if he preferred what he was waking to or the nightmare he left. By himself, in a hospital, in a town he'd never been before. *What am I gonna do?*

He shut his eyes, hoping he could put himself back in the dream. No matter what happened in the accident, being with her for one more second was enough to go through anything. He squeezed his eyes tightly and prayed to see her again. Only darkness with fuzzy light shaded rings where the room lights pushed their way through his eyelids. His brain held onto the memory of her smell and the feel of her hair.

When Joe would get uncomfortable in a social setting or when he had too many drinks, he could talk forever. Not Jody, though. She could navigate small talk without the awkward jokes and pointed truths that Joe offered, but she did not dwell in nostalgia. She was charming but never shared too deeply. Her connection to Joe was true and she loved him, but there were places she couldn't go. Jody spoke of her parents only a few times, even with some photos and memorabilia displayed in the house. After their first and only dog—a wonderfully dumb and loyal lab named Tucker—passed away, she and Joe were heartbroken and shared a bottle of wine over dinner reminiscing about their favorite Tucker stories.

Near the end of that evening, Jody began to talk about her parents. She was their only child and they adored her. She said her only real goal was to make them proud. Joe wanted to reassure her that he was sure they were proud of who she was, but he didn't want to interrupt the blessing of her sharing with him. Unlike so many moments before, he listened.

Her words came slowly. The night of her graduation from high school, her parents took her out to dinner at a nice restaurant in Binghamton. She hadn't decided on what college to go to yet, and her indecision came up at dinner. She had a high school boyfriend who her parents didn't think was the one, she was a kid and didn't know what to do, but her parents didn't want anything to interrupt her schooling. The euphoria of graduation and all the possibility that was ahead was running up against the overloaded mind of an eighteen-year-old. And her mom and dad gave her that look, like their hopes and dreams were bound to her and she needed to decide or risk disappointing them. She snapped in the silence of their waiting stares.

"I need to be able to make my own choices."

Those were the last words she would say to her parents, and those words stayed with Joe.

Jody and her parents drove home towards Remberg without a sound, until her mom's scream as the bright lights crossed the yellow lines. A drunk driver hit them head-on. Jody had some cuts and bruises but was fine. Her parents died instantly. Her tears flowed as she opened up to Joe. He held her as she sobbed. He never felt closer to her, until the very end, when he was by her side through the surgeries, the chemo, and all the pain. He didn't bring up the accident again and never asked to visit Remberg. Yet, here he was.

Joe would have never been able to forgive himself if he was drinking. After all his wallowing, he felt the shame of his drinking pile on top of his sorrow burying him into the hospital bed.

A gentle knock at the door broke Joe's stupor. "Mr. Barden, is it okay if I come in?"

"Come in." Joe's words stumbled out. "Dr. Alvarez?"

"Good morning. Are you alright?"

"I had a bad dream. Shook me up."

"That is fairly common after a traumatic accident. It's going to take you some time to get over the shock. But you're going to be okay. We have some prescriptions for your headaches. You do not have to take them if you don't need them. You may be sensitive to light, have some nausea, dizziness, or feel a little foggy for a few days. I want you to check back in with your doctor in a week or so. Do you have any questions for me?"

"I don't really have a doctor anymore and I'm hoping to be on a long trip. If I need anything, could I just call you? I honestly am not real comfortable with doctors. After all the time I spent in hospitals with my wife, I just..."

"Can I call you Joe?" Joe affirmed with a nod. "Listen, Remberg is a small town but we have some good doctors. I will leave you a recommendation of someone who I trust. He is my husband and has a general practice right in the town. I will leave my number if you get in an emergency or head out of town."

"Thank you, I can't begin..."

"No need to thank me. You'll find lots of kindness around here. That reminds me. Officer Baker stopped by and wants to take you to the garage to see your car and decide what to do. You're going to be alright. Take some time to get ready and once you open the door, Officer Baker will drive you to the garage. Take care, Joe."

"Thank you, Dr. Alvarez. I don't know how..."

"You're welcome, Mr. Barden. No words are needed."

27

Remberg

"Hello, Mr. Barden." Officer Baker greeted Joe at the entrance to the Emergency Room.

"Good morning, Officer Baker. You can call me Joe."

"Okay, Joe. You can call me Chuck. Good morning. So, I need to get you to your SUV. As I stated before, I took your vehicle to Stewart's Garage. Seth is a friend of mine. He does most of the work on the police fleet. You said your wife was from around here, right? Have you been here before?"

"Good memory. Yes, she grew up here. But no, I haven't been here before. She didn't want to visit...bad memories." Joe's eyes squinted as he adjusted to the late morning light. The hospital sat up on a hill over-looking the small town and the river that created a meandering border between the hotel and the town. It was a beautiful small town. A classic town composed of buildings with vernacular and Late Victorian style architecture. The view caused Joe to pause as he walked out of the hospital.

Chuck broke his appreciating gaze. "That's a shame. I'm sorry to hear that."

"No worries. Looks like I'll get to spend some time here now."

"My car is over to the left. Remberg's finest."

"Nice, thank you. I am glad I'm not being handcuffed in the back of the car right now." Joe laughed uncomfortably.

Chuck nodded. "Me, too."

Opening up the door of the police cruiser and sitting in the front seat was surreal.

"You know, I believe this is the first time I've ever been in a cop car."

"That's probably a very good thing."

"Yes, sir. Funny to me that we civilians have to use "hands-free" devices and you have this huge monitor right off the steering wheel."

"It takes some getting used to, and it can operate 'hands-free.' Do you want a ride or what?"

"Sorry. My wife, Jody, always told me that people didn't need to hear all my observations."

"I probably would've liked her more than you," Chuck said with a smile.

"Everybody did. Well almost. She could be sharp and righteous from time to time." Joe smiled remembering when Jody would give her doctors a hard time for being late to an appointment. "Time means a lot when you know it's short, Doctor," she would say.

The car pulled up to the traffic light from the hospital parking access road. The spot could serve as a town overlook or postcard photo. The town laid out before them with the three main east-west roads, with Main Street parallel and between Chase Alley and Valley Street. Four north-south streets intersected with each cross street.

"So, Joe. That there is Mill Creek between us and the town. It had suffered from bad pollution in the '70s and '80s. With the Clean Water Act, the old paper mill shut down and the water quality improved. They stocked it for a while, but about ten years ago it was designated as a natural trout water and it produces some good fish. It's really nice to fish and most town residents like to walk dogs and have picnics there in the park. It's gotten nice. No real crime to speak of either. The occasional kid stuff, breaking into a car, shoplifting, minor drug use, stuff like that. But it's a real amenity to have a stream like that through town. You may want to fish there while you're stuck here for a few days."

The light turned green and they drove down the hill along Grey Street. As they crossed over Mill Creek, Joe peeked off to the right. Dogwoods and willows grew in patches along the stream. A small trail paralleled the creek about five to ten feet north of the creek. Large boulders were exposed along the banks and throughout the bed. Fifty feet off the bridge, a steeper cascaded folded white water into a calming pool that crossed under the bridge. "Wow, that does look nice. Missed the nice view in the back of the ambulance."

"Yeah, you couldn't really enjoy the scenery last evening. The repair shop is right off of Chase Alley there, but I'll take you down Main Street first. I told you I'll give you the tour."

"Thanks, Chuck."

They turned right onto Main Street. An insurance broker, flower shop, small dance studio, a pizza shop, a diner, and a fly shop!

"Baker's Fly Shop?"

"Yup, it's my dad's shop. You should stop in."

"You didn't tell me you were a fly fisher."

"I'm not sure I completely qualify under that title. That's why it's my dad's shop. I like to go, but it's just not the same for me as the old man. It's a huge part of his life. For me, it's something I like to do from time to time."

"Gotcha."

Chuck pointed to the left. "You can't miss the focal point of the town: the County Courthouse. That's where you'll have to go for your ticket and the court date. I filed the paperwork first thing, so you should get a date pretty quickly."

The courthouse was dark red, adorned with flags and a prominent bell tower. The building has pronounced windows with round arches and a stunning gabled roof. "It's dead in the center of town, built in the 1860s, somewhere around there."

Joe admired the building. The design was eclectic and had a classic feel, with fantastic detail and thoughtful proportions.

"They don't build them like that anymore," Chuck quipped.

Joe chuckled. "Nope."

An ice cream shop, a general goods store, a law office, and the historic society rounded out the rest of Main Street. Chuck turned right onto Sullivan Street and they arrived at Stewart's Garage.

"Told you it was a quick tour. Let's go talk to Seth."

"This looks like a nice town."

"It is, for the most part."

28

Stuck

Three large bay doors dominated the facade of Stewarts Garage. The smell of gasoline, rubber, and oil filled the air as Joe and Chuck entered the office door. Seth emerged from the garage area through the door into the waiting area. He appeared quiet and reserved. His thin wire-rimmed glasses appeared smudged, and he continually wiped the hair from his forehead. A crew of three similarly appearing men all worked diligently behind Seth. As the door opened and closed, sounds from the garage speakers waffled in the waiting room., Oddly, it sounded like Miles Davis. It temporarily distracted Joe and induced a quick head turn.

"Hi, Chuck."

"Hey, Seth. This is Joe Barden, the unfortunate owner of that Chevy Tahoe we brought in last night."

"Wow. I didn't think whoever was driving that would get out of the hospital anytime soon. Feeling okay, Mr. Barden?" Seth turned to inspect Joe.

"Ehhh. I'm grateful to be here."

"I bet. Looks like it was scary as hell. Well, I'm glad you're up and moving around. There is a good bit of damage to the vehicle. I'll take you to have a look at it in a second. I wanted you to know that Chuck and I took out all your gear and stacked it up there. I can keep it here

77

for a few days, even a bit longer if need be. So have you thought about if you want me to do the work?"

Joe's head dropped. "I don't have any set plans anymore. I'd like it to get finished quickly. Do you have time to get it done? And you're sure it's not totaled?"

"The repairs will be expensive; there is a good amount of damage. But I doubt it will be totaled and I'm confident I can get all the parts and get it back like before the accident in three weeks or less. You'll have to reach out for your insurance, though. I can handle everything else once you get it started."

"Okay. I'll keep it here. Feels like this is fate telling me I'm stuck here for a bit. Plus, I've never met a mechanic who plays Miles Davis in his garage."

Seth looked up through his glasses.

"Joe, I trust Seth. He's a good man and a great mechanic."

"Thanks...I guess." Seth gave Chuck a sideways smile.

"Mr. Barden, I have the items from the SUV back here in the storage. I can give you a hand with what you need. As for the music, Pete over there loves metal and I just can't take it. I like staying calm. It's my garage, so jazz it is."

I'm not used to this. Are people actually this nice? Joe tilted his head as he walked to the neatly stacked pile of his gear.

The three men packed up some of Joe's gear, grabbed his duffle bag, computer bag, fishing supplies, and cooler and walked through the bay to the police cruiser.

Joe turned and looked at the SUV. The windshield and driver's side windows were destroyed and the whole front of the car looked like it had been squished and twisted by the Incredible Hulk.

"Looks worse than it is. Those things are built like tanks. You made a good choice to protect yourself there. I'll fix it up, good as new."

Joe shook his head. He had wanted to get a smaller vehicle. He just wanted four-wheel drive. Jody was hoping they could get a vehicle strong enough to tow a small pull-behind camper. The smaller SUVs were just not going to cut it. They never bought that camper, but the

Tahoe may have saved his life. *Jody would be thankful and maybe a little 'told you so' would be in her smile.* He tried to see her in his mind.

"You'll be ready to get back to your trip in no time. Let me take you over to the hotel. It's just a little up the hill."

"Thanks, Chuck."

Joe felt trapped and lost, but his brain quickly jumped. *Maybe Jody brought me here.*

"Alright, Joe. I called over to the Hill Top Motel. They have vacancies all the time and I was able to get you a discount."

"Thank you." Part of Joe felt like this was the perfect setup for a horror movie.

"I haven't been in the motel in quite some time. The beds and showers may not be the Ritz-Carlton, but the roof doesn't leak and I haven't been there on a call in years. It's not bad."

It could've been a motel anywhere. It looked exactly like all the stock photos you have ever seen for a motel, just a little lacking on the neon. Two stories, painted metal railings with repeated sets of two doors, two windows, and several feet of brick between each set.

This is a little depressing. Joe's face likely didn't hide his thoughts.

"Joe, the rooms are better than the outside looks, plus you're only three to four blocks from the whole town. You're going to need to be a pedestrian for a little bit. You can't rent a car unless you head over to Binghamton."

"Thanks. I'm just feeling a little silly, sore, and stuck. Walking around the town may do me some good."

29

The Diner

After getting checked in, he called Cindy and updated her on recent events. She was less excitable than normal and handled the news of the accident more calmly than Joe anticipated. Everything seemed okay with the house. She offered to come up and get him, but he decided to stick it out on his own.

Seeing the SUV in its current state was shocking. A big part of Joe wished he'd just died in the accident. He wasn't sure what waited on the other side for him.

Since Jody passed, Joe started to feel he would see her again. Years of Sunday school and confirmation didn't have the impact his parents intended. He'd seen too many people act out of power, control, or wickedness in the church he attended to feel like he was really in God's house. At best, he was a skeptical Christian. But he felt Jody around. She was there during the accident, in the hospital, and she was here now.

What am I doing? What stones am I meant to turn? I'm doing a bang-up job. I am barely holding on to my sanity.

He wished she was there. She could settle him down. Feeling drawn to a bottle was dangerous, and he knew it was one moment away. A stomach rumble broke his train of thought. *I need to go walk around and find some food. Keep moving. Don't let it take me over.*

Walking to the door, he checked his pockets, wallet, cell phone, keys. *Focus on the small things.* He slid the chain for the bolt latch as he left the room. Turning to lock the door, Joe felt odd. He missed her terribly, he felt lost.

Through the parking lot and onto the street, the town had some energy to it. His stomach rumbled again, and he focused on getting some food. *Didn't Chuck say something about a diner?* A couple blocks down the hill and a couple to the right and Joe was standing in front of Courthouse Diner with the courthouse across the street behind him. *Lots of very literal names in this town.*

The town had a good amount of energy and the diner was no different. About 10 a.m., Joe didn't know what day of the week it was, but it had to be a weekday, and the place was about half full.

"Hey, honey. Grab a seat where you like. I'll be right with you." A waitress in her late 50s called out to Joe. She had platinum blonde hair with purple streaks, looking as if she could've been the lead singer in an '80s rock band.

Joe watched his feet walk along the checkered floor. *Progress hasn't ruined everything.* He sat on a red-leather-topped swivel bar stool. All the chrome, bright colors, and neon lighting you would expect in a diner, with the gigantic menu to match. Joe always loved diners. Any restaurant that served breakfast all day was good by him. Pancakes, waffles, French toast, omelets, and traditional eggs all on one page of the menu. He preferred savory to sweet and quickly decided on the classic western omelet. Joe looked up from the menu to the sound of cracking gum.

"Hey, honey. My name is Georgia. You want some coffee or something else to drink?"

"Yes, please. Could I have coffee and water? Can I order now, too?

"Sure thing, sweetie."

"Western omelet with home fries."

"I'll get this right in."

"No hurry."

"You spend the night in the hospital?" Georgia said as she poured the coffee.

Joe blushed as he became aware that he still had the hospital bracelet attached to his wrist. *She is observant.* "Yeah."

"So, were you the one in that accident up on the highway?" Georgia hesitated. "I'm sorry. Sometimes my mouth gets ahead of my brain. It was just with the scratches on your face and the bracelet and a few folks this morning were talking…"

Side effects of a small town. Joe's brain spun.

"Well, I wasn't prepared to talk about that. But yes."

"Honey, we're glad you are okay and we're glad you are here. I apologize for my big mouth and my busy-body personality. I need to keep my flashlight on myself! Your food should be ready soon."

Joe looked down and took a deep breath. Oversharing was his nervous habit, but he felt exposed. The thought of people talking about him and the accident at the town diner right across from the court-house was unnerving. In the past, this could be a trigger for him to leave a restaurant, unlikely to return. Any level of embarrassment was so uncomfortable for Joe. He worked hard to always be ahead of others and be prepared. Breathing deeply, he tried to slow his heart and calm himself. He decided he'd sit in his discomfort. *I'm completely overreacting.* Joe tried to get out of his head.

Looking around the diner walls, they obviously were fans of Elvis. But there were also many photos of the town and people. Community events, school classes, and families were depicted all around the diner.

Georgia slid the overflowing plate across the counter to Joe.

"Here ya go, honey. I bet you are hungry. Good thing we have the best home fries for miles."

Joe smiled, relaxing a little bit. "Are they the only home fries for miles?"

Georgia snickered. "Something like that, but they are really good, no fibbin' here! Need me to top off your coffee? Anything else I can get ya?"

"More coffee and some hot sauce would be great." Joe could tell Georgia always moved a hundred miles an hour.

She poured the coffee and slowed her voice. "Honey, I know I'm a bit to handle, especially the morning after a car accident, but if you need anything or have questions about the town, just ask. I've been in Remberg since I was no taller than a dandelion. Went away for a bit, but couldn't stay away too long. So, really...If you have any questions about stuff to do in town, other places to eat, town gossip, whatever, I'm your girl."

"Good to know, thank you. I appreciate it. And you are right. These are good home fries." The warmth of the food in his stomach was making him comfortable and sleepy, but he had a fly shop to visit.

30

The Kid

The omelet and home fries filled Joe up and lightened his mind at the same time. He thanked Georgia for the food and friendly company. Feeling his pocket, he checked for his keys, wallet, and phone, and he also noticed the outline of a small three-inch by five-inch pad. On nature hikes or strolls through the city, Joe occasionally had been inspired to sketch out a building, feature, or setting that spoke to him. He collected those moments in folders in his office, like an idea Rolodex, where he could pull components together for the spaces and buildings he designed. He had tried to journal about his trip, but words didn't always flow easily for Joe. His brain would tire and divert before the thoughts could be put to sentences and paragraphs. He had a graphical mind. The layout and turn-of-the-century architecture of the town brought him back to his design mind and it was comforting. *Maybe I can try to sketch some today, or maybe pick up some watercolors.*

First stop was the fly shop. Baker's Fly Shop. Joe paused before he lifted his hand for the door handle. *Did Officer Baker tell his father about the accident? Does everyone know about me?*

The door felt heavy in his hands. Thick wood and glass with the name of the shop etched above a leaping trout adorned the glass pane. The shop was cozy but rugged, decorated like a hunting and fishing lodge, essentially like almost every other fly shop Joe had visited. Waders were lined up by the door next to the counter, with rows of enormous wading boots lining up neatly below where they hung. A large table divided into hundreds of small compartments held hundreds, if not thousands, of flies. It smelled like fishing. The combination of feathers, fur, and the plastic from waders made Joe smile. The door closed behind him and it was oddly quiet for a second.

A jingle announced the arrival of an energetic dog as it ran to inspect Joe. The older Brittany spaniel gave Joe a few sniffs and headed back to an office area.

"Don't mind him; he is a friendly pup! His name is Charlie." A strong voice emanated from the office. "Be right there!"

He named the dog the same name as his son?

"Hello, there! My name is Alan. Welcome to my fly shop! How can I help you, sir?"

Alan Baker, the shop owner, emerged from the office, walking through some carousels full of flannel and camo shirts and pants of different colors with various pockets, all looking like they could be called "tactical." He had gray hair and a gray beard and focused eyes. Alan walked like a man of discipline, likely with military training, but time had softened his smile and features.

I can see how Chuck became Officer Baker.

"Nice to meet you, Alan. My name is Joe."

"Wait…"

"Let me guess. You had breakfast at the diner this morning?"

Joe decided to own his story. He wanted to fish, not be embarrassed in each new place in town he entered.

"That's a hoot! Get my coffee there every morning. Can't help but catch some information from our version of 'social media.'"

"I figured either Georgia told you or Officer Baker did."

"Officer Baker's not much of a sharer. No worries there."

"Well, while I am waiting for the repairs, I figured I'd get some fishing in. I intend to get up to the West Branch of the Delaware River at some point, but for now I was looking for some tips on Mill Creek and other spots you may recommend in walking distance of town. Also looking for some tips on flies, techniques, stuff like that."

"You are in the right place, Joe. We are well into terrestrial season, so hoppers, beetles, ants are all fishing well. Dry droppers are producing, especially late mornings and early evenings. Luckily it hasn't gotten too hot this season. Are you an experienced angler?"

"I fished a lot as a kid, with my dad, and then got away from it. I've been trying to absorb as much as possible in the last few weeks. I remember most of the basics and I've watched hours of YouTube, whatever that's worth. But I like terrestrials, as I can see them and I can cast well enough to send a dry dropper. That sounds fantastic."

"Welcome back! Fly fishing never really lets you go you once it catches you. It's a good time to be an angler. Technology is so much better than when we were kids. It makes a ton of difference. Especially with the lines, leaders, and tippets. Much stronger and easier to cast."

"There's definitely a lot of stuff to buy. It's more overwhelming gear-wise than I remember. I did feel like I shook off at least some of my fishing rust quickly. So, what should I get fly wise?"

"For droppers, pheasant tails, Walt's worms, and Barr's emerger have been doing well. A sunken ant has been deadly, too. Hoppers, beetles, and ants are working great on top, but those foam hoppers are best for the dry-dropper rig. They float all day."

"I feel like I need to buy some of each and head out to the river."

"Well, have at it! There are some boxes there on the top. I'll point out the sizes for you and get you on your way."

Alan was surgical with tweezers, picking small flies from the large display, inspecting each one and placing it carefully in the small cardboard container. "That should get you going. Need any tippets or leaders?"

"I should be good for now. I loaded up a week or so ago."

A ding of a bell signaled the opening of the door. A shy looking teenage boy walked in the shop. Charlie greeted him and the boy bent down to pet the dog. Alan smiled at the boy and turned toward the counter near the front door. Joe followed Alan and paid for his flies.

"Let me show you some good access points for Mill Creek."

Alan grabbed a red Sharpie and a sheet from a pile of maps behind the counter. Out of the corner of his eye, Joe caught movement of the boy. He had grabbed a small bag of mallard feathers and quickly stuffed it into the waistband of his pants.

Joe's heartbeat spiked and he felt his fingertips getting warm. He thought about saying something immediately to Alan, but Alan broke the silence looking up after circling three areas in red on the map. "Need anything, Ethan?"

"No, sir." The boy's face flushed and he moved quickly to the door.

Pure instinct took over and Joe grabbed the boy's arm above the wrist.

"Alan, this boy shop..."

With a quick turn and upright yank of his wrist, the boy broke free and bolted through the door. Joe turned back to Alan.

"He stole a bag of mallard feathers! Should I chase him?"

"You ain't never going to catch that boy. You'll give yourself a heart attack. I'll work that out later. I really appreciate you calling it out, but these things have a way of working out."

"How can you be so calm?"

"Joe, I know that boy. His name is Ethan. Poor kid is having a go of it."

"But he's a thief," Joe said coldly.

"He's a kid. He's having a hard time. His mom passed away about a year ago. Overdose. Never had a dad. He's in foster care. Rough story."

"That is tough, but he's old enough he should know that's just wrong."

"Listen, Joe. I've raised kids, seen trouble come in and take them over. Once they get in the system, they hardly ever get out. If I learned anything parenting it's that some choices can impact you forever, especially in a negative way. But if life isn't a binary series of right versus wrong, good versus bad, you see that perspective can be expanded and your heart can open. I'm choosing not to hold on to the negative and choosing to help others see the positive. Too many rush to judgements these days."

"What? Is that some new age stuff?"

"Not at all. Who of us hasn't made mistakes?"

Joe looked down and Alan continued. "Kids need to feel loved, they need to feel seen and heard, and they need to have that foundation before they can establish a framework to build relationships, trust, and establish accountability for themselves. Some people never feel that or don't get it from people who are supposed to provide it. I don't want Ethan to get caught in that right-versus-wrong space just yet. He needs to shore up his foundation, and jail isn't the place for that."

"I can see that. You obviously work hard and take time to have a nice shop. People should not steal. That's hard for me to get around."

"Joe, Ethan just gave me a gift. Now I know he likes tying flies. That can help build his foundation. Build up, don't tear down...especially with kids."

31

The Dry Dropper

Joe took the map and the flies and headed up the hill to the hotel. He was amazed with Alan's patience and philosophies. Fly fishermen have been known to tell tales, but Alan seemed like a man full of integrity and positivity.

Joe packed the flies into his front vest pocket, grabbed his fly rod, and hung his waders over his shoulder. He locked the door, checking his pockets as he headed down the hill. Beyond the street crossings, between the buildings, Joe could make out the creek. He never quite knew the difference between a river, creek, stream, or hollow, but he was going to fish it today whatever it was called.

As Joe crossed Main Street and passed the end of the buildings and alley, the stream opened up in his view. Alders, willows, and arrow-wood grew in tight bunches. Joe wondered if part of the restoration of the creek was designed by a landscape architect. It looked beautiful and natural, but it didn't have the wild feel of Penns Creek or other wild streams he fished.

Large boulders were arranged in the channel bed in the shape of a U. Water poured over the boulders and scoured out a long, deep pool. Where the water fell over the obstruction, the water was turbulent and white capped. *There's gotta be a trout in there!*

Joe noticed a small trail that left the sidewalk and he headed towards the first boulder feature. The trail was as wide as one step, but the mud track framed by goldenrod and switchgrass looked exactly like an angler's trail or a very well-kept deer path. The water had the greenish tint that Joe associated with a trout stream. More of an emerald than a Granny Smith apple or Loblolly pine.

The trail was well worn to exactly the good spots to line up a clear cast to fishy-looking water. The first spot looked promising and none of the footprints in the muddy trail looked fresh, so Joe decided to give it a try. He carefully fed the leader through the guides of the fly rod and grabbed the tip of the line once it was entirely through. Joe checked to make sure it hadn't twisted and then added a few feet of 5X tippet to the end using a triple surgeon's knot he'd practiced last week. He had to concentrate and stare intently at the thin lines with each knot he tied. As a kid, his dad made him tie all his own knots after he turned eight, and he got to be fast and effective at a few of them. He couldn't remember all the names yet, but the muscle memory was rebuilding. *Fat old fingers and declining eyesight are not a friend to the fly fishermen.*

Today is the 25th of July. Joe hadn't thought about the day of the week or the specific date in two weeks. He was just getting through each day. Pulling up the waders, he really could feel the warmth of the day. *Should've just wet waded.* The summer months bring lower, warmer water conditions in many freshwater bodies of water. The seasonal changes allow grasses to grow on the edges of the streams where water flows in the winter and spring. The encroaching warm weather grasses present opportunities for the upland, terrestrial insects to get closer to the water when their life cycles are peaking. Ants, beetles, cicadas, inchworms, crickets, and grasshoppers are drawn closer to the streams, and many fall into the water, offering up a great meal to trout hiding in the cool waters below.

Joe followed Alan's recommendation of using a dry-dropper rig. The composition of the rig includes a dry fly floating on the surface that is connected to a "dropper" fly that is suspended below the dry fly in the water column. The dry fly needs to be buoyant enough to resist sinking below the surface with the combined weight/drag of the dropper fly (or flies) and the drag on the tippet that connects the rig below the water surface. Larger dry flies that simulate stoneflies, grasshoppers, and crickets are optimal dry flies for this type of setup. They are often tied with craft foam, or they use deer hair or dense overlapping feathers that help the flies shed water and remain buoyant. The dropper flies are usually meant to sink, tempting fish who are feeding below the surface on nymphs or sunken terrestrial flies like caddis flies or inchworms.

Joe knew this would test his rusty skills, such as casting two flies without tangling the flies or determining how long to make the dropper without it constantly hanging up on the stream bed.

He tied on a big foam dry fly and a bead-head nymph while he scanned the water.

A shallow riffle traversed the channel bottom, concentrating the current into a narrow boulder-strewn run where the water was deeper with the green tint. Joe sent out a few casts and barely managed to prevent the line from tangling and missed his mark by a few feet to the left. It took him about ten casts to get his rhythm. He paused and took a deep breath. *Settle.* He tried to calm himself.

His next cast landed softly with the nymph plunging into the water and the dry fly settling into a smooth, drag-free drift. With a quick gold flash on the left of his fly, his heart started to race. It seemed like an eternity. No strike came, and the flash was gone. Joe exhaled with disappointment as his eyes shifted to look back where he saw the flash when unexpectedly the foam fly was violently tugged below the water surface. The trout circled and took the nymph and went for a run. It was a strong fish, pulling the line through Joe's fingers quickly until the line was tight against the reel. The shrubs and boulders around Joe were like an obstacle course. He constantly changed the angle of the rod and rotated his hip left and right to keep the fish from pulling into tree roots and rock crevices. He reeled the line until he could see the end of the fly line pull from the water and get close to the tip of the rod. The large trout tired, so Joe was able to lift the rod and pull it to the surface. He quickly scooped the sparsely spotted golden bellied brown trout into his net.

"Woohoo!"

Every fish brought him back to his childhood. *No wonder so many flies have names that sound like a thirteen-year-old boy named them.*

32

Tying Some Flies

After a couple hours, Joe had caught a handful of trout, each more beautiful than the last. The stream was more manicured than he was used to, but it was the centerpiece of the town and needed to have a park appeal. There was a pavilion along the stream near the western limits of the town, up out of the floodplain near a small parking area. A mom and her two young children sat at a table having some snacks. *Bringing the built environment together with the natural environment connects people to a space.* Joe appreciated how the town embraced the stream and made it an amenity for the community, instead of a nuisance to be managed, or a flow path for waste to be delivered out of town.

Reaching the pavilion Joe decided to head back to the motel for a siesta. But before his nap, he wanted to stop in and thank Alan for the fishing advice and for helping him think a little differently. Joe slipped off the waders and hung them over his shoulder and walked along the path back to town. It was probably two in the afternoon and the town still had the same steady buzz of people driving and walking through town. Not overly crowded or hectic, but vibrant. Joe had thought these types of towns were only busy on holiday weekends or during special events, and nearly deserted most of the time. It was good to see a lively town and the energy helped Joe feel part of something without being put upon to be someone.

Joe broke down his rod so that it was back in the neat tube that fit nicely in the back of his vest and walked into town. Charlie ran to greet him as he pushed open the fly shop door. A quick rub behind the ears and it seemed like Joe was making a new friend.

"How'd it go down there, Joe?"

Alan's friendly voice lifted Joe's head from the attention of the dog.

"I caught a handful of beautiful trout, and your advice was right on, thank you."

"That's great! It's nice for folks to have a beautiful stream so close to town. The local Trout Unlimited Chapter did a great job raising money to fix it up and it turned out real nice. Good thing that the Clean Water Act passed in the '70s, too. Paper mills can make folks some money, but they can also make a mess of the streams."

"Well, it certainly integrates the lively downtown area with a fantastic natural park area. It's a great space and there are trout! That makes everything better for me!"

"No doubt!"

"Also, Alan, I just wanted to thank you for talking to me about the boy. I reacted but wasn't thinking about anything other than serving as the self-proclaimed sheriff of Big Town. You're a thoughtful fellow. I appreciate it. You got me thinking."

"Thank you. I've been through a lot myself, and with my boys I also went through a lot. I learned things the hard way. My kids taught me more than I taught them. Overreacting is part of the journey."

"My wife and I weren't able to have kids, so I don't have that experience, but I was thinking about what you said while I was fishing and I just wanted to thank you."

"You are welcome. Fly fishing is good for your soul and helps to get your mind right. Glad I could be a part of that. Hey, listen. Are you busy tomorrow?"

"Yeah, busy with nothing."

"We are having a free fly-tying class tomorrow at 5 p.m. It's pretty informal, but a few of the local fly tiers come by and sit around and tie some flies. You're invited to stop by. It's a nice gathering."

"I don't have a vice and I haven't tied in years, so…"

"Don't worry about that. I have extra vices and a bunch of materials you can use. Stop by. You may meet some interesting characters."

"Sounds good, thanks."

"Oh! Is there a place in town, within walking distance, where I can get a few art supplies? I was hoping to get a few things."

"Yes. It's called Creative Crafts, off Barn Street across from the Mill Theatre. It's about a five-minute walk. Everything in town is about a five-minute walk."

"The energy of the town is impressive. It's really amazing how many stores are here."

"About the time the stream project was undertaken, a family from New York invested in the theater and the town just got revitalized, building off the popularity of the theater. It's not common for most small towns, but the energy here has picked up and has stayed solid. It's a real success story. This place wasn't far from death in the late '80s early '90s. It's great."

"It is a great town. I hope to see you tomorrow. Thanks again for the flies."

"See you soon, Joe."

Joe stopped off at the art store and picked up a small pan set of watercolors, thin sketching pencils, a small sharpener, and three small synthetic brushes. He wanted to get back to the motel, paint his clearest memory of the day, and take a nap. His body still felt stiff from the accident and there were moments when his thoughts were still scattered. Joe noticed that his concentration felt improved after exerting the mental energy to track the flies while trying to have a drag-free drift. *Fly fishing is good for your soul.* Alan's words still lingered in Joe's mind.

Joe went to the sink, took the plastic wrap off of one the small plastic cups, and filled it a half an inch or so with water. He tore out a sheet from the back of the pack and divided it into four swatches, so he could test the colors. Sketching the arrangements of boulders and some flow paths of the water through the stream from memory gave Joe some artistic license. He felt pressure in trying to match the exact site in situ, but here in the motel, he was relaxing and reconnecting to his joy on the water.

His mind was completely clear as he made the quick painting. The last brush stroke was similar to the last cast in that his mind started racing and to dark places. *She is gone. What am I supposed to do?* He thought back to Cindy saying that Jody was helping him to find his purpose again. Painting and fishing were nice distractions, but were they just that? Distractions? *Maybe I can just add more distractions? Maybe I should tie some flies tomorrow.*

33

The Photo

The red light on the top right corner of the motel phone flashed before the phone rang, catching Joe's eyes and breaking the silence he was enjoying while finishing his painting.

"Joe?"

"Yes."

"This is Officer Baker. I have your paperwork and summons for the court case. I'm right around the corner. I was hoping to drop it off. Does that work for you?"

"Sure thing."

Nothing like a call from a cop about my pending court case to break my contemplation of a nice day fishing. The knock came within five minutes.

"Hey, Joe."

"Good afternoon, Officer Baker."

"I wanted to drop this off for you and explain anything, if you had any questions. I do have some good news."

"Says the man handing me a summons."

Chuck smiled at Joe's dry humor.

"I was able to get you on the docket for Monday. Fastest I've ever gotten a case in the system. You can hopefully get everything settled before your car is repaired."

"Do you think there is any chance I'll get jail time?"

"It's incredibly unlikely. I haven't seen it before on a first-time offense or for an open container citation, so don't be a jerk in court."

"Fair enough. Thanks for everything. Hey, I met your father today. He's quite the enlightened fellow."

"Ha! He wasn't always that way. That's a relatively recent transformation. Raising three boys after losing your wife will either kill you or help you grow. Thankfully for all of us, Dad followed the latter path."

"Oh, I'm sorry to hear about your mom. I had no idea."

"How would you know? She died when I was thirteen, so what is that, twenty-two years ago? Yeah, it was tough. Aged my dad, I wasn't sure he'd make it through. He just would say, 'I have to put one foot in front of the other. That's all I need to do.' I heard him muttering that over and over again. When one of us was getting in trouble and he needed to pick us up at school or the precinct, he would just keep saying that."

"I like him even more. You were a handful, huh?"

"Three boys. We were three boys full of piss and vinegar. He had his hands full, yeah. He's a good man. But he's still hard on me and my brothers. The other two moved out west, so we don't see them often. I think they needed a break from him. But we get together to fish once a year."

"Sounds fun and like family."

A loud chirp came over his two-way radio.

"Officer Baker, this is Dispatch."

"Alright, Joe. I have a call. I'll see ya soon."

Joe sat on the bed holding the summons. The paper felt sharp and rigid, not warm and soft like the watercolor paper. *I'll deal with this later. I need to go for a walk.*

Joe checked his pockets for his wallet, phone, and keys, and headed out. He wanted to explore the town, but he was also hungry and really felt like going back to the diner. Talking with someone he sort of knew was a better prospect than eating entirely alone. He hoped Georgia was still working. He wanted someone to talk to.

Opening the door, he saw she wasn't there. Elvis was playing from the jukebox and the crowd was more subdued than the sleepy but cheery morning patrons and wait staff. Even without a morning rush and Georgia directing traffic, it was still welcoming. With a menu bigger than the town phone book, Joe knew he wouldn't get bored eating here often, at least for a little bit. Even with Jody, Joe preferred the same three or four restaurants and often ordered the same thing at each spot.

Since Georgia wasn't there and he couldn't catch up on the news of the day, he decided to sit at one of the booths. There were photos from the town all along the wall of the booth. Easter egg hunts, football games, Fourth of July parades, grade school graduations…all seemingly distributed roughly by decade. He had no idea why it hadn't come to him before. *Jody may be in one of these photos.*

From the best he could tell, his booth featured photos from sometime in the '50s. A Chevrolet Bel Air was next to a '56 Corvette in one of the photos. He didn't know much about cars, but the '56 Corvette was always his dad's favorite. "That car is just sexy." He could hear his voice in his head. And that was the only time he ever heard his dad say that word.

Jody was born in 1969. She left the town when she was eighteen, so she'd have only been in the photos from the early 1970s to 1987. Joe wasn't sure if he'd recognize Jody as a young child; she literally had one photo of her and her parents, from her confirmation when she was fourteen years old. Now, his curiosity was overrunning him. He quickly ate his chicken parmigiana. The diner was clearing out and he asked his waitress if he could look around at the photos. She replied, "It's a free country," with all the charm the saying generates and then asked Joe if he could grab the ketchup bottles off the booths for him. She was not Georgia, but he grabbed the bottles to be polite.

A nervous anticipation was building as he looked through each booth. He otherwise may have felt some enjoyment looking through the pictorial history of the town and seeing the changes of the community over time. But now his brain had a focus.

He had gone through five booths and was tired of getting ketchup on his finger from the drippings on the bottles. One more to go. And there it was. She was probably in her late teens. It looked like a photo from a baseball game. She was with three other kids about her age. Two boys and one other young lady. He took a picture of the photo with his phone. Now he really had something to talk to Georgia about.

34

Coffee and Water

Joe is not a morning person. But today he woke up early around 6 a.m. Since his dinner last night and the discovery of a photo with Jody, his mind was running through scenarios of who the people were and what the backstory was. Suddenly he felt like a detective. He thought back to all the conversations he had with Jody about her childhood. She so rarely spoke about it that Joe knew very little about her before her time in college. She had no family, and no friends before she was 19 that were still in her life. There was a depth to her pain that was so intense when she described the car accident that took her parents, he didn't want to see her experience the trauma associated with those memories again.

So I am stranded in the town that she grew up in. A part of her life I know nothing about. I may need to turn over some stones.

The diner opened at 6:30. He was hoping Georgia was there. He hoped she could tell him about the photo and what she knew of Jody. His palms were sweaty. Each step down the sidewalk and across the street built his anxiety.

Joe got to the door right at 6:30.

"Sunshine!" Georgia opened the door with an overload of enthusiasm. An older gentleman was waiting for the diner to open as well.

"Good morning, Judge Perkins!" *Judge Perkins.* "The usual?"

"Yes, Georgia. Thank you."

The judge sat at the counter on the corner stool. Joe froze. *Will this be the judge that hears my case?*

"Howdy, Joe!"

"Hi there, Georgia. Is it okay if I sit in that booth?"

"Sure thing. I'll get you a menu in a second."

Joe sat nearly at the opposite end of the diner from the judge. Georgia handed Joe the menu.

"Coffee?"

"Yes, and water please."

"Oh, yeah right. Coming right up." She switched gears to talking to the judge while grabbing the pot of coffee.

"How are things going with your foster child there, Georgia?"

"He's a good kid, but taking some patience at the moment. Just trying to help him feel like someone cares about him."

"You are a treasure."

"Thanks, Judge. Your food will be up in a second."

Now Joe's mind was spinning. *Was Georgia the foster parent for the kid he grabbed at the Fly Shop? Let's stay focused.*

She dropped off the coffee.

"Hey, Georgia. I found a photo last night when I was in here for dinner."

"Dinner? You're becoming a regular already. I told you the home fries were good."

Joe started to get choked up. His breath skipped trying not to cry. Joe felt Georgia slow her voice and warm her eyes.

"Okay, Joe. What photo and what does it mean to you?

"It's in this booth...my wife..." Joe was struggling to find the words.

"It's okay, honey."

"She just passed away a few months ago. And there is a picture of her here, when she was a kid, well sort of a kid."

"Holy shit, Joe. I'm so sorry to hear of your loss. Which photo is it?"

Joe pointed to the photo. "Jody…"

"Jody Murphy?"

"Yes." *She knew Jody.*

"Holy shit, Joe. Let me…let me get the judge his food and I'll be right back."

The judge sat up more rigidly on his stool. It caught Joe's eye. It appeared as if the judge wanted to listen but refused to turn his head. Georgia grabbed the judge's food and slid it over to him on the counter with a small bottle of Tabasco.

"Looks good! Need anything else?"

"Nope. Thanks as always, Georgia."

"You're welcome, honey."

She scurried back to Joe's booth and sat across from Joe. He sat there, staring blankly at the coffee mug he was holding in both hands. A small plume of steam rose right between his eyes.

"She was your wife? Can you talk to me, Joe?" Georgia broke his stare.

"Jody." Joe slowly spoke. "She was my world. Breast cancer took her in May. She never really spoke about her childhood, but I knew she grew up here. All I know is that her parents died in a car accident and she never came back here. Did you know her? I feel like I'm walking back in time and I'm terrified of what I will find."

"Joe, I'm so sorry. I knew her, but not well. I will tell you all I know. I was ten years older than her, so I was out in the world and not here in Remberg when she was in high school. But I know some of her story. It was so tragic."

Joe was fighting back tears. "Can…can you share some with me…"

"Of course. I don't know the other girl and boy in the photo. They must've been friends with Jody. Jody is sitting next to her boyfriend. His name was Cody Franklin. He was a year older than Jody, I believe."

Georgia's breath slowed, and she looked intensely at Joe. All at once Joe felt like his life's course was going to be altered by the next words that Georgia uttered. Every breath felt heavy, like he was suffocating.

Georgia closed her eyes and pushed the story forward.

"He was a heck of a baseball player. A real big deal around here. That's a big part of why I know the story. Even when I was in California, my mom would mention how good of a pitcher he was, leading the school to the state finals and all that. He graduated and was drafted by the Brewers or the Cubs or something like that. Poor kid blew out his elbow in the first season in the minors. He came back to get an award for his high school accomplishments after the injury. I think that's when the photo was taken, about a year after he graduated. Well, he left to go back to the Midwest to rehab his injury, but he couldn't deal with it and he committed suicide."

Joe let out a deep breath. *What a traumatic event to process as a kid. I just wish she could've talked to me.* His chest tightened and his grip on the coffee mug did the same.

"It was awful; our community was devastated." Georgia paused. Joe looked up from the mug, and his eyes connected with Georgia. She looked terrified, commiserate with the devastating news she shared. It was so close to the look in the doctor's face when they heard the diagnosis.

"I can't imagine how Jody handled that at that age..." Joe's brain was trying to stay connected to what Georgia was saying, but the details were flooding him and he couldn't process how Jody shut this all out of her life with him.

Georgia shook and broke eye contact with Joe.

"I can't remember the exact timing of everything, but Jody's parents died within a few weeks of Cody in that car accident. They were hit by a drunk driver, I believe."

"That's the only detail I knew." Joe pushed the words out without taking a breath.

"Two awful tragedies stacked up on that girl within a month. From what my mom told me, Jody was such a sweet girl and so helpful around town. She especially was respectful of the older folks in the community. But after her parents died and Cody died, she just disappeared. Sold her parents' house and she was gone. Folks said she moved to New York City or was in Binghamton for a bit. But no one could blame her. Poor kid. Poor Cody's parents were so heart broken, within a few years they had both passed as well. Just one of the saddest situations ever."

Joe's eyes dropped back to the coffee. His right hand rubbed his forehead and he pressed his head down onto his hand. He wanted to wipe the pain away. It took all he had not to break down.

"Joe? Joe? You okay? I understand why she wouldn't want to talk about it."

Georgia's words were laden with sympathy. Joe knew his face must have been transparent to the gravity of how her words were impacting him. There was nothing he could do to conceal how many emotions flooded him. She got up and put her hand on Joe's shoulder. He burst into tears.

All that time. All that pain. I wish she would've told me. Joe teetered between devastating sadness and anger. *Could I have helped her? Did she really trust me? I can't even imagine the pain.*

"Listen. Joe. You're one of us now; you're connected to all of us. Okay? I'll help you learn whatever you want or nothing at all..."

"I just...I don't..."

"Joe, I just dumped a lifetime of pain on top of the lifetime of pain you just experienced. Maybe I shouldn't have shared like that."

"No...no...no...don't do that...I needed to know."

Georgia sat back down and reached for Joe's hand. The judge quietly left the cash for his bill on the counter and eased out the door. The kitchen was quiet. Joe stared at the picture and his heart broke for Jody. He wished he could hug her one more time. Georgia's hand felt like the only thing holding him from falling into a giant hole.

35

Beneath the Surface

Joe couldn't eat. His stomach was in knots. He sat with Georgia in silence for what felt like a lifetime. He made himself smile wondering if this was the longest Georgia had ever sat quietly. *Why do I always find the joke? I can never sit long in the pain.*

"Georgia, I don't think I can eat. I think I need to take a walk. I'll be back later."

"Coffee's on the house Joe. I insist. Don't even say anything."

"Thank you."

Each footstep felt like it was getting stuck in mud, gaining weight with each movement and dragging a trail of muck behind him. His head was spinning, his chest was tight, and his arms and legs were all on different rhythms. He needed to get to the river. The sound of the river drew him closer and helped him shake off the mud, clearing his mind. Joe let his mind wander and he heard his dad's voice quoting Heraclitus, "No man ever steps in the same river twice, for it's not the same river and he's not the same man."

Joe found a flat rock on the river's edge. He sat still staring at the water. After many minutes, he started to see activity in the water. Dozens of tiny fish darting, sometimes in pairs, other times in a solitary, continuous search. A crawfish scampered and propelled itself

106

backwards. With a puff of sediment, it was hidden under one of the many rocks interlocked in the stream bed.

Joe noticed the water surface changes, some abrupt and some subtle. The presence of underwater rocks and some large, exposed boulders created breaks in the smooth water surface. Underneath the surface, turbulence and current streams flowed by the irregular rocks that comprise the riverbed. Those irregularities produced pathways and hiding spots for everything that lives underneath the surface. Joe thought of Jody and how he saw her. *How did I not see what was below the surface?*

He thought back to the nights when they talked about having children. They tried for a short time. He remembered the night that Jody approached him and said she couldn't try anymore. "I'm not meant to be a mother," she would say when she had grit in her voice and sharpened eyes. "I don't want to share you with anyone else," she would say when she was light and playful. "I can't go through it, Joe. It's too much..." She never finished that sentence and he never pushed her.

It was too scary to push; he could tell it was her limit. He didn't want to live without her and now he wasn't sure he gave her all she needed. He wanted to be her rock, and he hoped he was. He wanted to be the love of her life, and he hoped he was. Now all he had was a story of their lives he wanted to hold onto. It was true to him when she said, "I do," and true when she died in his arms. It was true to him now.

His eyes went back to the river. He stared until his eyes blurred. His pulse slowed and his emotions diluted. A splash followed by a young voice yelling, "Oh, my god!" awoke Joe from his trance. Curiosity moved into the blank space his mind had created to distract him from his distress. With a quick turn of the head, he snapped back to consciousness. Joe pushed off the rock and got to his feet quickly. He moved in agile steps along the dry rock tops at the river's edge until he rounded the corner enough to gain vision of the downstream angler past the alders and dogwoods obstructing his view.

The young angler had their back turned to him. The rod was bent over and the line was taut, pulling quickly downstream of the fly fisher. The angler was moving the rod from one side of their body to the other, fighting the large fish with skill but they were giving ground. Joe thought the angler was younger so his "Don't mess with another angler" filter turned off, as if his age allowed him to tell someone younger what to do. "Don't let it get too far downstream of you! You won't be able to land it."

The head of the angler turned to see Joe heading down the river and quickly turned back to the line pulling away downstream. This was obviously a very large fish. Joe still couldn't make out the face or identity of the angler, but he felt compelled to help, even without an invitation to do so and continued moving downstream. "Move downstream of the fish!"

The angler furiously reeled in line and high stepped down the shallow margin of the stream to the head of the next pool, water splashing as they frantically moved to gain an advantageous position. Joe gained ground and was within feet of the young man.

"Want me to net the fish?"

The young man nodded and pulled his net from behind his back. He tossed the net to Joe. Joe bobbled the net and stumbled to his left but was able to keep his balance and get in position.

The fish pulled toward a large logjam against the stream bank. The angler dropped the rod to the lower position parallel to the water, putting side pressure on the head of the fish. If the fish made it to the large rootwad protruding from the accumulation of logs, there was a good chance the line would snap against the sharp roots. Joe gained ground and was within forty feet of the entangled pair. *Is this Evan? No, Ethan?* "Ethan?"

The angler turned his head with a look of panic. It was Ethan. He looked as if his hand was caught in the cookie jar and he contemplated running for the hills. Joe exclaimed, "Keep your eyes on that fish!"

Ethan turned back. Joe fired off more instructions.

"It's getting tired. As soon as it stops pulling, direct it over towards me and keep pressure on it and keep the head up!"

Ethan followed suit and led the fish to Joe. Joe dropped the net under the fish's head and quickly raised the net.

"Woohoo!"

Joe held the net in his left hand and raised his right hand to high five Ethan. Ethan's head tilted, confused at the whole scenario that just unfolded. He reluctantly slapped Joe's hand. Joe handed Ethan the net.

"Congratulations, young man. That's a fish of a lifetime. I've never caught one that big."

Ethan looked down at the fish, which looked every bit of twenty-four inches long. He dropped on his butt in the shallows of the stream, looking at the fish and then at Joe, shaking his head in amazed disbelief.

"Hi. I'm Joe. That's a hell of a fish."

36

Half Pint

The tail of the brown trout thrashed outside of the net. The golden yellow belly of the fish glowed like fireflies against the dark green water. As Ethan grabbed the tail and lifted it out of the net, Joe could tell it was a male, with its large, hooked jaw, commonly referred to as a kype. It looked medieval—dangerous and beautiful simultaneously.

"Do you mind taking a photo with my phone?" Ethan quietly asked, still shaking from the adrenaline rush of fighting such a large fish.

"Of course."

Joe carefully held the phone and took a few pictures, handing it back to the boy, making sure not to drop it in the water. Ethan was beaming. He then directed the fish's head into the current and held the fish in the water until it regained its strength and rapidly propelled itself back into the hidden depths of the stream.

"You've obviously caught quite a few fish."

Ethan nodded. Joe appreciated the skill and effort needed to catch and land this fish and was impressed by the respect Ethan gave the fish in such a gentle release.

Ethan looked back at Joe, the excitement of the catch was waning and suspicion edged back into his eyes. Joe noticed the fly Ethan was using. It was a streamer, meant to imitate a small baitfish or crawfish.

The fly was well constructed, with overlapping white and mustard colored mallard flank feathers. The light feathers bounced in the water and had some translucence looking to Joe like a juvenile brown trout or dace. Joe hadn't ever been able to tie a fly of that size, with that complexity and beauty, even after getting mangled by the biggest brown trout he'd ever seen.

"What kind of streamer is that? I've never seen one before." Joe inquired.

Ethan started to gather his gear and stepped backward from Joe.

"It's called a half-pint. Learned it on You-Tube. Did you call me Ethan?"

Joe felt caught. "Yes, is that your name?"

"Dude, this is creepy." Ethan took two more steps backward and turned to put more distance between himself and Joe.

"I was in the fly shop yesterday." Joe started to explain and Ethan bolted up the bank and onto the trail.

"That's a killer fly man!" Joe yelled as Ethan was out of sight, hoping there may be a chance for them to talk about that fish and fly eventually.

I couldn't even relate to many kids when I was their age, not sure why it would be easier now.

The excitement of the fish had cleared Joe's mind. *There is no way, I would've thought that big of a fish was lurking beneath the surface of the water. Fits the lesson of the day.*

Joe walked back upstream to the rock. In all the ruckus he'd left his drawing tablet and watercolors. His mind was now focused on Ethan. *It is very cool that he tied that beautiful fly. Unfortunately, he stole the feathers to make it.*

Why am I caring about this kid? He's obviously got artistic skill and passion for fishing. But even with skill and passion you can end up a thief or worse. "People shouldn't waste potential." Jody's words rang back in his mind and he said them out loud. Joe felt her back with him again. She always looked to help people in need, especially kids.

It was nice to get his mind off of the morning's conversation. And that fish! That was amazing. Joe looked at his inception of a watercolor sketch, gathered it up and all the supplies. *I was meant to learn more about her and I was meant to be here. She is with me. I can't give in to wallowing, I know where that leads. She wants more for me than that.*

Today was Friday. He had the weekend and then his court case. Joe's brain typically operated linearly, he had a task and he saw it through to the end. All his mental lists had evaporated, dissolved into a photo. There was a puzzle and he'd do his best to find the pieces, but he couldn't wallow. He knew he needed to prepare some for the court appearance, and he needed something to wear. He needed to get back on track.

Joe walked by Stewart's Garage and poked his head in one of the bays. "Seth?"

"Yessir!" Seth stepped out from behind a Ford Explorer, while John Coltrane played in the garage. "Mr. Barden. How ya doing?"

"Good, just wanted to check in. Any word on the parts you need?"

"Got a notification this morning. We're still about seven to eight days away from getting all we need and then it's probably another three or four days to put it together and get it all painted. That work for you? Oh, and all the insurance stuff went through, so all good there."

"That's good news. I don't really have a choice or anywhere to go, so the schedule works for me. Thanks for letting me pop in."

"No worries, anytime. Catch any today?"

"I was just sitting by the stream, but I saw the young man…Ethan I think is his name. He caught what must've been a twenty-four-inch brown. Just amazing fish."

"That kid is always fishing back through there. He's hooked. Ha! No pun intended, but I'll take it. Too bad fishing isn't a class in school."

"No doubt. Thanks, Seth."

Next stop was Baker's Fly Shop. It amazed Joe that within ten minutes he could walk to nearly any type of store he needed. Not having to drive was a nice plus. With a squeak the heavy door opened and he heard the jingle of Charlie's collar. "Howdy, Joe! Been on the river?"

"Saw Ethan hook a monster."

"So, you two are on a first name basis now?"

"Not quite. But I netted the fish. Had to be over twenty inches, maybe 2twenty-four. Male. Thing was a brute."

"There ain't many of those in there. That's quite the catch. I'd love a picture of that for the shop."

"Well, he's got one on his phone. I took it."

"You are on a first name basis there, Warden."

Joe chuckled, "Well, I don't think I'd mind him teaching me how to tie that fly. A streamer called the "Half Pint.""

"I'll have to look that one up. Come by at 5 tonight and we can try to tie it. I'll have some pizza, but no beer though. I can't be seen as serving here. Chuck takes that stuff seriously."

"Sure, sounds good. I'm good with pizza, but I don't drink anymore, so I'm better without beer around."

"Fair enough."

"Hey, is there a place where I can get a respectful jacket and khakis?"

"Well, there is a shop called Vintage Threads off Valley Street just two blocks west of the motel. You'll either look trendy or buy something you wore in 1995. Any type of larger store and you'll need a ride towards Binghamton."

"Vintage Threads it is. Thanks, Alan. I'll see you tonight."

"Sounds good, I'll look up that fly. Half Pint, right?"

"Indeed."

Back in the fresh air, it felt good to have some things to do and to have people to talk with. It felt like the longest day since the funeral, and it was only noon.

37

Tying Flies

Joe was able to find a sports coat, a pair of pants, and a collared shirt in the vintage store. He hadn't been in many of those types of stores, but it seemed like the owner spent more time picking out the furniture than the clothes they sold. He went back to the motel and opened up his laptop for the first time in days. Researching the court and the process of the hearing was sobering and helpful. He would tell the truth and see what happened. Judge Perkins oversaw the court in the County Seat and would hear the case. Whatever the result, Joe would face it. Tonight he was going to tie some flies and hopefully he could talk someone into taking him to the West Branch of the Delaware River over the weekend.

It had only been a few days, but Joe was enjoying walking through the town and he looked forward to being greeted by Charlie at the fly shop. The jingle of his collar was enough to put a smile on his face. He reached down to pet the spaniel and heard Alan's strong voice, "Good to see you, Joe."

"Alan, how are you, sir?"

"Good. Come back and join us. There's pizza on the table."

Joe looked up to see Chuck sitting next to Alan, each of them tying small dry flies in the jaws of two vices. On their left was Georgia and Ethan. "Howdy there, Joe!" Georgia's voice was warm and welcoming, but had a tint of gentleness, like a friend checking in on someone in pain.

"Hi, Georgia. I didn't expect to see you here."

"This is art and crafts for old fishermen and women, right?"

"Something like that," Alan chuckled.

"Joe, Ethan showed me that picture of the hog of a brown he caught. Best one I've seen in years."

"Best one I've ever seen." Joe couldn't help but add. Ethan blushed and frowned with his head down and eyes focused on spinning the thread around the hook securing the hackle feathers to the parachute-style fly.

"I'm used to the hot glue gun style of crafts and I got the fingers to prove it, but this is pretty fun!" Georgia had the timing down on when to rescue someone from embarrassment.

"I haven't tied a fly in about thirty-five years, so I'm going to need some help." Joe sat down at a table and fiddled with the vice.

"This is a no judgment zone, Joe, and we can help you." Alan pulled together a bobbin loaded with a brown thread, some small nymph hooks, a pack of hare's ear dubbing and some tinsel.

"Let's start with a Hare's Ear, a real simple one. Seriously though, Ethan, when any friend of the fly shop catches a trout twenty inches or greater, we put a picture up over the waders. Can you send me a photo of it? I want to credit you for the catch and show off for the customers."

Ethan looked up. "Sure, that's okay."

The door opened and a loud voice boomed, "Chuck! Good to see ya big man!"

Joe recognized the voice but couldn't quite place it until David stood up from petting Charlie.

"Joe, good to see you! How are you feeling?"

"David, likewise, good to see you. I'm feeling pretty good."

"Good, good. PIZZA!" David sounded like a grown-up Cookie Monster. Georgia shook her head with a sideways smile watching David devour a slice of pepperoni.

Joe watched Ethan carefully wrap thin olive thread around a size sixteen dry fly hook and surgically cut off the waste piece of the line. He clumped together some dubbing, separating the fibers and repeatedly stacking the fibers, getting them all aligned. Alan spoke up.

"Joe, Ethan is making the tail by a technique called 'carding.' It helps make a bushy tail."

"Thanks, Alan."

Joe appreciated the instruction. Ethan kept his head down, concentrating intensely on the fly, letting the attention fly right by him.

Joe tried to put a hook in the vice. There were new levers and a lot of time passed since he had last tied flies. He was embarrassed to ask anyone to help him. He felt completely inadequate. Georgia caught his eye and subtly motioned towards a small level off the back of the vice jaws, flipped the lever and took her hook out of the jaws, and then quickly put it back and lowered the lever. Joe smiled. She had a talent for helping people, no matter how small the need.

With a simple overlap of thread, it was bound to the hook with three or four wraps. Joe moved the thread covering the hook from the eye to the start of the bend. Georgia brought some of the rabbit's fur dubbing and set it in front of Joe.

"Take less than you think you need. Just enough to cover the line."

"Gotcha."

He picked up a wisp of the fur in his fingers. It had a translucent quality, with longer, thicker "guard hairs" mixed with the finer hair. Joe mimicked carding the fur as Ethan had done. Joe pinched the stacked fur and lashed it down at the end of the hook with four strong wraps. A smile came over his face. *I made a tail.* He looked up and everyone was smiling back at him in silence.

"Been a long time since I've done this. It's fun and less stressful than designing a library."

"I bet, Joe!" Chuck jumped in. "Now you have to tie in the gold tinsel and dubbing on the model. About two-thirds of the hook shank."

"Thanks Chuck." Joe smiled and followed the instructions.

Ethan was on to his next fly.

"Man, kiddo. You are good and quick!" Georgia doted on the young man. He didn't look up but he did offer a quiet, "Thanks."

Concentrating on the individual thread wraps and securing each material was very satisfying to Joe. David and Chuck continually gave each other a hard time, making the atmosphere light and funny. Joe learned that all the adults had left the town for a while and all made their ways back. They seemed to really care about each other and actually put forth effort to be friends. Besides Jody and his friends from high school, Joe found most people to be transactional. This was different and nice. He was even able to make Ethan smile by the end of the night. He didn't look up, but he smiled.

Approaching 10 p.m., Alan was calling it a night. Everyone was packing up the supplies and a vice if they brought one. Georgia's flies were voted the most likely to catch a fisherman by the group.

"I want a trophy for that!" she exclaimed.

"By the way boys, I have morning shift at the diner tomorrow. Anyone want to fish with Ethan in the morning?" Ethan looked at Georgia sideways, without turning his head.

"Not to be a pest, but I was also looking for a ride to try and hit the West Branch of the Delaware if possible." Joe decided not to be shy.

"Well, I think I could get my arm twisted into fishing the West Branch there, Chuck!" David jumped on the bandwagon.

Chuck's eyes moved back and forth between David and his father. Joe squinted while forcing a grin at Chuck.

"Don't look at me. I have a shop to run," Alan responded to his son's delayed response.

"I am coaching a youth baseball game at 3, so I have to go early. But I did hear there's been a 10 a.m. BWO hatch. Might be fun. I'll drive."

Joe saw a slight smile creep over Ethan's face, but he was being stingy with his eye contact. "What time, Chuck?"

"I'll pick you up at 5:45, Joe. Then get you, David. You're only a few blocks away. I'll stop and pick up Ethan around 6:15."

Georgia was appreciative, "Thank you so much. Chuck. That's right when I need to head to the diner. You're a peach."

"You're Georgia's Peach!" David couldn't resist the joke. Everyone laughed, except Ethan. Joe couldn't tell if he wasn't listening, didn't register the innuendo, or was just so grossed out that he refused to process it.

"Back in my day, boys!" Georgia was beaming as the center of attention.

"Easy, easy, Georgia." Alan was having no part of that joke continuing. Charlie rubbed up against Alan's leg.

"Alright all, I need to take Charlie for a walk and close up. See you all tomorrow. One more thing, I'll bet you all lunch at the diner that Ethan catches the biggest fish, and text me that photo!"

38

The Delaware

Over the course of the evening tying flies, Joe managed to throw enough fur and feathers on hooks to make five flies. He was proud of them: a couple Hare's Ears, a couple Pheasant Tails, and a wooly bugger. Joe was excited about fishing the Delaware. The whole point of his interrupted drive was to fish the West Branch. It was hard to admit, but the thought of having some fishing buddies, hell, any buddies at all, was enough to get Joe out of bed without snoozing the first alarm at 5:20 a.m. Maybe he could get Ethan to say more than two words at a time. Chuck would be there at 5:45 and Joe had to have his gear together. Joe also needed some coffee from the tiny motel coffee maker and he made that first.

A strong knock on the door startled Joe. Chuck was early. "Joe! The fish are biting!" Chuck's voice carried through the door.

"You're going to wake the neighbors, Chuck!"

"You don't have any neighbors, Joe! And this is a better way than how I wake up most people I have to visit early in the morning."

"I can only imagine. I bet you have some stories."

"Fish stories are the best stories. Grab your gear. I'm not awake enough yet for work stories."

Joe nearly forgot his coffee, running back to get it after sitting in the car. But Joe was able to get all his gear without forgetting anything and loaded it all into the back of Chuck's 4Runner. Chuck made another stop to pick up David, who wasn't quite as chipper.

"Late night?" Chuck inquired.

"I shouldn't have stopped at the pub after fly tying." David grumbled with his right hand holding his stomach.

"Well suck it up, buttercup. It's time to fish!" Chuck was busting David's balls.

"Listen, I'm going to pick up Ethan. Not sure how much of his back story you know. His mom, Kimberly, overdosed about 10 months ago. She was a real mess. I locked her up several times, all drug related. Child services got involved, whole deal. I don't ever remember seeing the dad. Kimberly said he was a real deadbeat."

David chipped in, "I remember her; she made a few visits to the ER."

"Yeah, personal care and responsibility didn't register with her as much as it should have. She loved the boy, got him to school, and he was on the T-ball and little league teams we helped coach. But she couldn't stay clean for long. Ethan was the one who found her. He's been sullen and quiet since then. Understandably, he is intolerant of drugs and alcohol at this point in his life, and I'm hoping he stays that way, but let's not make a thing out of the hangover."

"I feel like an ass. Didn't put two and two together." David sank into the back seat even further.

"You didn't know, but I wanted to warn you. Georgia and my dad have a real soft spot for him."

"We should treat him like a fisherman. After watching him fish and tie flies, he's a better angler than me. He's still a kid, but barely, and he's lived a lot of life already. But what do I know? I don't have kids," Joe chimed in.

"Treating him like one of the guys is a good idea. But don't try too hard. Kids can smell that a mile away," Chuck advised.

"Speaking of smell, crack a window, and you should probably move to the front seat when we pick him up." Joe jumped in to make fun of David's odor.

"Dude, three days ago I was wheeling you around an emergency room."

"I almost arrested him. Got you beat. We're here." The conversation lightened and they were laughing like old friends.

Before the three car doors opened, Georgia was three steps into her front yard.

"Morning boys! Here are some blueberry muffins. Ethan is ready to go and I have to get to work! Have fun."

"Thanks, Georgia!"

Joe took the muffins and headed back to the SUV. David opened the back hatch and helped Ethan load his gear.

"You ready, man?" David greeted Ethan.

"Yeah." Ethan was alert and awake but not ready for small talk.

Ethan got in the back seat next to Joe. Chuck and David hopped in and they headed off honking the horn to Georgia as they turned from the street.

"Have you fished the West Branch of the Delaware before?" Joe made another attempt at small talk.

"No, I've only fished at Mill Creek and the farm ponds," Ethan responded.

"Nice. You seem to have Mill Creek down. What are you thinking of using today, fly wise?"

"I'm going to nymph, probably a mop fly and a frenchie. But I'm going to check the bugs when I get there. I'll turn over some rocks."

Joe smiled. *Funny he used that phrase.* "Sounds good. I'll try that, too."

In another twenty minutes of driving, with only the occasional gastrointestinal noise from David as the soundtrack, they arrived at the river.

Looking out at the river, Joe's first thought was that it's much bigger than the streams he has fished in the past week. He couldn't remember fishing it as a child, but there was a photo in his album of his dad fishing somewhere along the banks. The river was approximately one-hundred feet wide near the parking area.

"Okay, boys." Chuck offered some advice. "I know it's bigger than Penns and Mill Creek by a bit. You just have to dissect larger streams into smaller sections and fish each small section. A few casts at a time and then find the next seam. There are BWO's and some caddis that may come off, so look for those and terrestrials should be good, especially beetles. Do you have any of those?"

"I have some ants and hoppers, but no beetles." Joe looked into his fly box.

"No worries. I'll get you some here in a second. Ethan, do you have any terrestrials?"

"Beetles and ants."

"Nice. We should stay within earshot or at least in sight of each other. Wading can be tricky. How about Joe and Ethan start near each other and keep an eye on each other?"

"I'm good with that. Are you, Ethan?"

"Sure."

David was dragging, getting his rod together and weaving the line through the guides. He must've dropped the leader back through the third guide four times before he could finish rigging the line. Chuck's brow furrowed as he glanced at David.

"I'll wait for molasses here and then we'll head downstream of you both a bit.

Joe looked across the stream and picked some specific zones to fish. Chuck handed him a beetle and Joe tied it on a long section of 5x tippet. Off the bend of the hook, he added a small pheasant tail dropper about eighteen inches below the beetle. Ethan set up a double nymph rig with a mop as the point fly and a frenchie off a tag, approximately eighteen inches above the mop.

With Joe's first step, his foot slid forward and he lost his balance. His right hand held the rod high and the left arm reached back missing the tree branch. Now flailing, he was headed for the ground with a crash. Water splashed on his face and chest, mud caked the left side of his hips and his left leg. His fall felt like it took thirty seconds, although he knew it was a second or two. Joe's cheeks flushed and he wasn't sure if his hip was bruised more than his ego. He counted to five to see if the pain shifted. David and Chuck reacted quickly, moving towards Joe. But Ethan was already there, reaching out his hand.

"You alright, Mr. Joe?"

Joe grabbed his hand.

"Thanks. I'm embarrassed and my ass hurts, but I'm okay. Thanks, man."

"You're welcome." Ethan smiled.

"Need to walk around or get checked or anything?" David was in nurse mode. "Also, great form protecting your fly rod."

"I'm good, thanks. Great start to the day."

"Well, you've scared all the fish for a bit, but I think a fall is good luck for big fish right?" David tried to inject some humor.

"Let's hope so." Joe's flushed cheeks started to cool.

Ethan moved upstream and waded out thirty-five feet along a seam. He pulled up his left sleeve and reached his bare arm down into the water, quickly pulling up a softball-sized rock. He turned it over and peered intensely at the scampering bugs.

"What are you seeing, Ethan?"

"Lots of size sixteen to eighteen small, dark mayflies and a few caddis, about the same size. Small pheasant tails and frenchies are probably good."

The kid knew his bugs.

Joe waded into a good position approximately twenty-five yards downstream of Ethan and took a deep breath, steadying his feet. He pulled fifteen feet of fly line from the reel and marked the spot he wanted to cast toward.

In a smooth motion, Joe lifted the fly line and rapidly backcasted. The line straightened behind him and then accelerated to a stop. The line tightly looped above his head and extended forward towards his target, rolling out like a carpet. The flies landed softly, but not as softly as he wanted. Joe whispered, "It's okay." The fly floats with the current toward the expected holding spot he is targeting. His chest tightens with excitement. A shadow moves and turns into a gold and brown submarine rising from the depths. *Now I know I'm holding my breath.* The trout rises to the fly, and *I'm ready*! Then it bumps the fly with its snout and retreats back to its hiding spot. In anticipation of the bite, Joe raised the rod quickly and pulled the line from the water abruptly. Ethan turned back towards Joe. *What went wrong?*

"Get one?" Ethan yelled down to Joe.

"Refused!" Joe hollered back.

"Bummer!" Ethan responded and then immediately lifted his rod. "Fish on!"

Joe looked up to see Ethan's line tight to the fish and the rod bent. It was a good fish. Ethan immediately turned the tip of the rod upstream with the rod parallel to the flow of the river. *Kid got side control already.* He kept the fish upstream of him and pulled it to his net in less than thirty seconds. *Man, that was good.* Ethan lifted the fish from the net and turned back to show Joe. He was beaming. "Wow, Ethan! That's a hoss!" Ethan put the fish back in his net, took a quick photo with his phone and released the fish quickly back to the water. *He's going to out fish us all.*

Joe felt a smile replace the grumpiness of his missed fish. Seeing the smile on Ethan's face was the best feeling he'd had since before Jody got sick.

"What was it on?"

"Frenchie." Ethan was still beaming.

"Nice!"

Joe looked back at the water in front of him. A good cast put his flies in a promising seam of moderate flow around a clast of boulders, and suddenly a bright flash of yellow captured his focus. An eighteen-inch brown trout had attacked the pheasant tail trailer and plowed upstream, putting a strong bend in his fly rod. *Fish on!* The flash made his heart jump, and he started the internal pep talk. *Don't lose this fish!* The fish pulled the slack line in the water in front of Joe through his hand and he got the fish on the reel.

"Whoa!" Ethan was excited looking back at Joe.

Slow down, slow down. Joe kept up the internal pep talk. *Side control, side control. Why do I always say things twice?* Joe scolded himself. He turned the rod upstream and the fish leapt from the water.

"Woohoo!" Ethan was cheering on Joe.

Deep breath, deep breath. Joe felt the fish ease up and he took the chance to lift the rod. The big brown slid into the net and Joe looked at the fish and then looked up towards the sky. He closed his eyes and exhaled. "Thank you," he said to whatever spirit helped him land that fish.

Ethan called out, "That's a big one, Mr. Joe!"

"Indeed! Looks like about eighteen. Hit the Pheasant Tail! And call me Joe! Woohoo!"

David called down from upstream, "Nice one, Jooooeeee!!!"

They fished for the next few hours and each caught a handful of fish. There were lots of "Woohoo's" and "Fish on" and "Killing it." Ethan and Joe caught each of their fish on the small mayfly imitations. Chuck had to get back for the baseball game and was rushing the rest of the guys to quickly pack up their gear.

As they got in the car to head home, Ethan talked through each of the fish he caught with Joe, David, and Chuck.

"There were a lot of fish holding in the linear troughs, where the darker green water was, there were large rocks on each side of the trough. Must be the feeding lies where they can get to cover."

"Ethan, I have a lot to learn from you, bud." Joe was amazed at Ethan's patience and observation.

Chuck dropped off Ethan and Joe at the diner.

"Nothing like walking into a diner with all your fishing gear!" Joe nodded at Ethan as they walked in.

"I've been doing it almost every day." Ethan smiled as he headed through the door.

39

Meatloaf Sandwich

"Boys!" Georgia was all smiles. "So did you catch the biggest fish, Ethan?"

"Not sure." Ethan was back to monotone.

"We all did pretty well. I learned a lot from him." Joe tried to boost him up and bail him out. Ethan cracked a slight smile. He couldn't hide that he had fun.

"Glad you all had fun! There's a meatloaf sandwich special. Can I get you each one?"

"Sure," Ethan replied.

"Sounds great." Joe directed them to a new booth. He didn't need to see Jody's picture at the moment.

Joe and Ethan sat across from each other.

"I've been dying to ask you. Ethan. How do you know all about aquatic insects?"

"I just read about 'em."

"An aquatic entomology book just fell from the sky into your backpack? That's not quite as easy to find as Harry Potter."

"At the library and..." Ethan trailed off.

"The library here in town? Were you going to say something else?"

Ethan looked at Joe. Joe felt like Ethan was deciding if he had the energy or trust to share anymore with Joe.

126

"You don't have to share, Ethan. I'm sorry. I'm not trying to be nosy."

Ethan looked down and after a few seconds his eyes lifted to meet Joe's.

"Before he died, my grandfather would take me fishing. I was little, but he talked about the flies a lot. He helped me know what a mayfly and caddis fly was. I liked the cases the caddis flies made. They're cool. After he died and my mom started having problems, she would drop me off at the library when she was at work. There was a section just on fly fishing, flies, bugs, that stuff. I read a lot of those books."

"Wow, that is impressive and pretty cool that you read all that."

"I was bored. Needed something to do."

"Well, it gives you a head start as one heck of a fly fisher."

"I guess."

"Here you go, boys!" Georgia slapped down two plates with open-faced meatloaf sandwiches with a side of mashed potatoes and gravy.

"Holy cow! Lunch and dinner!" Joe's eyes widened and he sat up straight grabbing the knife and fork.

"Mooo…" Ethan mimicked a cow.

Joe chuckled, "Quick wit, kid. Nice. Well done moo."

Being on the water all morning made Joe starving, but he didn't realize it until the heaping pile of meatloaf was piled before him. Ethan and Joe sat in silence scarfing down the overloaded plates in front of them.

Sitting back from the table, Joe rested his hands on the table and leaned back, stretching his stomach. He pressed his lips and exhaled, "Man, now I feel fat."

Ethan looked none the worse. *To have the metabolism of a thirteen-year-old.*

"Ethan, do you think we could fish again and you could teach me more about the bugs?"

"I don't know how to teach."

"I was hoping you could show me the bugs you know and how you match the hatch. And today was fun, and I don't have anyone to fish with."

"Okay."

"Well done work, boys. Anyone want dessert?" Georgia slid into the booth next to Ethan.

"Cherry pie?" Ethan wasn't shy about eating.

"Georgia, I am stuffed and I need to head back and prepare for tomorrow. I'll settle up."

"Sure thing. Joe. I'm glad you boys had a good time today."

"It was great." Joe smiled at Ethan.

"Yup." Ethan's words were retreating back into the hands hiding his face.

"See you soon."

Joe paid the bill and left a tip at the front counter. He looked back at Georgia doing her best to talk to Ethan. He was a good kid.

40

The Courthouse

Looking in the mirror was never comfortable for Joe. Today wasn't any different. The way other people saw him wasn't the way he saw himself. His self-doubt was a strong filter: dark, old, gruff. Putting on the sports coat and collared shirt brought back Joe to sadness. The last day of work and the funeral. Now a courtroom.

His memories of the accident were still so foggy. He knew there was a deer and he overreacted, turning the wheel so hard he lost control. And then he remembered looking down and seeing the burgundy cap of the bottle between his feet. Then the doubt. Complete confusion over if he was drinking. Blood tests saved his neck with Chuck and probably saved his sanity. He could've wound up in jail and instead he was in Remberg, discovering Jody all over again and catching some fish.

Back to the mirror. *Should I shave?* That thought hadn't crossed his mind in the last ten days. *It's the respectful thing to do. Nah, I'm going to be as I am.* He wasn't sure what to bring. *I should've asked Chuck some more questions. Why is my brain doing this again? Deep breath.*

Joe grabbed the summons and the ticket, checked for his wallet, phone, and keys and walked to the door of the motel. He wasn't sure if he could eat; even the slightest upset could send his stomach into unpleasantries. Each step was heavy and plodding. He walked by the diner, right across from the courthouse.

The red brick building could have been a perfect LEGO set. A beautiful building. A majestic white clocktower, a white marble staircase, and the prominent windows with round arches all drew Joe's eyes. It looked to be built in the late 1800s and its current condition was a testament to excellent craftsmanship. Standing, looking up at the staircase, pressure was building inside Joe. *I'm going to be okay.* He tried to console himself.

"Joe!"

"Officer Baker!"

"I'll walk you in and show you where to go. You okay?"

"Yup. Nervous, but okay."

"Yeah, listen, in court I'll be mostly business, okay."

"Yup."

"Judge Perkins has about fifteen cases on the docket today. Traffic violations are first. They don't post the list until the morning of, so I have no idea where you'll be, but probably you will be in the first hour or two."

"I don't have anything else to do and I'd like to look around the building a bit, so no worries."

"Okay. The judge is pretty serious, but he's kind and fair. What I'm saying is, don't joke around. I probably don't need to say it, but be nice. With fifteen cases he'll want to move fast and he doesn't tolerate bullshit."

"I understand."

Officer Baker pulled the large, white door open and motioned for Joe to walk through. The lobby was striking. Walnut wainscoting lined the base of all the walls, with bright white painted above. Historic photographs of the courthouse, and influential judges and county staff lined the walls. Now it was apparent to Joe why the diner was styled with the framed photos around each booth. Officer Baker was greeted with jokes by the security guards and ushered around the metal detectors and metal table that all entrants to the court were funneled through. Joe made his way through security without any issue. Court-rooms were on the second and third floors.

A large flat screen hung on the wall near the elevators and it listed the cases for the day and which courtroom would hear each case. Family Courts were on the third floor. Other county offices and judges' quarters were designated on the fourth floor. Barden, Joe - case 21-494 Room 202.

"There you go."

"Here I go."

The courts began hearing cases at 8:30, and Joe was second on the list.

"Do I just go to the courtroom and wait?"

"There is a small cafe back to the left. They sell danishes and bad coffee. We have about twenty minutes before the judge starts hearing cases. You can grab some coffee and then head up or head up now. I need to check in with the prosecutor. I'll see you in there."

"Thanks, Officer Baker."

"You're welcome, Joe."

Joe got a small coffee from the cafe. He wished he would've stopped and got coffee from the diner on his way. Georgia may have helped to settle him down or get him in a more positive mindset. He looked at the photos displayed in the lobby. The courthouse was constructed in 1892, and the architect was a local contractor who built several buildings in the town. Looking through the photos fed his love of architecture and activated his design brain. It was fun to think about the staging and construction of such a complicated building with the tools and technology of the 1890s. He looked down at his watch: 8:23. He finished his coffee and headed to the elevator.

The elevator opened to a long hallway with identical wainscoting. *This was built by a true craftsman.* The hallway had no pictures, furni-ture, or decorations. Only brass numbers and letters over each of the six doors along the hallway. At the very end of the hallway there were double doors with the number 202. The lobby downstairs was full of activity and the sounds of the shoes on the marble floor made it feel like Grand Central Station. This hallway was like a library—still, quiet, and reverent. Carpeted floors dampened any sound Joe's steps would make as he made his way down the hall.

Joe reached for the door handle and for a moment he envisioned that the door led to another world. Joe opened the door and was drawn to the ornate, elevated bench for the judge. A witness stand was to the right of the bench, and desks were placed in front of the judge's bench, with computer monitors in front of two seats. The rail that separated the public seating from the defendants' and plaintiffs' tables and the remainder of the court were built from the same walnut as the walls. The room was beautiful, but definitely intimidating and formal.

A uniformed officer stood near a door to the left of the judge's bench and a handful of people sat in the benches for public seating. Joe sat on the left side of the room near the outside wall. Conversations around him appeared to be between parents and children and attorneys and clients, all giving advice and worrying about outcomes to some degree. Joe sat in silence. He knew he would plead guilty and he didn't want an attorney.

Officer Baker came through the door, and two other officers were with him. They sat on the right side of the seating area. Joe wished Chuck sat with him, but he was Officer Baker this morning. The door opened behind Joe and he turned to see Amanda Jackson.

"Hi, Joe."

"Amanda? I wasn't expecting to see you."

"Chuck called me last night and I just wanted to be here to support you. After hitting your head like you did, I imagine that night might be fuzzy. So, if you want to call a witness, I'll stand up for you."

"Thank you. That's really nice. I'm not sure what to expect."

"You'll be asked for your plea. Sometimes if you plead not guilty, they'll have a discussion right there with the officer and prosecutor or you can have a trial date set if you are hiring an attorney. This should be pretty easy for you."

"That helps, thanks. I can't believe you came."

The bailiff opened the back door and Judge Perkins entered the courtroom.

"All rise."

Joe now noticed the courtroom was nearly full and the energy was closer to Grand Central Station than a library now.

At the diner, Judge Perkins' presence was smaller and older. As he entered the courtroom in his long black robe, he was regal and strong. Everyone in the courtroom stared in silence as he strode to the bench and sat down. The bailiff took a folder from the desk of the clerk and reporter and handed it to the judge.

The courtroom clerk rose and read the name of the defendant and the case number for the first case. A reckless driving charge for a younger man, he was wearing a suit that seemed one size too big for him and he walked with his head down. He was accompanied by his father, who glared at his son and then the prosecutor and police officer. The prosecutor, a tall, thin woman in her early forties briskly opened a folder and glanced at the older man and without any hesitation declared the State's charges against the young man, introduced Officer Wellough, and stated prior convictions of the defendant. The father gritted his teeth and shook his head.

The judge asked the defendant his name, with slow and clear enunciation. The father turned to the son, and he looked up as if waiting for permission to speak.

"Your honor, my name is Stephen Miller."

"Do you understand the charges against you?"

"Yes, sir."

The judge listed off the maximum penalties for the charges, which included sixty days in jail, a $5,000 fine, and court fees. The father clenched his right fist and shuffled his feet. The father seemed familiar to Joe, but he couldn't place him.

"Do you wish to enter a plea at this time?"

"Yes, sir. I wish to plead…" He looked back at his father. "Not guilty."

"Thank you, Mr. Miller. I will record your plea and we will set a time for your trial. Do you require an attorney to be provided for you?"

Stephen looked back at his father. "No, sir."

"The court date will be posted by noon today. Thank you."

Stephen and his father turned and walked through the gate at the rail and left the courtroom.

The courtroom clerk rose again and announced, "State of New York versus Joseph Barden. Case number 21-494. Mr. Barden, please approach the bench. Mr. Barden is charged with possession of an open container of alcohol in a motor vehicle."

Joe's chest tightened and he felt moisture on his palms. He stood and slowly approached the rail, pushing the gate and stepping through to a table on his right.

The prosecutor looked at Joe and smiled, a cold smile. Joe had seen smiles like that from clients who were about to tell him they went with someone else for a project.

Officer Baker followed Joe through the gate and stood next to the prosecutor.

"Mr. Barden. Can you confirm your name and place of residence?"

"Your honor, my name is Joseph Barden and I currently reside in Ellicott City, Maryland."

"I see you have no prior convictions. Possession of an open container of alcohol in a motor vehicle in the State of New York carries a maximum penalty of a $150 fine and up to 15 days in jail. Do you understand the charges against you?"

"Yes, your honor."

"Do you wish to enter a plea at this time?"

"Yes, your honor. I wish to plead guilty."

"Thank you, Mr. Barden. Counselor Campbell, do you have information regarding this case as I consider sentencing."

"Yes, your honor. On July 22nd at 7:08 p.m., Mr. Barden struck a deer and his vehicle veered from the road and hit a tree. Officer Charles Baker was deployed to the scene. EMTs also arrived at the scene. Officer Baker observed Mr. Barden had experienced a head injury and was confused at the accident scene. Upon inspection of the vehicle, an open bottle of Jameson Whiskey was found under the driver's seat.

Mr. Barden was taken, via ambulance, to Bracken General Hospital. A blood alcohol concentration test was administered at the hospital and Mr. Barden had a BAC of 0.0. Officer Baker reported that Mr. Barden was cooperative at the accident scene and at the hospital."

"Thank you, Counselor. Mr. Barden, do you have anything to share before I determine the sentencing?"

Joe's heart raced and his mind went blank. He looked at Officer Baker, who smiled and nodded. He looked back to Amanda, who's eyes widened and head shook slightly up and down encouraging him to offer some statement.

"Mr. Barden?"

Joe stammered. "Your honor…I had been going through a rough time." *Why am I talking?* Joe's words fell out of him. "I lost my wife almost three months ago. Without her, I was lost and I started drinking a lot. A week ago, I came to my senses and I stopped drinking. But I must have left that bottle under the seat at some point. I am guilty of the offense, but I wasn't drinking before I drove and I won't be drinking any more. I am sorry, I am ashamed, and I don't know what else to say."

Judge Perkins leaned forward.

"Mr. Barden, I am sorry to hear of your wife's passing. Grieving through a bottle will only continue your pain. You have broken the law and your actions prior to the accident endangered yourself and others. Alcohol-related traffic offenses are very serious."

"Yes, your honor."

"Mr. Barden, you will be sentenced to a $100 fine and in lieu of jail time I am assigning you twenty-four hours of community service to be performed at the Remberg Community Park."

"Thank you, your honor."

41

Cherry Pie

Walking down the courthouse steps, Joe's feet felt lighter. Sitting at the counter of the diner was really appealing. Joe needed to process what the judge said. Community service? *What would've happened if I kept my mouth shut? Why do I always overshare when I get nervous? Shit.*

"Joe! Joe!" Chuck's voice broke Joe's stupor.

"Officer Baker?"

"Joe, we're out of the courthouse. You can call me Chuck now."

"Okay. I said too much, didn't I?" Joe looked down, shaking his head.

Chuck smiled, "Well, the part about drinking and driving before, yeah that was not necessary, might've gotten you some more hours of community service. But, in the end that sentence is pretty good. Spending some time in the park isn't the end of the world and you're stuck here anyway."

"You're right. A few days of forced labor may be good for me. I certainly am glad to not have to serve any jail time, but I wasn't thinking I'd have to do any more than pay a fine. Look, I just want to have some coffee and eat some cherry pie. I'm not sure I'm ready to start planning out a service project."

"Yeah, sure Joe. I know that was stressful, so go have some pie. But you'll need to check in with the court clerk's office within two days to pay the fine and set up the service time."

"Thanks, Chuck. I appreciate you looking out for me."

Joe pushed the door open to the diner and within ten seconds Georgia hollered out a greeting.

"Morning, Joe!"

He had to admit that walking through a town and having several people already calling him by name felt good.

"Hi, Georgia!"

He couldn't help but think of "Cheers" and how everyone really knew Norm's name.

"Coffee and water, honey?"

"Thanks, Georgia. Any cherry pie?"

"You know it. Does that mean court went really poorly or well?"

"Both maybe? I got community service."

"Ha! Maybe the judge wants you to stick around, too."

"Always the comedian."

"One of my many talents." Georgia winked at Joe.

Hmm. Who wants me to stick around? Maybe I am becoming Norm.

Joe sat and stared at the pie. *What am I doing? Why am I here? I was supposed to be on a fishing trip, clearing my mind, writing some, drawing, and painting some watercolors. Now I'm serving community service in the town my wife ran from and never looked back.*

"You okay, Joe?" Georgia stopped momentarily from her constant motion to make eye contact with Joe.

"Yeah, I'm just contemplating where my life is headed. Being a drama queen in my head." He took a bite of the pie and smiled.

"Sometimes, Joe, you need to appreciate the present. You know it's a gift. That's my cheesy advice for the day, free of charge."

"Thanks."

"You know, my little kleptomaniac has community service at the moment, too. At the Community Park."

"That's funny. That's what the judge assigned me. What's Ethan doing there?"

"He's picking up trash, mowing, weeding, that sort of stuff. I think they're going to do some repairs and paint the pavilion. Looks like you'll have a chain gang buddy."

"More comedy."

"Free of charge, like I said."

After the pie, Joe went back and paid his fine and registered for community service. Starting tomorrow seemed like the best way to get it over with quickly. He would much rather spend his time fishing, but he had to take care of his mess. *You're never done until you've cleaned up your mess.* Joe's father's words drifted back into his mind.

Joe was drawn to the park. He'd walked along the stream and fished, when he saw Ethan land that monster, but he hadn't really seen much else of the park. There were two parking areas at each end of the park. The western side of the park had a smaller parking area next to a large pavilion with two tennis courts and a basketball court. The pavilion was elevated on the northern floodplain, allowing the vantage point of the town to the north and the stream valley to the south. The eastern side of the park continued past Sullivan Street, where two baseball fields occupied the southern floodplain. The larger field with marked fences and some aluminum stands behind each bench area had a large sign on the backstop. Franklin Field. *I guess that's for Cody Franklin. Very sad, but I'm not sure I would've liked him. Jesus, I'm jealous of a dead guy and my wife isn't even here anymore.*

Ethan emerged from a trail along the stream channel, wearing a fluorescent yellow vest with silver reflectors, rubber gloves, and carrying a trash bag that appeared to be about half full.

"Hey, Ethan."

Ethan appeared startled and more than a little embarrassed.

"Hi, Mr. Barden. What are you doing here?"

"I will be joining you tomorrow. I hadn't seen the whole park yet, so I wanted to see it before tomorrow."

"You're joining me? What does that mean? What did you do?"

"Something I shouldn't have. I have to serve twenty-four hours of community service here at the park."

"I only have twenty hours left after today," Ethan said. "It's not too bad."

"That's good."

"I have to go. I need to bring this trash back to the office and clock out. See you tomorrow."

"Yep! Bright and early."

42

Dark Blue and Gold

Waking to an alarm knowing you have a day of work ahead felt good to Joe. He wasn't ever a morning person but without a job or any reason to wake, he suddenly felt pride in getting up early. It didn't hurt that in the heat of the summer the fishing is almost always better just before the sun rises.

Joe made a cup of coffee and got dressed. He thought it was funny that virtually all of the clothes in his duffel bag could be worn for performing manual labor, but he had to go to a second-hand shop to look presentable in court. As a teenager, he had various summer jobs as a laborer for landscape crews and carpenters. It taught him some practical skills and the value of an education to avoid the consistent pains of physical labor. He also saw the choices and flexibility working with your mind gives you over working only with your back. However, the respect he had for the commitment to hard, physical work never left Joe. He was looking forward to feeling the satisfaction again, even if it was forced punishment for his errors.

Ethan was leaving the diner as Joe walked down Apple Alley to Main Street. Joe waited at the corner, as Ethan noticed and picked up his pace.

"Morning, sir."

"Morning, Mr. Barden."

"Ethan, now that we're working together, you have to call me Joe."

"Okay, Mr. Joe."

"Did you get that from your grandfather, too?"

"What's that? What do you mean?"

"Respect for your elders?"

"Yeah. He always said 'Pay people respect until they show you that they don't deserve it.'"

"Sounds like a wise man."

"Yeah." Ethan looked down and shrugged his shoulders. Joe worried he was pushing into something Ethan didn't want to talk about and the two walked in silence to the park.

They arrived at the park office, which was a windowless room attached to a garage that housed two large mowers and a tractor. A balding, middle-aged man sat at an army-green metal desk. He was typing on a computer that looked like it still had a floppy disk drive.

"Ethan Bennett. Coming down the home stretch, are we?"

"Morning, Mr. Hunter."

"And are you Joseph Barden?"

Earl Hunter gave Joe an up and down look and a scowl replaced the jovial smile that greeted Ethan.

"Yes, nice to meet you."

"Hmm. I wonder why Judge Perkins assigned you to me? What do you do for a living?"

"I'm an architect."

"One of those, huh? You super anal?"

"Maybe you're thinking of engineers?

"Same thing. You're the ones that say we have to have only one kind of dark blue to paint the pavilion…some branding bullshit."

"I guess I fit into that category a bit."

"Good. Now you're going to get used to NY Park Dark Blue and Gold. Sign the form here and clock in."

Earl looked back at the glowing screen and pushed a paper and a pen on a clipboard towards Ethan and Joe.

"I hope you're both okay on ladders. I want to finish this before you're both done with your time and it needs at least two coats."

Earl walked them around to the garage and pointed out several five-gallon buckets of paint and some paint brushes, rollers, and tarps.

"I've been asking for a paint sprayer or two for years, but somehow Judge Perkins always finds some wayward souls, like you two, every time the pavilion needs a paint job. So have at it. The pillars are gold, the rails and benches are blue. Oh, yeah, and that top part—one of you will have to get up there—is gold."

"The central hub and cupola finial?"

Joe decided to throw out some anal technical terms. Ethan smiled.

"What? Yeah. Whatever, Mr. Architect." Earl was not amused. "I'll be back in about an hour to check on progress."

Joe and Ethan chuckled and then got to work laying out the tarps. "You painted much before, Ethan?"

"Not really. I just painted my room at Georgia's house."

"Well, that's something. I think we should start with the blue."

"New York Dark Blue." Ethan corrected Joe.

"Ha. You're either a comedian like Georgia or on your way to be an anal architect like me."

They worked together to lay out the tarps and prepare the painting supplies. It was apparent to Joe that Ethan was thoughtful and good at making decisions.

"You *have* done this before."

"I think I'd like to be a fisherman or something about fly fishing." Ethan blurted it out like he was building up courage to speak.

"Me too. When I grow up. All jokes aside, you could be a guide or own a fly shop or a writer. Lots of things are connected to fishing. It's good to have some passion in life and stay connected to it. There are lots of good ways to creatively make a living these days."

Ethan smiled and nodded.

After an hour and a half, they had painted all the rails. Earl was happy with their progress and left them after a quick inspection with a, "Keep at it."

They each were in their own minds as they started to paint the benches and Ethan paused to drink some water.

"Mr. Joe, you didn't tell me what you did to get community service."

"No, I didn't. I am embarrassed about it."

"Sorry. I just…"

"Don't worry about it, Ethan. I guess I need to own it right?"

"You don't have to…"

"I think I do. I had an open bottle of whiskey in my car and I had an accident. Officer Baker found it and I was convicted of having an open container in a moving vehicle. I should've known better and done better."

"Were you drunk driving?" Ethan's voice was shaking.

"No, no, no, not then. But I had been a week or so before."

Joe looked up from the dark blue bench and looked at Ethan. He was intently staring at him.

"I'm really ashamed about it, Ethan. Alcohol is like fire. For some people at some times, it's like a fun bonfire, bringing people together and having fun. For others, it burns your whole house down; it's uncontrollable. I guess for me, my house caught on fire, and maybe it still is smoldering. I don't know. Some lessons are hard to learn."

"My mom caught on fire."

"I'm sorry, Ethan. I can't imagine how hard that was for you."

"It was like you said. If I could've helped her…" He paused and his voice began to break up.

"Can we just finish painting?"

"Sure thing."

They finished the first coat of blue. It was bright and clean.

"We did a good job on that, Ethan."

"Yeah, it looks better."

"I think you're going to go up on that roof tomorrow to paint the cupola. My old ass isn't getting up there."

"It'll be a nice view of the stream up there. Cupola…is that the little top part up there?"

"Yes. They typically help add natural light or ventilation to the area under a roof. Without good ventilation, roofs can get overheated and break down quickly. The finial is the ornamental top of the cupola meant to emphasize the point of the roofline."

"Hmm. Thanks. I never heard of that before."

"Learn something new every day, right? Now you have to teach me more about aquatic insects. Want to go fishing later this afternoon?"

"Sure."

43

Fishing Dreams

"Where would you go to fish if you could fish anywhere?" Ethan asked.

"I don't always like these sorts of questions, but I'll play along because I like you. I tend to break things into categories, making it easier to arrange. So, I'll stick with trout first. I haven't fished out west yet. I grew up listening to a folk singer named John Denver and he sang about how beautiful Colorado was, so I have that in my head from when I was a kid, wanting to go there. I was trying to get to Colorado first, be like John Denver, and then maybe Montana. So all the storied streams like the South Platte, Frying Pan, Madison, Yellowstone, Gallatin. I'd like to fish those first. Then maybe start fishing the salt for tarpon and bonefish, stuff like that. How about you?"

"Every time I read a fishing magazine, I think of a new place. All those places you list sound good. But my grandfather always talked about how he wanted to take me to the Beaverkill River and how it had the best fly fishing in New York. And so many flies were invented in the Catskills. I want to go there."

"Ethan, that's only an hour from here. We can definitely go there. I thought you were going to say New Zealand or something like that."

"I can't drive and I haven't been to many places before. I've never been far from here. My grandfather worked all the time."

145

"I wasn't making fun of you. That wasn't my intent. I just want you to have big dreams!"

"I just want to finish painting the gazebo. Never mind."

I'm good at ending conversations awkwardly.

They finished the gold on the pillars in silence. Earl arrived just as they were finishing, almost like he was watching them from somewhere.

"That's enough for today, guys. Looks pretty good. You can start with the roof tomorrow. Bring back the supplies and sign yourselves out and you're free to go."

They grabbed the five-gallon buckets, tarps, rollers and brushes and headed back to the garage. Ethan and Joe were about to head back to the diner, when Earl stopped Joe.

"Four hours down, huh? Twenty to go, Mr. Barden. Listen, I have a highly irregular request for you. But I'd like to ask you a question in confidence. Is that okay with you?"

"Yes, Mr. Hunter."

Joe turned with a nervous smile towards Ethan. "I'll see you later. Can I meet you at the diner?"

"Okay." Ethan uncomfortably backed away and left the park office.

"Mr. Barden, according to your file here, you were a practicing architect for about 30 years."

"That's correct."

"Can you give me some background on what types of projects you worked on? We may need to ask you for some guidance on a problem."

"I guess so. This does seem a little odd."

"Up to you, but we may be able to use a portion of your time advising the County and not all manual labor at the park."

"Okay. I have mainly worked on public buildings and historic buildings. I specialized in libraries and historic church renovations. I've designed at least a dozen libraries in Maryland, Virginia, and Pennsylvania."

"Thank you. Ed Williams is the director of Public Works. I had a meeting with him today. He's having an issue reviewing some architectural information and needs an expert to ask some questions. I think you may qualify. Are you up for helping the County for a few hours?"

"Of course." Joe reluctantly agreed, narrowing his eyes as he looked at Earl.

"Okay, Mr. Barden, Mr. Williams is free at 1:30 at the County office on Main Street. It's right next to the courthouse. Can you meet him then? In about an hour."

"Sure."

"He's in office 304, and he'll be expecting you at 1:30."

"Okay."

Joe lingered, wanting to ask more questions, but he was thrown off and his mind was spinning. Earl looked back up at Joe.

"Did you have another question, Mr. Barden? Mr. Williams will clear this up. They are his questions and not mine, so he can help you."

"Thanks, Mr. Hunter."

Instead of going to the diner, Joe wandered around the town for a bit. He was suddenly nervous, similar to how he felt before the court appearance. He hadn't thought much about work since he was asked to leave. It had been less than two weeks since his conversation with Jacob. It felt like a lifetime ago. Keeping track of time wasn't a priority to start the fishing trip and then the accident just blew it all to hell. Ten days or so and his truck would be repaired. Four to six days and he'd be done with community service. Those were the days he was tracking now. Not the number of chemotherapy treatments. Not even the submissions to complete the latest project at work.

Now I'm wandering around Remberg. I am wandering. His brain went back to the conversation with Ethan. *Where do I want to go fishing and why did I want to go on this trip?* Joe laughs to himself as he starts to hum John Denver.

Now he walks in quiet solitude, the forest and the streams
Seeking grace in every step he takes
His sight has turned inside himself to try and understand

The serenity of a clear, blue mountain lake

Solitude, grace, understanding, and serenity. Thinking of this song, each word filled him with hope. He connected to it. *Why do some songs feel like they're written to teach me a life lesson? Why do I think so much?* More John Denver popped in his head.

Life ain't nothing but a funny, funny riddle.

Joe looked at his phone with a smile: 1:15. Time to meet Mr. Williams. It was nice that every walk in town only took ten minutes at most. The County office building was immediately next to the courthouse. The brick was likely selected to match the courthouse, but it appeared newer and built with the burden of more modern, practical thought. *Most modern architecture can be really boring. This is not bad.* County Administration Building in large block letters adorned the facade of the building above a large glass entrance way and below a large American flag and New York Flag. Sets of five large windows on each of the two top floors looked out onto Main Street.

He was sensing a theme. Inside the lobby, a security guard sat behind a small chest-high counter with a marble railing. Pictures of the community were nicely framed and distributed around the lobby. He stopped at the station and notified the guard that he had a meeting with Mr. Williams at 1:30. It felt like visiting a client.

Joe showed his driver's license, signed a simple ledger, and headed towards the elevator. He caught a glimpse of himself in the chrome of the elevator. *Shit. I never changed my clothes. Won't be the last time I feel underdressed.*

The elevator opened to a room he felt he'd seen before. Light brown cubicles filled the interior of the space, kitschy signs and house plants were distributed to various degrees in the cubes, and there was an equal representation of college and professional team banners throughout the room. Offices on the outside walls, which he assumed were for managers, kept the natural light from entering the space. *Designed by an old man.*

A middle-aged woman with dyed hair and glasses approached Joe, looking to direct the dirty man back to the lobby. "You looking for grading permits?"

"No, ma'am. I have a meeting with Ed Williams. Can you point me in the direction of office 304?"

She looked skeptical. Joe gave his cheesiest grin and decided to be irreverent.

"I apologize for my appearance. I just finished my community service at the park when I was requested to meet with Mr. Williams."

Now she seemed unsettled and pointed him quickly down the hall. As soon as he passed her desk, Joe heard her sit and pick up her phone. "Did you hear that?" she whispered to whomever was on the other line. It felt good to stir the pot a little.

He approached the door to office 304 and he heard a booming voice.

"God Dammit, Mike! I need that traffic study done to request that funding. Get that back on track!" Ed Williams slammed down the phone and grumbled. Joe knocked on the open door.

"Mr. Williams? I'm Joe Barden."

44

Redacted

"Mr. Barden! Nice to meet you. Sorry about my language there. Gotta keep things moving. Time is our enemy. How was your morning with Earl?"

Ed Williams sat back with a pronounced thud. His chest was puffed out more than appeared natural and it highlighted the bright orange and blue striped tie against his white button-down shirt. A golden shovel and oversized scissors sat in the corner of the office below several framed pictures of ribbon cuttings for various public works projects. There were over a dozen ribbon cutting photos of roads, schools, parks, bridges, and other projects indecipherable from the photos throughout the office. Ed was in each photo. Ed was balding and older than Joe, and the tattoo on his forearm was only partially covered by his rolled sleeve.

"I'm not sure how to answer that, but honestly it is satisfying to see the progress made by my hands and to see how new life is given back to the pavilion with a coat of fresh paint."

Joe couldn't get comfortable in the chair. He had a nervous habit of lifting himself up to slide his left foot under his right knee. He fought the urge. Jody always told him it made him look like a scared teenager. Joe wasn't sure why he was in this office and Ed was loud and aggressive enough to be entertaining but unsettling.

"Spoken like a true idealistic architect! Not a cynical bureaucrat like myself." Ed's irreverent humor kept some pressure on Joe.

"Everyone has their role, right? It takes a lot of organizing and effort to run a Public Works Group. By the look of these photographs, you have gotten a tremendous number of projects done." Joe tried flattery to make the conversation more comfortable.

"Maybe you're a politician?" Ed chuckled. He was having fun. "Okay Joe. Enough dancing. I don't want to waste either of our time. I need some help and God may have brought you to my doorstep."

"How can I help you?"

"We are renovating our library. I applied for and received a large grant to assist with funding most of the renovation. A key criterion of this grant was to ensure that the library can be LEED certified upon completion. You know, all that sustainability crap?"

"Yes, I am aware of that."

"What I am asking you to help with is a bit awkward within our procurement world, but a friend mentioned that you are experienced in designing libraries, a skilled architect, and in debt to the State and County due to a traffic infraction. I checked with the court clerk and it is allowed to transfer a portion of your community service hours if you choose to help the County. Well, really help me, understand the complexities of some architectural proposals and bids we received for this project. It would be a huge accomplishment for me and I'm over my head. I'm a former landscape manager. I know plants and construction but I don't know anything about LEED. Our review panel is a structural engineer, a transportation engineer and a wastewater engineer. And we're all old. We got a lot of money from this grant and it's gotten more attention than normal."

"From the pictures, it looks like you may be selling yourself short. What exactly do you need? Also, I should disclose that I am currently "on leave," or maybe I was let go from an architectural firm that likely bid on this project."

"Don't worry about that. I have redacted copies that remove references to the firms. Procurement requirement for the County. But I need help verifying that the scope items listed in the proposals match the LEED requirements for certification. Are you experienced in that?"

"Yes, I'm LEED-certified myself and I mainly worked on libraries, both new construction and renovation. As long as I'm not getting anyone in trouble, I'd love to help. Never been on this side of the review before."

"I don't think this is getting anyone in trouble, but I'd rather you not talk about this. In fact, all the County employees have to sign an NDA to review it. Are you willing to sign an NDA?"

Joe chuckled, "I'll have to have my attorney review it."

Ed's quick wit retorted, "Still have one on retainer from traffic court?"

"Touché." Joe recognized it was fun but not a winning strategy to verbally spar with Ed.

"And it has to be an hour for an hour on your service time. I can't hire you as a contractual employee in time, especially if you're still employed and I can't have it be a professional hour versus labor hour sort of thing for the court. But I need this contract to go well. Earl told me today you may just be the uppity architect I need to help me translate all this jargon."

"Okay. I'm up for it. How many bids did you receive?"

"Eight. And you have to do all the reviews here in my office at that round table there. Can you start now? I'll print off an NDA for you."

"I can start. Can I get something to eat first?"

"I'll get you some food. The proposals are on the table and the checklist for our scope is in the tan folder. I'll order you a sandwich. Want a Coke?"

"Root beer?"

"Will do. Give me five minutes and I'll start asking you some questions. Please read over the checklist."

Ed left the office quickly after patting Joe on the shoulder. It occurred to Joe that Ed may be more of a type-A personality than any other public works director he ever met.

Reading through the evaluation criteria, Joe was impressed. It was clearly organized and focused on the applicant defining the steps of the project and sequencing actions with very detailed precision. This wasn't a proposal that could be faked or had fluff thrown at. There were plenty of jobs Joe went after that just counted buzz words or years of experience from the key staff. This criteria and request for proposal required the respondent to show their experience and thoughtfulness for the specific project. It couldn't be phoned in or faked. Joe found the mistake on the fifth page. The request for the LEED certification referred to the incorrect LEED version scorecard. *This guy, or his team, is very thorough but that is a weird oversight.* Joe looked around the office and quickly noticed the Landscape Architecture degree from Syracuse. *The tie.*

As an architect, Joe learned early that landscape architects (LA's for short) were the optimistic idealists who were annoyingly detailed, and Joe liked details. He liked to pick on LA's, but Ed was obviously very thoughtful.

"So, can you help me? Chicken salad okay? And the root beer?"

"Yes. Yes. Thank you. I found something little that would be good to see if people notice." Joe was proud he had something to quickly offer.

"The version scorecard reference?" Joe was caught off guard by Ed's response. "I saw that this morning. I read that about ten times. Too close I guess; sometimes you need a fresh set of eyes or…my trick this morning was to read it out loud."

Joe's mouth moved faster than his mind.

"What do you need me for?"

Ed smiled. "I realized when I saw the mistake that the firms responding could have missed it, exploited it, or pointed it out clearly. And I wanted to be ahead of anyone who tried to underbid that item thinking they could exploit us for an extra work order later. I want to compare apples to apples. I need this to go well."

"I will help you the best I can. Here is the signed NDA. Can I ask why this is so important?" The look on Ed's face showed Joe he overreached.

"Like I said before, a lot of grant money. And the library is important to my family."

Joe felt like he intruded, but he was still inquisitive. Letting go of the questions was a good idea at this point.

"Here are the redacted proposals with the sections of the LEED certification highlighted. Can you read them through and find clues on how the firms are viewing it?"

"Yes, and thanks for the food. I read fast so this should only be a few hours." Joe was interested in the proposals and also wanted to stop talking before he got into trouble with Ed.

"Take your time."

After three hours, Joe had read through all eight proposals. He could tell from the page formatting that his old firm had submitted on the project. He was thankful that they pointed out that a newer certification form was required. Three other firms each pointed it out. It was nice to see that integrity still existed. The remaining respondents repeated the requirement from the RFP. Joe didn't see the entire proposals or the costs, but he was hoping his old firm would win the bid.

Joe stacked the proposals neatly. He placed Post-it notes on each page marking his notes and left his handwritten notes on a pad next to the stack. Joe hesitated before looking up to let Ed know he was done with his review. He had looked at these proposals for the past three hours and the name of the library never registered with him. *The Murphy Memorial Library of Remberg, New York.*

Murphy. Joe needed to go to the library.

"Ed, I've read through all the proposals and I made some notes to help you compare apples. Half of the group called it out, the other half did not." Joe's voice broke.

"Thank you. That is a huge help. We are picking a short list and holding interviews next week, so I appreciate your help. And jumping right on it."

Joe shifted in his chair. He felt his heart rate accelerating and his face was getting warm.

"You okay, Joe?"

"Do...Do...you know who the library is named after?" Joe couldn't look up.

"I do. My wife, Sarah, has been the librarian for the past twenty-five years. Lilian Murphy was the librarian there from when we were in grade school through college. She was the kindest woman and she is the reason Sarah became a librarian. Lilian tragically died in a car accident around thirty-five years ago. The library is important to my family."

Joe sat glassy eyed. "I can see that it would be important."

"You okay?" Ed was still and settled comfortably into his chair. Joe smiled, trying not to cry. He couldn't find any words he could say without tears.

Joe took a deep breath. "Good luck with the interviews. Thank you. I'm going to go now."

"Thank you, Mr. Barden."

"Thank you, Mr. Williams."

Joe shook Ed's hand and quickly made eye contact with a nod and smile.

45

The Librarian

Joe walked slowly, with his head down, to the elevator and out into the lobby. As the elevator doors opened, he looked up to see people scampering in through the glass doors, covering their heads with umbrellas or just their arms, retreating from a summer thunderstorm that was soaking the town in a quick, intense burst. There was a playfulness of the people as they shook off the wetness, like they just got off the log flume ride at an amusement park.

The silliness of the wet pedestrians brought a smile to Joe's ruminating face. *Should I walk to the library? Or try to find Ethan to fish the evening hatches and fish my emotions away? Leave no stone unturned, huh? Jody left a lot of stones laying around this town.*

Somehow the lobby scene lightened Joe's mood and gave him the courage to walk to the library. After one step through the doors, he had the instinct to run the block and half. But he just walked. *A summer rain doesn't have a sting like a cold winter rain. It's exhilarating and I can feel my body.* His aches, pains, strength, and agility, and even the heavier parts felt cleansed and awakened.

Walking into the library like a wet dog, the shift from concern to disapproval in the eyes of the librarian caused Joe to blush. *Already off on the wrong foot with Mrs. Williams and she doesn't even know my name.*

Joe turned left and right to scout for pictures. Sure enough, there was a series of framed photos along the left wall around the desk where Mrs. Williams stood, along with another librarian to answer questions and help people check out books.

He always liked libraries. No wonder he liked to design them. The quiet nature appealed the most, but oddly his favorite sections of libraries were always the children's sections. They always were the loudest area in the quiet space; even just the shushing of an excited child increased the decibels. Joe always wanted to design a library that was one big kid's section, even for the adults. Why couldn't the whole building appear magical? Big characters and bright colors, oversized furniture and building blocks on the floor. Stuffy and academic won the day most times. Lately technology was changing every space into an IT lab.

Approaching the photos meant approaching the desk. He wasn't quite dripping, but he was saturated. Joe feared taking too many steps, which may leave a watery trail and further put him at risk from a scolding from Mrs. Williams. She kept an eye on Joe, but continued to help a mother and child at the counter.

He decided it was too awkward to turn around and leave, plus it was still raining buckets. The first few photos were from the early 1900s. Everyone dressed formally with great hat selections. He was going to have to cross Mrs. Williams line of sight at the counter to get to any photos likely to have Jody's mom featured.

The mother and child gathered their books and left the counter. Joe walked up to the desk, wishing his clothes were dry. "Good afternoon. Are you Mrs. Williams?"

"Yes, how can I help you?"

"My name is Joe Barden. I just spent the afternoon speaking with your husband." Joe took a deep breath. Getting any words out about Jody came with a tightness in his chest and the fear that he would emotionally and uncontrollably overshare.

"Lucky you!" Sarah Williams' eyes softened and her cheeks rose to form an impish smile. "What did you do to deserve that honor?"

"I was helping him with some things. I'm not sure what I can say. I signed a Non-Disclosure Agreement and I already can't remember what it said I'm allowed to talk about." Joe shuffled his feet. *Talking with her makes me feel as awkward as talking with Ed.*

"He'll probably tell me all about it tonight. But good for you! Honorable!" She replied with the encouraging voice of an Elementary School Teacher.

Sarah Williams had short, graying, dark brown hair and her blue eyes were kind but stern. She wore a light blue striped button-down shirt and a thin, black vest. A bright green lanyard held a plastic card case with an ID badge and a key card.

"He did let me know that the library is being rededicated as the Murphy Memorial Library." He was powering through but his voice was shaky.

"Yes! After Lilian Murphy, the librarian from my youth through my college years. She meant the world to me and helped me grow my love for literature and reading. She was taken too soon." She paused and looked to the left.

"How did you know Lilian?"

Joe felt tears welling in his eyes. *Keep it together.* "I never met her. But I married her daughter."

"Oh, my God! Jody! How is that sweet girl?" Sarah's smile widened.

"Unfortunately, she passed away in May." Joe still had trouble believing it when he said it.

Her face shifted from welcoming to shockingly saddened. "I'm so sorry. I haven't seen her since her parents' funeral. I'm so sorry. Was she sick?"

"Yes. Cancer."

"Poor child. I can't believe it. Joe, right, it is Joe?"

"Yes, Joe. Joe Barden."

"Oh, my god, Joe. I want to hug you. I am shaken up. I was just talking about her with Ed last week. Once the library renovation project got underway, I was going to try and track Jody down to see if she would come to the dedication. Sweet girl left and never came back after the accident. I felt like it would be great for her to be there."

"That would've been nice. I wish she was here and able to see all this. Honestly, I am at a loss, because she hardly even spoke about the town or her parents. When Ed mentioned Lilian, I couldn't even talk about it. I walked right from his office here. I wanted to see if there are any pictures of her here."

"Of course, dear." She hurried from around the counter and motioned to her co-worker to cover her position at the desk. Sarah grabbed Joe's arm and squeezed it, like an aunt who hadn't seen her nephew in years.

"I think there is even a picture of Jody in Elementary School."

Joe put his hand on Sarah's hand and took a deep breath. She led him around the corner of the desk and past a large display of political books. Along the wall before the many stacks created a labyrinth, a series of a dozen photographs were displayed. The first few photos were from the 1950s and '60s.

"Lilian was the head librarian from 1970 until she died in 1985." The fifth photo there is from 1970."

"And there she is. Beautiful, wasn't she?"

Jody looked so much like her mom. Joe stood in silence. He'd only seen a few photos of her parents, at their wedding, Jody's confirmation, and maybe one other event. He never looked at them enough to really digest the similarities.

"She was beautiful. They looked identical. At this age, Lilian looks exactly like Jody when I met her. It's uncanny."

Sarah squeezed his arm tightly. "Jody would have been just a baby or toddler when this was taken, right?"

Joe couldn't stop staring. "Yes, Jody was born in 1968."

"There are two more to the left. I think that may be Jody in the background of that second one. She's sitting in that rocking chair."

"She always loved the rocking chair at our house. That's where she always read and looked out the window at the birds."

Joe's emotions were so tangled. He felt blessed to discover this part of Jody's life, but he missed her so much. His mind wanted to record every detail of each photograph but his heart wanted to run to the river.

"This photo looks like it's from 1976, maybe she was in second or third grade?"

"I've never seen a photo of her before her confirmation as a teenager. I'm a little in shock. Thank you so much, Mrs. Williams."

"Please call me Sarah. And you are welcome."

46

Crickets

After a few more minutes chatting with Sarah, Joe left the library to take another walk. He walked a lot in this town. It certainly helped that he was days away from having a working car. But a town that had everything you needed in walking distance was both odd and a tremendous relief to Joe. Interacting with people was something that Joe generally avoided, but now he liked watching people, who were already appearing familiar, going about their daily activities. He sat on a bench outside of the diner. Only some puddles and wet sidewalks were left from the rain. A cityscape isn't like a stream valley, which holds signs and scars from the rain for hours, days, and sometimes years. The cityscape just looks a little wet and even a little cleaned up.

Joe was caught in the space between the cityscape and the stream valley. Scars from his loss hadn't quite healed over. The recessed place in his mind that latched on to any feeling of inadequacy got activated each time he thought of the buried world that Jody kept from him.

How much did I really know her if she hid all these things from me? Did she really trust me? Was I a stop along the way that could have been erased? Did I make her feel unsafe to share? How much did she really love me?

Joe's mind raced on that bench. *I bet her mom was sweet and tough like she was. I wish Jody would've let me in more. Did I let her in? What could I have done differently? What would I say to her if I could see her one more time?*

The door to the diner flung open. Ethan stomped out of the door.

"Hey, Ethan. You okay?" Joe stood and stepped towards Ethan.

"I waited in there for you for hours. You said we would go fishing."

"Shit. Ethan, I'm sorry. I was asked to meet with Mr. Williams in Public Works and it took a long time, then I..."

"Whatever, man."

"Wait, Ethan!" Joe shouted as Ethan ran off down the street.

"Shit." *Well people say they'll do stuff and don't do it all the time. Why would he get that upset?*

Joe turned and walked into the diner. He scanned for Georgia and his eyes met her glare. She tilted her head to the side pointing Joe towards a seat at the counter. Joe felt like he just got called to the principal's office.

"Hey, Joe. I guess you saw Ethan on your way in? Coffee and a water?"

"Yes, and please."

She turned and grabbed the coffee pot. As she poured, her face tightened. "If you tell a kid who feels abandoned that you're going to do something with him, you need to do it."

"Georgia, I..."

"Listen, Joe. I know you probably had a good reason, but he sat here waiting, even though I encouraged him and Alan encouraged him just to go fishing and if you could you'd meet him on the river. He's in a tough space. He likes you and he feels let down."

"Shit. I really had a heck of an afternoon. I just didn't check back. I don't have his cell phone number."

"He saw you walk by twice and then he got really pissed when you were just sitting outside on the bench. He's a teenager who's been through a lot. You're going to have to talk to him once he calms down."

"I don't have his cell number."

"I'll let you get that from him if he wants to give it."

"Fair enough."

The pause was beginning to be awkward. Joe could tell that Georgia was upset that Ethan was upset. Joe didn't like the tension.

"Are there any dinner specials?" he asked with the most sheepish voice he could muster.

"None for you. Linguini with meatballs."

"I know. I'm sorry and I'll take it."

The silent treatment from Georgia was still more conversation than Joe was used to. She always was good-hearted and always made people feel welcome, even when she was irritated. Joe ate his dinner and struggled to tell if he really learned his lesson. Georgia couldn't tell either. His urge was to buy Ethan some feathers for a new fly and apologize in the morning. *That is a bad dad thing to do. Don't really understand how to change Just buy them something.* He chuckled to himself, trying not to let Georgia see his smile. There was lots he needed to learn.

He left the diner intending on another walk, maybe wandering along the stream. The summer evenings were beautiful and the sunlight held on until nearly 9:30, making a nightly stroll pleasant. The door to the fly shop was open and Charlie sat in the entrance. He sat up and walked to Joe as he walked by.

"Charlie!" Alan's voice bellowed from inside the shop somewhere.

"Alan!"

"Is that you, Joe?"

"Yessir."

"Come on in! You doing okay? I heard you went missin'." Alan nudged Joe. *Word gets around quick.*

"I don't know about all that. I was delinquent in letting Ethan know I was occupied at the Department of Public Works. I did get to meet both Ed and Sarah Williams." Real nice folks."

"Yes, they are. What was Sarah doing at the DPW?"

"Oh, I went to the library after I worked a few hours helping Ed. Found some interesting things there."

"Sounds like you had quite the day.

Unfortunately, I am closing up soon. Can I help you with something or are you just stopping by?" Alan rubbed his hands together and smiled at Joe.

Joe looked down and turned to the fly supplies. "Well, I was thinking…"

"That you'd buy something to say you're sorry to Ethan?" Alan quickly finished Joe's sentence, chuckling as he said it.

"Been down this road, huh?" Joe could feel the dampness in his shoes, which added to his growing discomfort.

"Not quite like drinking too much and staying out too late for your wife, but leaving a bereaved thirteen-year-old stuck at a diner for four hours, not so good."

Joe's face began to flush. "I was getting used to people not caring what I say or wear I go, so him being pissed didn't even register. I feel bad. It just didn't cross my mind."

"He will get over it. He's just got a lot to deal with. You just have to be mindful to do what you say you will when you talk with him."

"Got a recommendation on how to break the ice?"

Joe understood but part of him was tired of feeling lectured to, even the good-natured ones. *I've got a lot to deal with, too.*

Alan scratched his head and walked toward the rack of animal hair.

"He asked me about cricket patterns the other day. That takes black deer hair and a black hackle. He should have the hooks."

"Okay, load me up."

47

Heights

The morning light reflecting off the ceramic tiles in the small round table near the window radiated yellow, blue, and orange streaks across the bed. Joe woke and looked down and laughed. *I'm at the end of the rainbow.*

Joe found sitting in a hotel room by himself was far lonelier than driving, camping, or even being at the house. He was stuck with just his thoughts and all the questions. No affirmation or even familiar spaces safe enough to mope. The questions would never have answers. Finding humor, wherever he could find it, helped to keep him sane. *Time to wake up, get dressed, grab some coffee, say I'm sorry to Ethan, and paint a gazebo.*

He wasn't sure why, but he felt lighter this morning. The morning sun was bright and hadn't quite burned off all the rain, and a thin mist hovered overhead. When facing an awkward conversation in the past, he'd always thought about it incessantly and practiced what he would say. Once he got in the moment and any emotion entered him, his chest tightened, his words left or just fell out all over the place and he folded.

He arrived at the park office before Earl and Ethan. The pavilion looked very dark blue after the first coat and the gold looked almost white in comparison. Ethan walked by and headed towards the office without looking at Joe.

"Hey, Ethan."

Ethan pretended he didn't hear Joe.

"Ethan," Joe called out louder.

Ethan kept walking. Joe picked up his pace. Good thing they weren't far from the office. Ethan sat on the front step of the office.

"Hey man. I wanted to apologize for yesterday. Can I talk to you quick?"

"I guess. I mean we have four hours together, right? It doesn't have to be quick." Ethan emphasized "right" with the tone you'd expect.

Kid is a smart aleck. Reminds me of me.

"I'm sorry about yesterday. I can tell you what happened if that matters, but I really should've found a way to tell you that I got held up at the Public Works office and wouldn't be free for a few hours. And I didn't find a way and you waited for me at the diner for hours. That's not cool. And I'm sorry."

"I felt like a dork sitting there waiting for you. I thought we were going fishing."

"I wish I could make it up to you, really. Georgia gave me a hard time, too. I was a donkey. I would like to go fishing today if you can. And I got you something."

"Trying to make up for ditching me?"

"Yes, I was a donkey. You want it or do you just want to give me a hard time? You're a heck of a fishing buddy. I never had a fishing buddy and I didn't treat you respectfully." Joe held out his hand. "Apology accepted?"

"What did you get me?"

"Black hackle and deer hair for crickets."

Ethan tried to hide his excitement.

"Thanks, that's cool. Yeah, apology accepted. You trying to get me to tie you some flies?"

"I'll take 'em if you're giving them away." Joe smiled and reached down to shake Ethan's hand while pulling him to his feet. "We've got to be eye to eye for it to be official. Man code stuff."

An old white pickup truck with faded green lettering for New York State Parks pulled into the gravel lot next to the weathered Park Office and Maintenance Garage.

"Morning, gentlemen." Earl emerged from the vehicle holding his coffee. "I grabbed a better ladder for you two this morning. One of you has to climb up there and paint the cupola finial."

Joe smiled and laughed as he and Ethan walked to the back of the truck to grab the ladder.

"Yes, I listen, Mr. Architect. Ha!"

Ethan laughed and tried to heave the ladder by himself. His face strained as he struggled to gain the leverage and his left foot lifted off the ground. Joe reached the end of the ladder and lifted it to Ethan's outstretched hand to help him regain his balance. They lifted it together and moved towards the gazebo.

"I'm glad to see you're both here early and ready to go. Have at it."

Joe set his end of the ladder down and Ethan alternated his hands to push the ladder up against the roof line of the pavilion.

"Joe, why do ladders always seem bigger on the ground than when they're up against a building?"

"Not sure exactly what you mean. You can extend this one by lifting the slide rail and catching it on the rung locks."

"I get that part, I think. It just looks smaller laying down."

"Probably just perspective, Ethan. Comparing length to height makes the height seem smaller. My bet is once you get on that roof it'll seem a lot higher. I'm scared of heights, so it sure will feel high to me."

"Scared of heights?"

"I don't know who said it first, but I'm really scared of falling. I get this feeling that I'm going to be pulled off and fall. Now I'm not trying to scare you; that's just me. I think a lot of people aren't bothered one bit by heights."

"One way to find out."

"I can hand you the paint once you get up there."

Ethan quickly climbed each rung and crawled onto the roof of the pavilion.

"Joe, I can see a lot from up here. I can see lots of the stream from here."

"See any fish?"

Ethan held onto the central hub and looked intently at the stream.

"Don't think so."

"What about a paint brush?"

"You're about as funny as Earl."

Joe cracked up and handed Ethan the painting supplies. They worked the next few hours, with Joe painting the pillars as Ethan took his time enjoying the view and painting the cupola. They finished up the gold coat and brought everything back to the shop where Earl was closing up.

"Thanks, guys. I'll need you to empty the trash cans. Ethan knows the drill, and then you can sign out and be done for the day."

There were five receptacles distributed through the park. Joe and Ethan walked along the trail making fun of each other and goofing off as they grabbed the bags and replaced them with empty ones. They dropped the full bags at the office and signed out.

"Can you show me more about the bugs today, Ethan? It's going to be better weather than yesterday anyway. I'll head home and we can just meet up at the river." They exchanged cell numbers and headed back to get their gear and hit the river.

48

The Hopper Pool

Joe was fighting the urge to nap when his phone vibrated. The notification was a text from Ethan: "Let's go!" *Why does he say that so much? I am becoming a grumpy old man too soon.*

Another buzz. "Meet you at the pavilion in ten minutes."

Buzz. "Cool?"

Maybe I shouldn't have given him my number.

"Sounds good."

Wearing waders through town still felt a little embarrassing, but carrying them back and forth was too much effort. Joe arrived at the gazebo and Ethan was already there.

"Guess what?" Ethan was beaming.

"Chicken butt?" The joke never got old to Joe.

"That's really bad. No. I tied two crickets during lunch. You can use one." Ethan held up a size ten fly that clearly looked like a black cricket with a chartreuse green hot spot. He handed it to Joe.

Holding it close to his eyes, Joe could see the black deer hair spun around the hook and trimmed to emulate the head of a cricket. Turkey feathers formed the wings and pheasant tail fibers were knotted to resemble the back legs of a cricket. The hackle fibers were palmered around what was to be the thorax of the artificial insect. "Holy shit,

Ethan. This looks great! You tied two of these and ate lunch in the last forty-five minutes?"

"I wasn't hungry, just had some yogurt, and yes. Oh, I had knotted the PT before, using it for some hoppers. They look pretty good right?"

"Indeed. Awesome. It's almost too pretty to fish it."

"Oh, we will fish them." Ethan was nearly giddy. "Let's go!"

"You say that a lot!" Old man was coming out of Joe.

"You say shit a lot." Smart ass was coming out of Ethan.

"Touché." Joe chuckled. "You are quick, kid. But I also wanted you to teach me some things about aquatic insects, since you are an expert."

"No cap. Let's go turn over some rocks."

"What?" Joe was startled by the phrase.

"That means no doubt or for real. I'll show you some bugs and we'll pick which nymph to use as the dropper."

"Let's go!" Joe liked being able to poke back at Ethan and he felt Jody was near to him. It was going to be a good afternoon.

At the stream, Ethan took a step in and bent to pick up a rock about twice the size of his hand. It teetered as he tried to balance the large stone and advised, "You need to get closer. They move fast!"

Joe peered over Ethan's shoulder. Ethan pointed to a small tan and dark brown speckled nymph with flaring gills on the abdomen, dark circular eyes, and two splayed tails.

"I'm pretty sure this is a flathead mayfly. *Heptageniidae* is the family name. This is a sulphur nymph. You can see the wing buds are getting darker. These are hatching now. This one looks like it's going to hatch soon."

Joe was shocked and impressed. "Are you making that up?"

"I may be wrong, but I don't think so, and I'm not making it up."

"Impressive, Ethan. What's this one?" Joe pointed to a larger insect. It was reddish brown, with three tails and light-colored gills fluttering along the elongated abdomen.

"That's a cool one. That's a slate drake; the scientific name is *Isonychia bicolor*. When they are about to hatch, they can get a white line down the center of their bodies. They are good swimmers."

"I remember fishing slate drakes with my dad a very long time ago. Several of your lifetimes ago. They get pretty big from what I remember."

"Yup, oooh, but not as big as this one. It's a *Perlidae*. They are predatory stoneflies. I think this one is the Golden Stonefly. That is what I use the Pat's rubber legs fly for." I haven't seen one here before."

The large insect was over half the length of Ethan's pinky and looked like a yellow insect in a storm trooper costume.

"There are lots of other bugs on here and some scuds. This stream is very healthy and has so many insects. That's why the fish get big. My grandfather called it a "Bug Factory." Once it got cleaned up, lots of the bugs came back."

"Ethan, you are a knowledgeable stream ecologist and entomologist already. This is super impressive."

Ethan blushed and set the rock carefully back in the stream. "You just want me to tie more flies for you."

"Well, I told you I'll take them if you're giving them away. You do a great job. But I'm serious. That's a lot of knowledge you've gathered. Ready to fish?"

"Yup! You know with all those sulphurs in there being close to hatching, we should tie on a size sixteen pheasant tail with a yellow thorax for the dropper. Do you have any of those?"

Joe reached into his vest and grabbed a foam box full of flies. He held it up about a foot from his face to make out the small flies snuggly fit in the foam dividers. "No, just straight up pheasant tails."

"Those should work, but I have a few if you need them."

"If you start crushing me, I may ask you for one."

"Then you'll have to buy it! Two bucks a nymph." Ethan quipped.

"Deal! You're a hustler. Was there anywhere on the stream you particularly wanted to fish today?"

Ethan clenched his fists and looked up as his eyes widened. He started talking as fast as an infomercial.

"Yeah, yeah, there is an undercut bank downstream of Sullivan Street a little ways. I haven't fished it yet. The baseball outfield isn't mowed that often and I think there are lots of crickets and hoppers there. I want to try to cast my new fly and have it drift under the undercut. I think there's another big fish in there. I want to try to catch it."

"Man, you've been scoping it out. That's cool. Let's head down there." It was nice to see Ethan so excited.

Ethan paused. "Joe, can I ask you a favor?"

"Of course?"

"Can you video me casting and getting a drift under the tree? You can use my phone."

"I guess so. Not sure how great of a photographer I am, but I'll try. What do you need a video for?"

"I want to start a YouTube channel for fly fishing."

Now Joe's eyes got wide and he picked up the pace of his speech. "What? That's cool. You'll need to get a good camera, at least a GoPro. Do you have a computer?"

"Georgia lets me use hers and I have one for school, but I can't use YouTube on it. I need a camera."

"You're going to need to save up some money there, buddy."

"No cap. That's something else I wanted to ask you…the whole hustler joke."

"What?" Joe couldn't keep up with the slang. He was amused but not sure he could follow Ethan.

"Do you think I could sell my flies?" Ethan stopped and looked dead serious, like his whole future depended on this answer.

"I'd buy them for sure. You should ask Alan if you could tie for the store. Those streamers are probably worth a few bucks each."

"He sells them for five dollars each. Shouldn't I be able to get that much?"

"Ethan, he needs to make a profit and pay for the store and everything else that goes into running a business. So he marks up the cost of the flies. He probably buys them from a wholesaler at two or three bucks a fly. That's how it works. But your story and making quality products may get you more than that. You should talk to him."

"Okay. That's kinda scary."

"Only the first time. Then you'll be on your way to being a world-renown fly tier! Let's go to the hopper pool."

Ethan began to whisper, like he was stalking prey. He directed Joe where to stand and what angle to film from.

"Man, you're all Hollywood already!"

"Don't mess me up, man. I've been thinking about this for over a week." Ethan raised his voice slightly to show he meant business.

Joe grinned, impressed by Ethan's focus. "Okay, okay, sorry Ethan."

Ethan tied on the cricket and a small pheasant tail nymph dropper with a light-yellow collar.

"Here goes."

Joe couldn't tell if Ethan was talking to himself or to Joe. It didn't matter.

Ethan pulled line from the reel and aligned his feet with where he wanted to cast. He practiced two false casts straight ahead to measure the amount of line out of the reel. With a slight turn of his waist, he directed the back cast straight behind him and then accelerated his arm forward to a quick stop. The line formed a tight loop and laid out on the water softly. It was a beautiful cast, unfortunately it was about four feet too close to him.

"Crap."

Ethan let the fly drift with a look of apprehension that he didn't want to catch a small fish and blow up the pool.

He lightly picked up the fly and with an efficient pull of the line during the back cast, his second cast landed a few feet upstream of the pool along a trajectory to drift just under the overhanging tree roots. Joe held his breath trying to keep the phone steady. He focused in on the fly the best he could after having a wider shot to show Ethan's cast. As the fly drifted three feet under the edge of the undercut, Ethan shifted his arm to a side arm position to keep the line from hitting the outreaching roots. Joe almost turned to look at Ethan when a swirl of water underneath the cricket flushed the fly downward in a violent motion. A flash of bright yellow and a large, dotted tail slashed the water.

"Fish on!" Ethan exclaimed in a joyful burst.

"Woohoo!"

Joe couldn't control his excitement. He did his best to track the line pulled tight underwater and then panned back to show Ethan lifting the rod and moving his arms back and forth to keep pressure on the fish and to avoid getting hung up on the tree. A minute or two into the fight and Ethan was able to scoop the large brown trout into the net. He kneeled in the water and stared at the fish with the widest smile.

"You now have caught the two biggest brown trout I have ever seen. I'll take a picture now. Do you want to hold it for the hero shot or just have it in the net?"

"I'll hold it." Ethan was glowing.

"I can't tell if that's the reflection off the fish or your excitement, man! You are glowing!"

"Both! And you got it on video?"

"I did. I'm no Quentin Tarantino but I think I did well. So begins the legend of Ethan Bennett."

"That was lit! Who's Quentin Tarantino?"

49

Archives

Joe felt his age trying to keep up with Ethan, both in the language difference and his energy levels. At the same time, Joe was invigorated by the conversation, the activity, the knowledge, and the friendship Ethan generously gave. Ethan left the river around 6 p.m. to meet Georgia for dinner, leaving Joe to sit on the bank and create a watercolor. Joe wanted to remember this afternoon for as long as possible. *This may be the first time when seeing someone else catch a fish was more fun than catching one myself.*

Joe thought back to Ethan turning over the rock and being able to identify most of the bugs crawling around. *That was super impressive. That kid is super sharp.*

The library was calling Joe back. It was open until nine o'clock and this town was creating lots of questions and Joe didn't like not having answers.

Sarah wasn't at the counter when Joe walked through the library doors. *Probably better off, so I can focus on research and avoid a long emotional conversation.* He stopped and asked the librarian on duty which computers would have access to a newspaper archive. Cody Franklin, Kimberly Bennett, Lilian Murphy. That was the unknown cast of characters Joe's interactions had generated in the eight days he had been in Remberg.

I should leave Cody Franklin alone. *No use chasing the ghost of a dead boyfriend. But curiosity.* Joe kept disciplined and pecked out K i m b e r l y B e nn e tt on the keyboard. He set the search to the newspapers within fifty miles of Remberg.

The obituary was the first article to be listed, followed by several police record reports, all for drug offenses. Kimberly passed on September 8th. *Ten days before we found out Jody was sick.* Kimberly was predeceased by her parents Michael, two years prior, and Debra Bennett, six years prior, of Remberg New York. Survived by son Ethan Bennett. *All the loss that kid has experienced at such a young age.* Kimberly competed in figure skating and loved the outdoors. Her favorite activity was reading books and spending time with her son. No other family. No one else mentioned. *He has no one but Georgia.*

All of Kimberly's arrests came after her father passed away. Possession of narcotics and driving under the influence. *Poor kid just unraveled.*

Lilian Murphy. An article in *The Remberg Independent* was the first listing.

Beloved Teacher and Librarian Killed in Car Accident. Nicholas Murphy, 46, and Lilian Murphy, 45, suffered fatal injuries in a car crash along Old Route 17 outside of Remberg, NY. Jody Murphy, 18, was transported to Bracken General Hospital with non-life-threatening injuries. The other driver, Robert Sheffield, 24, of Horseheads, NY, was arrested at the scene under suspicion of driving under the influence. No other details of the crash were released; the sheriff released a statement that the accident is under investigation.

Joe had forgotten that Nick Murphy was a teacher. He knew so little about Jody's parents. There were a half a dozen articles on events at the library with quotes from Lilian, always exuding positivity and a love of reading. A notice for the funeral service was also listed, indicating the service was held at the Methodist church in Remberg.

What am I looking for? What do I want to know?

Joe sat staring blankly at the computer screen. *All these people are gone. What is there to learn? What was left behind?* He wanted to feel closer to Jody. He wanted to discover the pieces of her he never saw. He wanted to see what there was to find. So far since being in Remberg, he had learned more about her childhood than he learned in the twenty-two years they were together.

Nicholas Murphy. The same articles popped up and a story about a science fair he judged. A science teacher and a librarian. Joe never quite understood how Jody became a medical illustrator, but the daughter of a science teacher and librarian seemed likely to become someone to draw incredibly detailed illustrations of cells and body parts. There were not many articles about Nick, other than two articles describing the accident.

After finding and reading each article, Joe would find it hard to go on to the next. Staring blankly at a library computer screen, Joe felt lost. He normally cherished quiet, but this silence was different; it was alarming, and alone. He missed the sounds of the stream. A young woman with her arms full of books emerged from the stacks and broke the silence.

"Sir, we will be closing in about ten minutes. Please let me know if you need any assistance."

"Thank you."

Joe's vacant expression hid his grieving and spiraling mind. He wanted a drink. His fingers froze at the keyboard and his breath quickened. *Why didn't she tell me about her parents? About Cody? What was it about me and our relationship?* He wished the computer could answer all his questions, but there was nothing but a blank screen and he had no idea what to search for.

"Miss?" Joe turned away from the screen and called out to the librarian.

Startled, she looked back and dropped several books off the edge of the counter. "Oh, my. Yes, can I help you?"

Joe cringed and quickly left the chair to help her pick up the books.

"Jeez, I'm so sorry. I didn't mean to cause you to drop the books."

"No worries, that was on me. What did you need help with?"

The librarian stood after collecting some of the books off the floor, with more remaining around her feet. Her lanyard and key card swung as she rose and she steadied it with her left hand while setting the books on the counter.

"I was hoping to find a book about how to deal with grief?"

"Those are in the self-help section. There may be some on the end cap of aisle seventeen."

"Thanks." Joe looked down and smiled. "I think I'll just check out this one. Can I apply for a card real quick?" Joe helped her put the remaining books back on the counter.

"Oh, that system is down. Can you come back tomorrow?"

"Sure." Looking back at the book in his hands, he laughed out loud. The title was *It's Not About You.*

50

Responsible

Joe's alarm went off at 6:04 a.m. He batted his eyes and pressed his lips together. No headache, no tacky mouth. Clear head and settled stomach. He breathed a sigh of relief. He had to repeat, "It's not about me" all the way from the library to the motel to avoid going to the pub. It was the first time since the accident that he felt like he couldn't resist the pull towards a drink. His mantra kept him on track, but he held onto Jody...and Ethan...in his mind to keep him on track. He decided his reward would be home fries and a potential word overload from Georgia.

He got dressed, checked for his wallet and keys, and headed for the diner. The morning felt like a victory. Eggs Benedict felt like a celebration. The bell rang as the door opened and he smiled as he was greeted by the neon lights above the counter.

"Morning, Joe." Georgia's smile and warm greeting alleviated Joe's mind from his fear of relapse. "Coffee and water?"

"Thanks, Georgia."

"Today is Ethan's last day painting with you."

"Oh, yeah, I forgot. I still have two more days left. That's great for him. More time to fish, tie flies and make YouTube videos. Summer for an addicted fly fishing thirteen-year-old."

"What is it with those videos?"

"Better than those incessant TikTok dance videos."

Georgia rolled her eyes and giggled. "Ha. I don't get that either. But I wanted to thank you. You made up for ditching him that day in a big way. You've helped him focus and have excitement about his future. Thank you."

"You are welcome. It's only been a few days, but I appreciate him. He is very intelligent and tenacious. He has taught me a lot."

"That's very nice to say. What did you want for breakfast?"

Without looking at the menu, Joe flicks the edges with his thumbs. "Eggs Benedict."

"Oooh…fancy. Coming up." Georgia turned and slid the ticket into the kitchen.

"I wanted to ask you a question when you get a second." Joe lifted the coffee cup from the saucer and gently blew on the surface to cool the drink.

"Yes, give me a second." Georgia scrunched her nose and narrowed her eyebrows.

"Okay, so what's the question?" She looked nervously at Joe.

Joe took a deep breath. "It struck me last night that maybe Jody didn't tell me about the town and her parents, not because of my relationship with her, but because of something with her and her relationships with her parents. I can't think of possibly what that would be? But maybe it's not about me."

Georgia froze in place. Her constant motion was halted. Her smile shifted to flat, tense lips. "Something that deep isn't likely about your relationship; that's probably a good way to think of it." Georgia rubbed her hands together. "What would it take for me to bury the memory of my parents and my whole childhood? What would it take for me to erase my mom's memory?" A tear fell from her eye. "That's so sad to me, it's hard to even think about. Maybe their last conversation was a difficult argument and she felt like she disappointed or hurt them and could never make it up. Maybe she felt like she distracted them or she felt responsible for their death in some other way. It would have to be something tragic and intense."

The bell rattles against the door and Judge Perkins enters.

"Morning, Judge." Georgia switched instantly to a smile. "Usual?"

"Morning, Georgia. Yes, please. Good morning, Mr. Barden."

Joe's head turned, caught by surprise from the greeting for the judge.

"Good morning, sir."

"I wanted to tell you the pavilion looks great. I appreciate the care and effort you and Ethan have put in on it. I can tell you're taking your time and doing a good job."

"Thank you, sir."

"You are welcome." Joe felt a surprising level of pride from Judge Perkins compliments.

"I thought Ethan may be a good partner for you."

Joe couldn't restrain his response.

"Why do you think that, sir?"

Judge Perkins took his seat at the counter. He stopped himself from speaking and took a slow sip from the hot coffee that Georgia placed at his seat. His words were measured.

"I overhead you the last time we were in the diner together. I heard the love and reverence you have for your wife who passed. That kindness and devotion is very important for an imperiled young man like Ethan. I believe God put me on this Earth to do His will and the freedom of my decisions is how I try to fulfill that mission and it is one of the benefits of being a judge in a community like ours. You have something to share and cherish. Don't waste it."

Joe didn't know how to process this statement from the judge. His words fell out without polish or any filter.

"Judge Perkins, I don't know what to say. I don't know if I should say thank you or..."

"You don't have to say anything. Let's enjoy our breakfast and the day." Judge Perkins looked down at the breakfast that Georgia slid across the counter towards him.

The knife felt heavy in his hand. The Canadian bacon resisted the sharp edge as Joe's vision blurs, staring at the mix of egg, hollandaise sauce and English muffin. He cuts through and lifts to take a bite of his breakfast. *Felt responsible for their death.* The words rolled through his mind over and over again.

Joe finished the food and placed the knife and fork across the plate. Georgia made eye contact.

"Finished Joe? About time for you to meet Ethan and finish up the painting?"

Joe looked up at the clock, surrounded by neon lights and nodded.

"Do you have any pastries or donuts I could bring to Ethan and Earl to celebrate his last day?"

"Aren't you sweet? Sure, I'll pull some together."

"Thank you."

He carried the box as he walked towards the park office at a quickened pace.

"Joe, you were almost late." Ethan sat next to the front door, smiling.

"I come bearing gifts. A send-off breakfast for the end of your masterclass in pavilion painting."

Joe handed the box to Ethan.

"Let's go! From the diner?" Ethan's eyes widened.

"Yup. We should share some with Earl. Seen him yet?"

Joe grabbed the handle of the door and looked back at Ethan.

"Not yet."

Earl walked through the door with a box of donuts in his hands, startling Joe as he stumbled past the door.

"Happy Last Day, Ethan!"

Earl's words slightly trailed off. "Great minds huh?" He was slightly disappointed he wasn't the only one with an idea to celebrate. "Let's gather up the supplies and sit in the pavilion and have some breakfast. I did make some coffee inside, too, if either of you drink it."

The three of them sat on the blue benches drinking bad coffee from white Styrofoam cups, eating donuts and pastries. It reminded Joe of his first summer job as a laborer for a carpenter framing houses many years ago. Each Friday they would have coffee and donuts. He fondly remembered those days. Earl and Joe told stories about their first summer jobs as they ate and laughed. Ethan ate more than Joe thought was possible and laughed at the "old men" telling their stories. Then they got to painting.

51

Practice

"I was thinking we should paint the blue today, Joe." Ethan said with a mischievous smile.

"Not a chance my, friend." Joe side-eyed Ethan as he opened the gold paint.

"Ha! I was kidding. I know you want no part of getting on that roof." Ethan was proud of his joke.

"Earl would have to get up there or wait until some other heathen got community service to finish that off if I had to do it."

"You could do it, Joe. I have faith in you."

Joe paused. He felt like Ethan truly meant it. It struck Joe that he wasn't sure what he did to deserve that faith.

"Thanks, Ethan. I don't have faith in myself, though. I shake just thinking of being up on that roof."

"Are you going to Baker's tonight for fly tying?"

"I forgot it's Friday! I don't have plans to do anything other than fish and get some food. It was fun last time. Feels like last Friday was a long time ago."

"This week definitely went faster with you around. Last week took forever. Thanks, Joe."

"You are welcome. I enjoyed it too. I do have to say that I really hope we don't have to be serving community service to hang out from now on. No more court-mandated community service, okay? Deal?"

"Deal. No cap. I don't want that either. I may get more than community service if I get in trouble again. I don't want any part of that."

"Good to hear. I'll hold the ladder. You ready?

"Yup. Thanks."

After a few hours of painting with a belly full of eggs Benedict and pastries and a mind swirling around Jody, Joe was ready for a nap. Ethan, however, was not ready for a nap. At least a half a dozen times over the morning he asked Joe to fish with him in the afternoon and each time Joe answered, "I may need a siesta before hitting the river, young man."

They finished up the second coat of gold paint and packed up the supplies. They lifted opposite ends of the ladder and headed back to the shop.

"Any ideas what you're going to tie tonight?"

"I have been having luck with those crickets. I think I should have some more. And…" Ethan's voice weakened and cracked.

Joe craned his head to look back at Ethan.

"What is it, E.?"

"I want to ask Mr. Baker about selling some of my flies and I wanted to show him my crickets. I thought they would be good to sell since I've caught some big fish on them and they look pretty good."

Joe stopped walking and while switching his hands on the ladder, turned to face Ethan.

"Listen, Ethan. Alan is very supportive of you. So is Georgia. So am I, for that matter. We are in your corner and ready to support you. To be taken seriously you need to self-advocate. So ask him, face to face, man to man. I know it's scary, but once you talk to him, you'll know the answer and be able to move ahead. Would you want to practice with me? I bet Alan's easier to talk to than I am."

"How do I practice that?

"You ask me and pretend I'm Alan. When you ask you should be confident but not arrogant. Make eye contact but don't stare. Be yourself and be strong. Then see what happens. Be respectful of his response." Joe spoke quickly and with strength. "Give it a try. Remember everyone else, even adults, are just people. Ready?"

"What? Now?" Ethan started to get flustered.

"Yes. Now. No pressure intended, just trying to help." Joe tried to soften his tone.

"Joe, I was hoping…"

"Alan. My name is Alan Baker."

"What? Yes. Okay. Sorry."

"Mr. Baker, I was wondering if you would want to buy some of my flies to sell in your store. If not, no worries."

"Strong." Joe reinforced. "Can I see them? Are the eyes clear? How many do you have and what did you want to sell them for?"

"That was a lot of questions."

"Sorry, I was getting into my role. Answer what you can. Remember, be confident."

"Mr. Baker, so far I've tied about a dozen crickets in sizes 12, 10 and 8. I can tie streamers, nymphs and dry flies, too. So, I can make more, maybe a few dozen a day if need be. Here they are?" Ethan's voice inflected oddly.

"Is that a question?" Joe chuckled as he peered closely at the flies. "Dude, they look good."

"You think he's going to say 'Dude'?" Ethan tilted his head and the left side of his mouth scrunched.

"Sorry, I do think they look good. You'll have to answer how much you want to get paid for them."

"I don't know what to say."

"You could ask what he pays for the other flies or make an offer. I'm excited. You'll do great. Worst thing he can say is no."

"That would suck." Ethan looked down.

"Be positive and you'll do fine. Confident and respectful. Sometimes you get the bear and sometimes the bear gets you."

"What?" Ethan gave Joe a puzzling look.

"Something my dad used to say to me. Sometimes things work out, sometimes they don't, just keep moving forward."

"I don't want to get eaten by a bear."

"Learn to run fast." Joe laughed and put his arm around Ethan's shoulder. "Seriously, you'll do great. Don't chicken out."

"Okay. Thanks. But I am freaking out a little."

The shop door opened and Earl emerged.

"Mr. Bennett! You are now released from your service to the great state of New York. I need you to sign out today and then you will keep one copy for yourself and take the other to the courthouse clerk's office. I don't expect to see you back here. Oh, let me change that. I don't want to see you back for community service, but if you ever need a summer job, stop by and see me. You're a good worker. Thank you."

"Thank you, Mr. Hunter." Ethan shuffled his feet and looked down.

Earl reached out his hand for a handshake. Ethan brought his eyes up to meet him and shook his hand.

"Take care of yourself. And Mr. Barden, sign yourself out there and I will see you on Monday."

"Thanks, Earl. Have a good weekend." Joe smiled and felt proud of Ethan. Joe and Ethan headed back towards town. Ethan looked back at the pavilion.

"Looks a lot better, huh?"

"Indeed. One more coat of the 'park' blue and it'll be good for a few years." Joe paused for a moment.

"Ethan, I'm going to need a few hours before I can fish, but I do want to fish. I need to rest a little and take care of some things. Want me to text you when I'm done and see if you want to fish at all?"

"Yeah, that would be good. I want to tie some flies to bring to Mr. Baker. I should eat, too."

"How are you hungry?"

"I don't know. I'm a teenager?" Ethan shrugged his shoulders and smiled a bashful smile.

Joe smiled and muffled a laugh. "True, true. You know when I was teenager…"

"Forever ago?" Ethan let out a loud "Ha!"

"Smart ass. When I was a kid, my dad owned a lighting store. They sold chandeliers, lamps, specialty lighting, things like that. I spent a lot of time at that shop. Next door to the shop was a bakery, the Pastry Shack. God, I loved that place. Anyway, on Fridays my dad would buy donuts or pastries for the employees and customers. Two dozen every Friday. When I was done with school I would walk to the store, and as long as I didn't tell my mom, I could finish the pastries that were left over. I loved Fridays. Well, when I was thirteen, a dozen donuts were left over. My dad was a serious guy normally, but he dared me to eat all the donuts. So I did. He laughed so hard. I can't remember seeing him laugh that hard before. But then I was sick for the rest of the night. My stomach was not happy. But my dad sure was, and he laughed about that for the rest of his life."

"That's a lot of donuts! Maybe I can try next week!"

"I wouldn't recommend it, but you probably had six today, so I believe you. Let's not try that."

"Probably a bad idea. Text me later, okay? I definitely want to go fishing."

"Sure thing. And practice some more flies!"

52

The Guardian Angel

Sitting on the edge of his bed, Joe slipped off his right shoe and then the left. His toes wiggled in his socks and his brain whirled. One more day of community service. A few more days and his truck would be in working order. He was waylaid in the town his wife grew up in and never mentioned. He was turning over stones.

He searched through his bags for his journal. He found the list of supplies and the itinerary. Scribbled notes from the first day at Penns Creek outlined what camp site he stayed at, a description of the reach he fished, the flies he used. Joe nearly had forgotten the last note penciled in the journal before drifting off to sleep. "I feel alive."

He was finding joy and connection; things he wasn't sure he'd find after losing Jody. The mystery of the town created an uneasiness. Joe wished that Jody had shared more with him. Putting together a puzzle without a picture or all the pieces kept him on edge. Her parents died in an accident with a drunk driver, Jody was with them, and she could have as easily died in the accident. It was an accident.

Joe's mind jumped to the flash of brown that distracted him and caused him to lose control of his truck. *What if she distracted them? What if she caused or felt like she caused the accident? Who would have known her then? Maybe I need to seek them out? Or should I just move on? Leave no stone unturned.*

Maybe Sarah would know more about her friends? Jody would have needed help to recover from the accident, handle her parents' estate, and to sell the home. A doctor, a lawyer, a real estate agent, family friends, someone. There are people here that knew her then. I need to find them. Courthouse records were likely filed for the deed transfer. I need another trip to the library and probably the courthouse.

He drew three circles, like the beginnings of a family tree. Joe lettered neatly; it was beaten into him in college. He wrote, "Nicholas Murphy" underlined with "Teacher" placed under his name in the first circle. "Lilian Murphy,", underlined "Librarian" was within the second circle. He connected the circles with a line and extended a line orthogonally downward for the third circle, "Jody Barden."

Along the bottom of the page he wrote, "Real Estate Agent? Property Search / Family Friends?" Doctors and lawyers will likely not have public records. But the sale of the house will be publicly recorded. Maybe Sarah knows who family friends may be?

Joe's stomach growled. The mission made him hungry, but at the same time he felt like he didn't have time to eat. Then he thought of Ethan. He needed to text him. "E - I need to go to the library. Not sure if I'll have time to fish. Will stay in touch. Tight Lines!" Joe didn't want to let Ethan down, but his brain needed progress on the questions.

Grabbing his wallet and keys, he nearly forgot to put his shoes on before heading out of the door. He made it to the library in record time. As he reached for the door, his pocket vibrated. It was Ethan.

"Alr."

Huh? "Huh?"

"Alright, Old Man!"

Joe smiled and slid the phone back in his pocket.

Sarah wasn't at the front desk. Joe decided to sit at a computer close to the front desk, hoping he would see her. Sitting in front of the computer, he realized he didn't even know the address. The property research website allowed you to search by address. It took some digging but he was able to query zip code and year sold, which he assumed was 1989. It turns out it was late November 1989. Nicholas and Lilian Murphy's home at 970 North Gray Street was transferred to the Murphy Estate in August of 1989 and sold to Ernest and Amelia Stewart. In 2010, the property was transferred to Seth Stewart. *The mechanic?* He owns Jody's house. This world is getting smaller.

The startled librarian from the other night is at the front desk. Joe looks over.

"Hi! Is Sarah here tonight?"

"She left today at lunch time. She will be back on Monday. Oh, that's you from the other night. Did you want to get a library card?"

"I'm not a county resident."

"Are you a New York resident?"

"No. Although it feels like it."

She smiled. "Unfortunately, that means you can't get a card, but you're more than welcome to use our resources here."

"Thank you."

Back to the mechanic. No record of the real estate agents, but maybe Seth has some information or paperwork. Joe wrote down the dates of the house sales into the journal and cleared the search. *Time to check on the truck and try to ask Seth some questions without being too weird about it.*

Joe walked by the diner quickly, to avoid getting talked into fishing for the afternoon. The smell of cherry pie wafted through the door and turned Joe's head, reminding his belly that he forgot to eat. My belly can wait, or I'll get stuck there for the rest of the day. *I wonder what music Seth will be playing today?*

Joe passed Apple Alley and turned right onto Sullivan Street. He could hear a slow jazz bass, a high hat, and saxophone. Then a piano. Seth's glasses were perched on the tip of his nose as he peered down at the computer keyboard. The music was loud enough it masked the sound of the door opening.

"Is this Coltrane?"

"Mr. Barden! Yessir. With Thelonious Monk. I dig it."

"Nice. You are quite the jazz connoisseur!"

"It's all my parents played in the house growing up. I hated it in middle and high school, but I guess it wore off on me. I've found it helps me to focus. Kinda soothing. Plus, then no one fights over what to play in the shop and I don't need to hear metal all day. I guess you're coming to check on the car and not talk about jazz?"

"Yes. But I also have a weird question for you."

"I like weird questions. Let's start on the Tahoe. I have one last part I'm waiting on. It's in transit and tracking says I should have it on Monday. So, you'll be good to go on Tuesday, Wednesday at the latest. You can hit the road again."

"I was beginning to think I'd be here for the rest of my life."

"Works for me. Also, just because you have a car doesn't mean you have to leave."

Joe chuckled.

"True, true. Can I ask you that question?"

"Fire away."

"This requires a slight introduction. My wife, Jody, grew up in Remberg and lived here until she was 17 or 18. She passed away in May." Joe took a breath. *Try not to get weird.*

"I'm sorry, Mr. Barden."

"Thanks. Please call me Joe. This is where the question becomes a little odd. Jody never spoke about her life here in Remberg. I know her parents died in a car accident and she was injured and traumatized."

"Wait, your wife was Jody Murphy?"

"Yes."

"I live in her parents' house."

"That's what I wanted to ask you about."

"Man, this is a small world."

"No kidding. Do you know anything about the sale of the house to your parents? I was hoping to find someone who knew about Jody's parents and Jody's life here growing up."

"Man, this is so crazy." Seth pushed his glasses up to the bridge of his nose.

"I was six years old when we bought the house. My mom and dad lived in an apartment above the shop before then, now it's storage, it's small. They'd been looking to stay in town, but nothing was affordable. When the Murphy's were killed in the accident, there was an estate sale. What wasn't sold or taken by Jody was left with the house. I still have some of their furniture. I don't remember anything about the sale. I was too young."

"Would your parents remember?"

"Unfortunately, my dad passed away five years ago and my mom has Alzheimer's. She's at a home in Binghamton. She barely remembers me these days."

"Do you have any records or heard any stories or anything?"

Seth cocked his head sideways and touched his chin.

"You're certainly welcome to come to the house and look around. I don't remember much and I'm fairly sure I don't have records other than the deed."

"Thanks Seth."

"Hold on Mr. Barden…I mean Joe. You know what? I can remember one thing. There was a lawyer who presided over the estate sale and handled the sale of the house. My parents would always joke that he was the 'Guardian Angel' of the town and helped them find an affordable place to stick around. He's still around himself. Ken Perkins."

"Judge Perkins?"

"Yessir."

53

Turkey Club

Judge Perkins? Joe couldn't wrap his head around it. *A guardian angel? Seems like a grumpy, old man. In some way, is he looking out for me…or Ethan? That seems more likely.*

Joe looked at his phone. It was a quarter to 4. He texted Ethan: "Sorry, Ethan. I hope you're fishing. I've been held up on some stuff. See you at fly tying?" Joe's phone buzzed right back.

"No prob. I've been tying some flies to try to sell to Mr. B. C U then. #confident"

Joe was relieved he didn't leave Ethan hanging. *What is it with the hashtags?*

Joe wasn't sure he could wait until 5 to eat at Baker's. He decided the diner may be a good place to eat, think, and maybe Georgia would have some ideas. Judge Perkins would not be allowed to disclose any items that fell into client confidentiality. He seemed like a man of principle and Joe didn't want to step into any conversation that seemed improper with the judge. *What was there to find out?*

"Hi, Joe! Too late for coffee?"

Joe sat at the counter and took the menu from Georgia.

"Good to see you. Never too late for coffee and…"

"Water, I know, I know."

"Thanks! You going to Baker's for fly tying night?"

"Yes, and I hear you're giving Ethan advice on how to pitch to Alan on selling his flies."

"Trying to help if I can. He ties great flies. It's a real talent. I hope it works out."

"I have a feeling Alan will jump on it, if Ethan musters up the courage to ask."

"Sounds like you may have more than a feeling." Joe sensed Georgia was taking an active role in Ethan's job prospects.

"I may have started the conversation already, but maybe not." Georgia winked at Joe.

"You are awesome."

"Thanks! You're coming along yourself." Georgia winked at Joe as she slid a saucer and full coffee cup.

"A work in progress, Jody used to say," Joe said with a smile.

"What can I get you, honey?" Georgia took out her guest check pad.

"Turkey club, crispy bacon, and a small side salad."

"Coming up!"

"I also wanted to ask you a question."

"There's an upcharge for that, especially with *your* questions."

"Put it on the tab."

"Sure thing. I'll be right back."

The steam from the coffee tickled Joe's nose. He took a deep breath. *What do I even ask her? What do I really want to know?*

"What did you want to ask?"

"I discovered today that Seth Stewart's family bought Jody's parents' house after they passed. I spoke to Seth. He said that Judge Perkins was the 'Guardian Angel' of the town and helped them buy the house and stay in the town. I don't know exactly what to ask. I know he comes in many mornings, so you probably know him well. Is he the 'Guardian Angel' of the town?"

"This one is absolutely going on your tab. Long ago, Judge Perkins was a young attorney who then became a public defender, who then became the district attorney, who then became the District Court judge. When it's only the two of us in the diner, he's more talkative. I've asked him a few questions about his career, he doesn't offer too much up. He's been coming here as long as I have worked here, so I've gotten to ask him lots of questions. I know he is an honorable man and cares about this town and community. If there's a legal matter that's impacted this town over the past forty to fifty years, he's been involved in it. He convinced me to become a foster parent and helped me with the process. He suggested I meet Ethan and foster him. More coffee?"

"Yes, please. Need to take a breath?"

"Ha! Not me. So I would say that he has done a lot of good for a lot of people. He held people accountable and helped them see a better way. He probably is a guardian angel."

"He definitely seems to be taking care of the people in this community."

"I'd say so. Looks like your sandwich is up. Be right back."

"Thanks."

"Here ya go."

"So how does the foster parent thing work?"

"Adding more to the tab there, Buster. I don't have all the details memorized. I may need Google. I filled out a long application, submitted for a background check, got interviewed by a caseworker, met with Ethan, and here I am. One thing is weird about it. They placed him with me for 15 months. I can adopt him or another family or parent can as well. He's been with me for 11 months. I'm sixty years old. I do wonder if it's the best thing for a thirteen-year-old boy to be with a sixty-year-old woman."

"You're great with him. I can tell how much you care about him."

"Thank you. I love the kid. But he still got arrested while he was under my care and was still getting into trouble. Without Alan, Chuck, and now you looking out for him, he'd likely be in more trouble."

"Maybe he's turned the corner and feels more confident and stable and cared for...hopefully he can work something out with Alan."

"Hopefully I can work something out with Alan!"

"Oh, yeah, wow. Good for you."

"I've had a crush on him for years. He is a handsome man and he is his whole self. I love a mindful man with beautiful lips. Mouth and eyes say it all, Joe. You are rubbing off on me. Now I'm oversharing! Please don't say anything."

"No worries Thank you for sharing. Honestly, I'm a little shocked you've kept *that* a secret. I hope that works out. We all deserve to be happy."

"Ain't that the truth, honey. I talk a lot, but when it comes to romance, I don't like to throw that stuff around. Too personal, you know? But I'm getting too old to not say what's on my mind and it's been too long since I had a date!"

"Understood! Life can change quickly and time can be short. So are you coming to the fly-tying night? Might be a good chance to ask Alan out?"

"I am. I'd rather not say something like that in front of a crowd, though."

"Fair enough."

"Eat your sandwich. I'll leave you be."

"Do you think Judge Perkins would share anything about Jody's family with me?"

"He takes his commitments to the court and his clients religiously. I think that's unlikely."

"I feel like I only know a small portion of her story. I want to know more. It's driving me a bit crazy."

"Maybe I can think up some ideas"

"I'd appreciate anything."

54

Maneater

Joe got back to the motel and took out the notebook while sitting at the small circular table. Under the house sales notes, he wrote Judge Richard Perkins - Guardian Angel. Attorney -> Defender -> Prosecutor -> Judge.

How will I learn anything from Judge Perkins? When should I leave Remberg? Where will I go?

There were so many questions. He wrote additional notes: Ethan Bennett -> Kimberly Bennett. -> Michael and Debra Bennett. *Is there a connection between Judge Perkins and the Bennett's?*

The alarm on the phone surprised Joe. It is time to go to fly tying. There was nothing else to write down at the moment, but his mind spun. *Maybe tying some flies will focus my mind.*

Joe appreciated the walks through town. There were always a few people out and about who were happy to say hi but busy enough to not linger in awkward conversations. Turning onto Main Street, he was greeted by a blaring voice on the loudspeaker.

"Welcome to First Friday!"

A large man in an ill-fitting brown suit stood on a small stage. Two teetering towers of speakers flanked the stage in front of the courthouse. A drum set and keyboard occupied the courthouse side of the stage. Groups of elementary-aged school children rode bikes on the closed off blocks of Main Street. A dozen younger adults, who appeared to be parents of the school-aged children, sat on portable chairs. "Tonight we are lucky to have the Dynamic Rockers with us all the way from Ithaca! They play all our favorite hits from the 1980s! Let's give them a warm Remberg welcome."

Joe felt like he was walking back in time. A smattering of applause and a handful of squeals from kids on bikes brought the band of balding fifty- year-olds to the stage. They had a wardrobe style that was a mix between Def Leopard and a golf foursome.

"Hello, Remberg! We are the Dynamic Rockers!"

Joe never wanted to get into a store so badly. Charlie greeted him at the door and Alan quickly yelled, "Close the door please! Oh, hey Joe!"

"Made it just in time!" Joe looked up at Alan while rubbing Charlie's belly until he got the leg kick.

"You boys! That takes courage to get up there! They're not so bad!" Georgia playfully scolded Alan and Joe.

"It probably takes Liquid Courage." Chuck Baker lifted his head from the vise to greet Joe.

"Hi, Chuck!" Joe was happy to see him.

"Good evening, Joe!"

"Come on, Charlie, let Joe in the door." Alan patted his leg, calling Charlie back to the tables where the vises were set up. "We're going to tie some ants, beetles, and green weenies tonight, Joe."

"How many weenie jokes have been made so far?"

David spoke up. "What did you call me? Ha! That covers all of them. You missed at least a dozen of them! Howdy, Joe!"

"Howdy there, Dave! And who is this guy?" Joe pushed on Ethan's shoulder.

Alan spoke before Ethan could look up from the cricket he was tying.

"That's the newest professional fly tier in Remberg!"

"No fooling!" Joe grabbed both of Ethan's shoulders. "Congratulations, Ethan and to you, Alan. This kid ties great flies!"

Ethan beamed. Alan spoke in a very bad Marlon Brando accent, "He made me an offer I couldn't refuse. I'm excited for him to help me. He may even work here in the shop once he's old enough to get a work permit."

"That is fantastic!"

Ethan resisted looking up, but Joe could see the huge smile as Ethan peered at his fly.

"Joe looked around at the vises in front of Chuck, Dave, Ethan, and Georgia. Black foam was lashed onto size 12 hooks, with an underbody that appeared to be peacock herl. Thin black plastic tubes lay beside each vise.

"We decided fly tying beetles would be our protest against the whatever Men Without Hats or Rick Astley crap they start playing out there."

"So, tying terrestrials of Beetles is your protest inferring Beatles with an A?" Joe laughed.

Chuck stepped in. "This is all Dave's ramblings, but he obviously knows a lot more about '80s music than the rest of us, and I have seen him karaoke "Celebration" reasonably well after a few drinks."

Dave responded quickly. "Hey, you promised you wouldn't repeat that!"

"You're lucky I don't post the video online. So keep your yap shut!" Chuck retorted.

"Well, everyone loves Kool and The Gang, anyway." Dave had to have the last word.

"Here, sit next to Ethan and follow his lead. These flies have been deadly at Mill Creek and on the Delaware the past week. Ants are doing well, too. I'll get out some supplies for those, too." Alan directed Joe to his seat and vise with a neat stack of supplies.

"Wow, what a great set up. Thank you." Joe was impressed with the organization of materials.

"Well, I had some help today. Georgia and Ethan came over early to help me set up. Also, on the First Fridays I keep the shop open longer since so many folks are walking about. So, I need to be able to help any customers that straggle in." Alan glanced at Georgia and smiled.

The door of the shop opened as two middle-aged men quickly entered the store, chased by, "Oh, oh, here she comes…" Charlie greeted them at the door and they closed the door behind them to shut out the music.

An oddly familiar voice asked, "Are there always strange men singing Hall and Oates around here?"

Alan stood up to greet the men. "Welcome, gentlemen. We are having a tying night tonight and the First Friday celebration only treats us to marginal cover bands in town once a month during the warmer months."

Joe craned his neck to see the face that went with the voice. He couldn't believe it. Jacob Miller, his old boss, was walking toward him, along with the father of the boy who was in court before him. Joe froze.

"Joe Barden, is that you?" Jacob walked towards Joe.

"Man. Joe. Are you famous everywhere?" Dave kidded.

"Jacob, what are you doing here?" Joe rose from the chair and slid around the table, outstretching his arm to shake hands.

Jacob grabbed his hand and pulled Joe in for a half hug. He couldn't remember a time Jacob ever hugged him. Joe wondered if Jacob had consumed a drink or two before wondering into the fly shop.

"Well, we are shortlisted for the library project and we have a presentation on Monday. Kind of short notice, but you know how it goes. And this is my brother Matt. He doesn't live too far away and I haven't visited in a while. So, we decided to make a weekend out of it."

Joe shook hands with Matt, who didn't seem to remember him from the courthouse.

"Nice to meet you, Joe."

"Likewise."

"Joe is one of the best architects I've ever worked with., Man, it is good to see you."

He definitely had a drink. Jacob was not one to effuse praise.

"Good to see you, too. I wasn't sure I'd see you anytime soon."

"Did you guys want to tie any flies?" Alan interjected, feeling an awkward moment from Joe coming on.

"No, no. We have to get back home, but we were going to hit the West Branch of the Delaware tomorrow and needed to pick up some flies and some tippet. Also, my brother needs to get a New York license," Matt interjected.

"Sounds good! Well, Jacob. Follow me over to the desk to get your license, and Ethan, do you mind helping Matt pick out some good flies?"

"Yessir."

"Ethan is our ace in the hole. He's an entomologist in training and out fishes all of us constantly. He will put you on the hot flies." Alan motioned towards Ethan.

Ethan blushed and headed to the long, wooden table full of compartments loaded with flies.

"Are you looking for dry flies or nymphs or streamers?"

Joe sat back down at the vise. His heart raced and he felt awkward and out of place. Remembering the walk from Jacob's office after he had been put on a leave of absence felt like a lifetime ago. An embarrassing lifetime ago. He knew he deserved to lose his job and left Jacob with no alternative but to let him go. He was grateful that Jacob left the door open for him to return, but he didn't anticipate ever seeing Jacob after he left his office. The comradery of the fly tying was upset by the arrival of the customers and everyone could sense it. Georgia started to hum the tune to "Maneater" and Chuck and Dave looked up. "No!" They shouted in unison.

"How can you not like Hall and Oates?" Georgia quipped.

"Easily," Dave responded.

"She's a rich girl..." Joe softly sang to break his building tension. Chuck, Dave, and Georgia erupted into laughter.

"Quick! Get the microphone!" Chuck prodded Joe.

Alan, Matt, Jacob, and Ethan conferred at the counter. Jacob looked over at Joe and lifted his head.

"Hey, Joe. Ethan is trying to convince us to fish Mill Creek on Sunday. We have a float scheduled for tomorrow, but Alan's saying Ethan would be a great guide as he knows where all the big fish live. Ethan said he would guide us as long as you came with us. Are you up for that? It would be good to fish with you!"

Joe looked at Ethan who had the look of a puppy begging for food. Joe turned to Georgia. She could see the struggle in Joe's face and gave a wincing smile while lifting her shoulders. Ugh. Fishing with my boss who fired me and the asshole dad of the kid in traffic court. How better to spend my Sunday. Joe looked back at Ethan. His eyes pleaded with Joe. Getting hired to tie flies for a fly shop and as a guide all in one day, this could be one of the best days of his life. Joe couldn't refuse no matter how awkward it may be. *This may be a maneater.*

"Sure! The kid is a wizard. Sounds like a fun day!" Joe put on his best consultant smile.

55

Wet Feet

Joe tied a handful of beetles to avoid any deeper conversations about why he wasn't still working with Jacob. Ethan was bouncing off the walls for most of the night. Alan and Ethan talked through how many flies to have for clients, what knots and leaders he would have to know, and how to help people who may not know they need to be helped.

"The basics of guiding is listening to people and offering ways for them to learn. It makes it much easier if you can put them on fish, and easier fish to catch."

The group of tiers talked through good places to fish and importantly places not to share, their own "honey holes."

"Fly fishers always try to keep some really good spots to themselves or at least to good friends," Alan reminded Ethan. Georgia offered to put together bag lunches for everyone and Joe would carry a small soft cooler in his vest. Ethan understood his game plan and was excited to be a fly-fishing guide.

A couple of slices of pizza and a root beer filled Joe's belly and brought on his exhaustion. His eyes were feeling heavy. They had successfully tied flies through the entire set of the Dynamic Rockers. It was safe to enter the streets again. The darkening skies coincided with the end of the music and people dispersed. Food vendors were closing down and the city crew was taking down the stage. Joe said his good-byes and walked back to the hotel.

As he sat back on the edge of the bed to take off his shoes, Joe tried to think through his plan for the following day. He felt pulled to talk to Sarah Williams, to learn more about Lilian and Nicolas Murphy. *Something didn't add up. What possibly could have made Jody suppress the memories of her family?* Seth Stewart invited Joe to visit the house. Joe wanted to stop by, but it also felt invasive. *Would Jody want me to be there? Well, she told me to turn over some stones and find my way.*

Ethan was going to spend his day tying some flies for Sunday and scouting out the path he wanted to take his first "clients." *It was nice to see him so excited.* Joe drifted off into a deep sleep.

"Don't go chasing waterfalls, please stick to the rivers and the lakes that you're used to..." Jody didn't like to hear her singing voice, but she loved '90s R&B music. She said it reminded her of freshman year of college when her life was expanding. Expanding. She would always say that word slowly with a sly smile and bright eyes as she moved her hands apart. Joe loved to hear her sing and watch her smile. He reached to touch her hair. She leaned her head against his hand.

Suddenly, the windshield shattered and Joe lost control of the truck. They were spinning off the road and tumbling down the embankment. He couldn't take his eyes off her. The truck came to rest at the bottom of the slope. Glass, dirt, blood and debris covered the dashboard. Her head was still and laid to the side. A gash in her forehead dripped blood over the left side of her face. Her eyes were closed. His chest was tight and his face felt warm and wet. He didn't want to move. Joe looked ahead and looked out at the matted vegetation and mud. He turned to look back at Jody and her eyes were blankly staring at him. "I didn't tell you..."

Joe's eyes bolted open in a panic. He was dripping in sweat and his heart was racing. *What is she trying to tell me?* Joe went and grabbed a glass of water, trying to settle his nerves and cool himself down. *I don't want any more car accident dreams.*

Joe ended his fitful night of sleep as the sun came up. 5:47. The diner didn't open until 7 on weekends. He decided to take his notebook and watercolor tablet down to Mill Creek. *Starting the day with some nature and art may do me some good, since I can't go back to sleep.*

The town was not quite awake. The city crew had cleaned up well after the festivities, as Main Street looked bright and ready for the day. As Joe walked toward the stream, a deer bounded across Sullivan Street and through the ball fields. He found a large, exposed boulder on the northern stream bank and took off his shoes, letting his feet dangle in the water as he sat on the flat surface of the boulder.

He dipped the small brush into the stream and started his water-color. Joe printed Mill Creek Sunrise on the bottom of the tablet after the first few strokes. The bright green of the grasses mixed with the light green of the willow leaves provided a soothing background. Clumps of dark purple irises and red cardinal flowers accented the lush riparian corridor. Years after the restoration it would be hard for many people to determine all the work needed to return this area to a naturalized condition. White foam and frothing water tumbled below the steep rocks; their gray and black edges added an angular element to the flowing and pulsing movements of the vegetation and water.

"Morning, Joe." Ethan emerged from behind a thicket of alder.

"Good morning, Mr. Fly Fishing Guide."

"I couldn't sleep, I was so excited." Ethan's smile hadn't faded from last night.

"I couldn't sleep, but for other reasons."

"Oh, yeah? Need to talk about anything?" Ethan genuinely seemed interested.

"That's a dangerous question. Probably best for another day. I do need to tell you something about Jacob Miller."

"Is it going to ruin tomorrow?"

"I don't think so. But something may come up. Jacob used to be my boss. He gave me a leave of absence a couple months ago because I was struggling."

"Because of the drinking?"

"Yeah."

"Well, you don't drink anymore, so don't worry about it."

Joe smiled. *Is it that easy?*

"I will try. I didn't want there to be any surprises to mess up your first day. So, you need to tell me what you need me to help with."

"I need to think out the plan more, but I definitely want to talk with you later if that's cool."

"Sure thing."

Ethan headed off upstream. Within fifty feet he was hidden by the foliage, like he disappeared into a fog. Joe sat and looked at the river. *Stream ninja.* Joe chuckled to himself. Sitting on the rock, dangling his feet back in the cool water, Joe took in his surroundings. He smiled and finished the watercolor painting. Time had flown by. It was 8 am. The library would be open and Joe was hoping to talk with Sarah. He moved his toes in the water and took a deep breath. After a couple shakes of his feet, he slid his feet back in his shoes and was on his way back to town.

Joe appreciated the heavy doors of the buildings in town. They had preserved so much of the character and workmanship of the original buildings. He was hoping the library door would remain following the renovation.

Sarah was at the front desk as Joe entered. She looked down at her notes, up at him, and smiled. Her lanyard swung against her chest. She grabbed her pass and looked down at Joe's feet. "Morning, Joe. Why is it you always have wet feet?"

"Funny. Isn't there a saying about if you don't get your feet wet, you'll never know?" Joe scratched his chin and felt his stubble, a bit coarser than he was used to.

"I don't know that one."

"That's because you have dry feet." Joe grinned.

Sarah smirked, "No wonder you got along with Ed. You're both too clever for your own good. What can I help you with this morning?"

"I'm still trying to put together a puzzle of Lilian, Nicolas, and Jody. I don't know how many pieces or the picture I'm trying to match."

"That is a dilemma. I knew them, but I don't know what to share. Also, I may get interrupted to help folks coming in. It's generally pretty quiet until 9 a.m. when the children's Harry Potter club comes in. What do you know so far?"

"I know Jody wasn't into Harry Potter."

"Clever again."

"I know where they lived and that the Stewarts bought their house. Seth Stewart still lives there. Seth also told me that Judge Perkins helped facilitate the sale and that he helped Jody with the estate. I believe Judge Perkins is prevented by attorney-client privilege to discuss anything about the estate. Seth also referred to the judge as a "guardian angel.""

"Wow, you get right to it." Sarah's eyebrows furrowed.

"That's funny. I've never heard anyone call the judge a guardian angel, but he's helped a lot of people in Remberg. I did remember he helped Jody. After the accident, she was in the hospital in Binghamton for a bit. She had some injuries and what have you. But she ended up staying there for a bit."

"In the hospital?"

"Uhhh…I don't think her injuries were too bad, because she was around for the funeral. She had some bruising, but she was moving around okay. I don't really know the extent of her injuries. Maybe she was seeing a therapist? She just wasn't around after the funeral. I did help the judge with a small estate sale after Jody took a few things. But she didn't take much; it was nearly a fully furnished house. I think she took some personal records and family pictures, maybe a little of Lilian's jewelry."

"I don't think I could've handled all of it at that age."

"Definitely a hard situation. And then that poor boy committed suicide, just awful."

"Did you know anything about Cody?"

"Just that he was a star baseball player, best ever to come out of Remberg, according to Ed. He got injured and his career was threatened and…"

"Very sad."

"Yes. I remember Lilian was worried that they were too close and they were so young, typical mom stuff. She wanted Jody to go to college and not pine after some boy who was galivanting around playing baseball. Nicolas, even more so. They wanted her to be independent and educated. Really what most parents want I guess."

"I guess so. Not being a parent myself, I don't really know."

"Hey, do you still have those records? Did Jody keep them?"

"I don't really know. She had a few boxes, but we moved into our house over twenty years ago. Jody handled finances and paperwork, so I didn't pay attention."

"Well, you may have some records at your house."

"Why didn't I think of that?"

56

Beloved

A young girl with long brown hair pushed past her mother as she opened the door to the library and ran toward Sarah. She was wearing a long, black cloak and had a mustard yellow and burgundy scarf around her neck. Sarah squared her body to the onrushing girl with a careful eye on a small wooden wand.

"Good morning, Mrs. Williams!"

"Good morning, Mackenzie! Are you excited for the Harry Potter club this morning?"

"Yes, oh, yes! And guess what?" She took no time for a response. "Mommy got me a latte this morning!"

Sarah's eyes widened. "Wow, aren't you lucky!" Sarah turned and grinned at Joe.

Her mother approached with a sheepish smile. "Please say you're sorry for interrupting Mrs. Williams' conversation, Mackenzie."

"What? Oh…I'm sorry. I wanted to tell you about the latte!"

"No worries, dear."

"Good to see you, Joe. I need to make sure everything is set up for the club right now. You can stop by later if you have anything you want to chat about. I'm here until 3."

Two young boys dressed as wizards with red "Z"s painted on their foreheads rushed to join Mackenizie.

"Thanks, Sarah. Have fun today." Joe smiled with a slight wince.

Sarah smiled, nodded, and headed off to join the gathering.

Joe stepped out of the library and the town bustled with energy. Joe found a bench near the courthouse steps and sat to jot down some thoughts in his notebook. *Where would Jody have stored old boxes of records?* He couldn't remember. There were boxes of photos, college notebooks, and other items in the storage cabinets in the basement. Not that he paid attention to things like that, but nothing popped in his mind as a treasure trove of documents where all his questions would be answered. *I am five hours away from my house, with no car and no idea what could possibly be in any records, or if Jody even kept any records. But I have a cell phone.*

"Cindy!"

"Joe, it's been a while. How's my big brother?"

"On a roller coaster, figuratively."

"Well, I can't wait to hear about it, but I'm headed into the theater. You okay? Can I call you later to catch up or do you need to talk right now?"

"Um…I guess so. I was hoping you could run by the house and look through some stuff for me?"

"I would. I mean, I will. But I'm in Branson, Missouri, for a week. Don't worry, all is good with the house. I don't want to be late for the Dolly Parton Tribute Concert."

"Wow, that sounds awful. I mean right up your alley. I'll call you tomorrow."

"Love you, bro."

"Thanks. Love you, too."

Another incomplete step toward the unknown. Joe hated waiting. He looked back at his phone. It was 11:45 and Seth said he'd be home at noon. Maybe a walk would clear his head. Not that he had any other option.

Joe stretched his legs and walked along Main Street. The shops were busy and smiling faces greeted him near each store front. A small dance studio must have had a change in classes as a dozen young girls and a handful of boys spilled onto the sidewalk. Parents parked along the street or sitting on benches waved to the young dancers. Joe's steps lightened. The excitement of the children and the smiles of the parents were contagious. *Why am I holding onto so much stress? She wanted me to explore and expand, I think, not become stressed and paranoid.*

He reached Gray Street and headed north. Beyond Valley Street, Gray Street became a charming and steep cobblestone lane. Victorian-style houses with long, narrow yards were separated by various fences and hedgerows. There were some white picket fences, but when Joe reached 970 North Gray Street, three blocks north of town, a black wrought iron fence delineated the yard. He felt the sweat pulling his shirt against his skin and wiped his forehead as he opened the gate.

"Son of a Son of a Sailor" could be heard through the windows of the house. A large transom window let light in above the ornate wooden door. Fish scale shingles adorned the mansard roof with three dormer windows along the top floor. A sunburst sat above the bracketed portico framing the front door. A black iron knocker brought Joe's eye to the center of the door and two full-length windows framed the door. Joe lifted the knocker and let it fall. It was heavier in his hand than he anticipated and the drop was abrupt. The door opened quickly.

"Welcome, Mr. Barden. Sorry, I mean Joe! I'm a slow learner."

"Thanks for inviting me over. Sorry if I didn't give you enough time to settle down after your morning."

"All good, Joe. How 'bout that tour? Did you want a drink or anything? Water? Lemonade?"

"No, I'm good, thank you. I'd love the tour though. Your home is beautiful."

"Thanks."

Seth led Joe to an ornate wooden banister leading to a stairway that rose from the left side of the home to a small balcony on the second floor. The dining room was in a room to the left with a large bay window that added brightness to the red walls and dark wood setting. A large, round Oriental rug drew Joe's eye. Seth stood on the first step.

"So, what do you want to see first? A butler's pantry connects the dining room to the kitchen in the back of the house. The living room is straight back beyond the staircase. There is a bathroom off the kitchen and one upstairs."

The artistry of the woodwork was impressive.

"This is a work of art Seth, really."

"Thanks. I haven't had to do much to keep it up. I added a new knocker to the door and replaced the fence, with some work in the kitchen and bathrooms, but I loved the woodwork. You know the saying, 'They don't build things like this anymore.'"

"No kidding, this town seems like it was built by talented artisans."

"It really was. There are so many beautiful buildings here. I'll show you upstairs first, if that's okay."

"Sounds good."

Photos of Seth's family were hung along the staircase as well as photos showing the evolution of the shop. Joe loved the old signs; the neon and porcelain sign work was classic and expressive. Each upstairs bedroom doorway was a master class in hand-carved framing. Crown molding outlined every ceiling and floor surface. The house wasn't large, but it was beautiful.

"Do you know which room was Jody's?"

Seth turned and pointed down the hallway. "The room in the back of the house looked like it was yellow at one point, so I'm assuming that was her room. But I don't know for sure." He pointed to the center room, which was currently an extra bedroom. "This room was an office when I was growing up, so I assumed it was always that way. Now I use the back room as my office so I can look out the back window when I'm bored of looking at my computer."

"I always wanted a window near all my offices too. It helps you feel like you're outside when you're stuck inside all day."

"I totally agree. So I kept some of the furniture but my parents switched out some furniture in my room because I had a tendency to jump and climb on furniture. I broke more than a few things in my youth. They had their hands full."

"I understand that. I was a handful, too."

"Oh, one of the coolest parts of the house is downstairs. The sitting room is also a library. People say I should make it into a more modern entertaining space. But I just love it. Books were important to my mom. That was her room growing up. And I believe Mrs. Murphy was the town librarian, too. I think a lot of the books were from her, too. I don't think that room has really changed at all. I broke a side-table when I was a teenager, kicking a soccer ball through the house. Mom went through the roof! I thought she was going to kick me out for that one."

"Ouch. Yeah, I'd love to see the sitting room."

A large fireplace centered the left wall and a large window faced into the yard from the library.

"Is this walnut?"

"Yup. Isn't it nice? It was available around here, far more affordable than mahogany. Such rich tones."

"It is very nice."

Built-in shelving was stacked upon a row of walnut cabinetry at the ground level. The ceiling was twelve feet high and books filled every space on every shelf. Two large chairs and a loveseat were arranged facing the fireplace. A black iron rail with a wheeled ladder was a nice touch. "I just ran into a group of mini-wizards at the library who would love this room. It looks like a mini Hogwarts castle."

"Ha! Maybe I should offer it up for a meeting."

"That would be a hit. You could serve lattes."

"Lattes? Is that a Harry Potter thing?"

"Maybe just a ten-year-old thing." Joe didn't feel like explaining the whole story but smiled to himself at his joke.

"You sure I can't get you anything?"

"I'll take some lemonade. Thanks, Seth."

"Sure thing."

As Seth went to the kitchen, Joe looked through the books. Many classic books. *A Tale of Two Cities*, *Moby Dick*, and others filled one panel. Another panel was filled with many science books. The third panel was filled with more modern novels. As he was looking through the titles, a white spine with red lettering caught his eye. *Beloved.* Morrison. This was one of Jody's favorite books. She had at least three copies in their house.

Joe picked up the book and wiped a thin layer of dust from the spine. In his clumsiness, he knocked the book from his hand and it landed open, face down on the floor.

"All okay in there?"

"Who left this soccer ball in here? Just kidding. I dropped a book. It looks okay. Sorry!"

"No worries!"

As Joe lifted the book, a receipt fell from the book. He picked up the receipt in his right hand: S&C Books and Brew - $8.99 - May 25, 1988'

Huh, it doesn't seem like inflation hit the book market. Joe flipped over the receipt. A stick figure picture was drawn in pencil. His heart stopped.

57

Oversharing

It felt like the longest possible amount of time to pour lemonade. Joe sat staring at the receipt. Jody obviously drew this. Cody Franklin was her boyfriend at the time. A baby? Was this a daydream or whimsical sketch? Two sets of initials, twins or one male and one female?

"Here you go, Joe. I squeezed the lemons myself. My mom loved Arnold Palmers, so I make a lot of iced tea and lemonade. Kind of my thing now."

"Thank you. Looks good." Joe was obviously distracted.

"You okay?"

Joe put the receipt back in the book and closed the book.

"Yes. I was looking through your books and I saw *Beloved* by Toni Morrison. Jody loved this book. I picked it up and found a receipt. It looks like it was purchased a few weeks before she left town. I think she may have bought it. I'm feeling a little emotional and connected to this. Would it be okay if I have this book?"

"Of course. It is likely from when she lived here. Most of the books my mom added were to the right of the fireplace. Was that on the left side?"

"Yes."

"Of course, you can have it. I can imagine this is like walking back in time with you, being in Remberg."

"It does feel like that. It's been nice, but also stressful, like secrets are everywhere I look. It feels like everyone knows a secret I don't know."

"I get it. That sounds unsettling."

Joe took a sip of lemonade. "This is really good. Thank you. I also really appreciate you showing me your house."

"You're welcome."

Joe felt an urge to find Georgia as soon as possible. She could help him make sense of this. Or at least feel better and rationalize away the paranoia. "You probably have a lot to do. I feel like I've taken a lot of your time already. Again, I really appreciate everything. I will talk to you soon."

"You're more than welcome. Oh, and by the way, everything should be good to go on the Tahoe by Tuesday.

"Thanks, Seth. I will see you on Tuesday."

Joe put his hands on the arms of the chair and pushed himself up. He took a long look around the library along with a deep breath. Books, art, and science filled the house. It definitely seemed like a good setting to grow up.

Walking out of the door and down the stairs he held onto the book tightly. Joe's eyes were open guiding him back to the diner, but he wasn't present in each foot step. He was a ghost. His mind was in the book and imagining Jody reading it. *Beloved*, a book about the atrocities of slavery. A story, based on a true story, where the level of suffering and trauma is so severe that a mother killed her own daughter so she wouldn't have the same fate. And this sketch. *Did she get pregnant? Did she abort the baby? This certainly could destroy a relationship with her parents.* He needed to talk with Georgia.

The bell hanging from the diner door brought Joe back to his eyes. His gaze met Georgia's. Very quickly her greeting smile shifted to a furrowed brow. "Booth at the end."

Her intuition was ridiculous. Honed by years of truly listening to people, she could read Joe's look of dead-eyed panic immediately. She didn't ask if he wanted a coffee and a water. She just brought it to him. There were only a few customers spread throughout the diner. She slid the coffee over the table and sat across from Joe. He set the book on the table and looked up at Georgia.

"*Beloved?*" Her eyes narrowed and her head tilted.

"Open the front cover."

She opened the cover slowly, like she was trying to avoid anything jumping out and scaring her. She subtly shook her head looking at the receipt.

"Flip it over."

She took a deep breath.

"Joe, do you know how many times I wrote my first name and some boy's last name on sheets of paper? This could be something any girl scribbled."

"Did you ever pick kids' names?"

"Not with a last name, but I daydreamed of what I would name my children all the time. And I never was very motherly or interested in anything other than a steamy romance."

"Could a pregnancy or..." Joe lowered his voice while looking to see if anyone was sitting close enough to overhear. "...an abortion really damage her relationship with her parents? Maybe cause her to feel responsible for their death, like you mentioned?"

"That definitely would be an awful strain for two parents focused on raising a scholar. You're making a huge leap here. This could be nothing."

"You know the story of the book, right?"

"No." She looked around to see if any of the customers needed anything. They all seemed content.

"Read the summary on the back cover. It's short."

She flipped the book and quickly read the summary. Her eyes widened and the edges of her mouth dropped.

"This is weird. But it could be a book she wanted to read and just a coincidence. I can see this would throw you. But don't linger on it too long."

She paused. "No doctor or lawyer that she may have interacted with could ever share anything like this and they more than likely would be very old or passed. This may be a black hole with no bottom."

Joe took a deep breath. Georgia had always listened, always helped him feel a little less crazy. He couldn't tell if she was cleverly trying to protect him from a painful truth or if she was kindly pushing him away from paranoia. The fact that his brain was processing her motives alarmed Joe. This was different. He looked at her differently for a second, getting out of his own head.

"Georgia, are you okay?"

She looked right to scan the diner. All the patrons were eating or involved in their conversations.

"I'm not quite myself today, Joe." Her chin began to shake and her eyes welled. "Alan has prostate cancer. He told me last night. After I told him I really cared for him."

Tears fell over her lashes and down her cheek.

"I feel like I found someone and they may not be here for long."

"Whoa. I don't know what to say. That is heartbreaking and terrifying."

"The doctor's think they caught it early, and hopefully they can take care of it quickly, but it has shaken me up. I am sensitive to share this with you, knowing what you've experienced. I'm just on autopilot today. I couldn't talk about it until just now."

"I am concerned about you and Alan. But my brain is also processing the excitement that you told him how you felt about him. That is a big deal and very brave. What did you say?"

She brushed her cheek and cracked a soft smile. "I asked him what it was going to take for him to ask me out." She chuckled to herself and let out a breath. "I've not thought about it because of how it ended. But it was a big deal."

"Can you tell me more?"

"I started off by thanking him for helping Ethan and being so thoughtful to him. I kept talking and I kept sharing more. You may be rubbing off on me Joe." She paused and smiled.

"I told him I knew he was an amazing man, an amazing husband, and that over the last few years I began to care for him deeply. He blushed and didn't know what to say at first. He told me that he hadn't asked anyone out since his wife passed away many years ago. I told him that we'd been having coffee multiple times a week and that we'd been essentially dating for years. That I looked forward to seeing him more than anyone I've ever known. Then he started to get teary and he told me about the cancer."

Joe's eyes were now full of tears.

"That is incredibly sweet, Georgia You can't let him go, no matter what. It is so precious to have that love. Fight for it. Even if the time is limited, it is still time with love."

She nodded her head and a patron caught her attention.

"Thank you, Joe. I need to get back to work. Girls daydream about romance. Even when they are old waitresses. Don't get lost in the picture or the receipt. And thank you for helping Ethan tomorrow."

Joe nodded and smiled.

58

Guide Service

"Morning, Ethan!" Joe called out as he entered the diner.

Ethan was pacing at the counter. "Oh, hey Joe."

"You waiting on the sandwiches? You are going to do great today. I'll be with you the whole way."

Joe settled his voice into a soft tone. "Morning, Georgia. Good to see you."

"Want a coffee to go, Joe?"

"Yes, please. You doing okay?"

"I'm always okay, Joe." She lied. "I woke up and found Ethan sitting at the kitchen table. He made me oatmeal. What a great way to start the day. And it's his first day ever as a professional fishing guide. It's a big and exciting day."

"Indeed, it is." Joe looked at Ethan, who was still pacing. He stopped, rubbed his hands together and smiled.

"We're meeting at the pavilion, right?"

"Yessir."

"Okay, Ethan. I want to ask you two things. You ready to listen?" Joe heard his tone and tilted his head. "I said that too abruptly. I wanted to ask you two favors. Is that okay?"

Ethan stopped in his tracks, trying to process Joe's words. "Sure."

Joe thought about his requests and how he could articulate his thoughts without overwhelming the boy.

"I appreciate you being polite. And it is good to be polite to your elders. It is respectful. But you are going to be a professional, and you know fishing, especially Mill Creek, better than most folks. So today don't defer to me or your clients on what you recommend. You can be strong without being rude. Clients can always follow their own way, but you are the guide. Offer your ideas with confidence. You have earned the right to your opinion already. So when you're the guide, you don't need to say 'yessir.'"

"Okay. I get it. Be confident."

"Yes. You are knowledgeable and you are the guide. Don't forget it. The second favor is more personal to me." Joe paused and debated in his mind if he should keep talking.

"I know Jacob Miller well. He was my boss. It would help me preserve my dignity a bit if you didn't mention that we were working together on community service. I'm learning that oversharing isn't always a good thing."

"Okay. I understand."

Georgia took a roll of wax paper and cut four sheets large enough to wrap the sandwiches. She creased lines into the paper and folded the paper around the sandwiches like she was wrapping a special gift. "Okay, boys. Here you go. Two turkey and bacon and two pastrami. I gave you boys a choice."

"Thanks, Georgia." Ethan gathered the sandwiches in a small, soft cooler with an ice pack and four bottles of water.

"Ethan, I am so proud of you. You will be great. Can I hug you?" Georgia leaned forward with a cautious smile.

"Yeah, thank you." Ethan took a step and Georgia took several quick steps around the counter to hug him. She grabbed him tightly, and tears ran down her face. The tears weren't just for Ethan, but it touched Joe. Georgia wiped her eyes and shook her head.

"Go get 'em, boys."

"Let's do it." Joe put his hand on Ethan's shoulder and they headed out the door.

They made sure to get to the pavilion about twenty minutes ahead of the agreed meet-up time. Joe put the rods together and tied the tippets onto the leaders. Ethan checked the stream conditions and flipped over some rocks. He decided his clients would start the day with some micro streamers, and when the sun cleared the trees, he would likely switch to a dry dropper rig.

Jacob and Matt Miller drove up in a Toyota 4Runner and parked at the park office. The crunch of the gravel half made Joe think Earl Hunter had pulled up. Jacob got out first.

"Morning, Ethan! Morning, Joe! We brought extra coffee if you want some."

Joe perked up. "I'll take one. Thank you."

Matt lumbered out of the car. Jacob looked back at him.

"Old man Matt wrenched his back a little there yesterday. He will be moving slow today. He made it all the way to the end of the day and took a weird step getting out of the drift boat."

"Ouch. Sorry to hear that, Matt. I'm probably more your speed today then. I can stick with you. Ethan, did you want to give the rundown of what you wanted to do today?"

"Yes..." Joe shot him a glance to interrupt the sir that may follow. Ethan caught the hint. "Yes, I'm thinking we'll split up and hit some of the larger pools first thing in the morning with small streamers, as the terrestrials don't get moving until the sun hits their wings. We'll switch to a dry dropper with a beetle or cricket up top, and a pheasant tail or hare's ear trailing once the sun clears the trees. It's harder to fish the streamers together, but if you want to come back together for the late morning, we can do that."

Matt chimed in half jokingly, "Jacob and I spent all day together yesterday on a small drift boat, a break from me may be a relief to him."

Jacob laughed. "I haven't seen you in over a year, so I can handle a few days."

"Ready?" For a thirteen-year-old, Ethan was setting a nice professional tone.

Matt and Joe slowly walked downstream and found the run-pool transition that Ethan had mapped out for them.

"So, I'm assuming you are an experienced angler? I don't want to give you guidance you don't want to hear or anything. Ethan has been having success jigging these micro streamers through the pools. He casts it upstream and leads it though the pool with a subtle jigging motion. You can also do the quartered downstream and retrieve. Slower retrieves have been working better lately. Normal small stream holding lies, undercut banks, and overhanging logs. You may be surprised at the size of some of the fish lurking in these pools."

"Fun stuff. I've been fly fishing since I was a kid, but I don't go all that often and I mainly just fished dries. My dad was a strict purist. Like Reverend Maclean in *A River Runs Through It.* So we followed suit. Didn't you ever wonder why Jacob was so uptight?"

Joe nearly spit out his coffee and laughed a deep belly laugh. He may get along with Matt after all.

The weight of the streamer interrupted the typical motion of Matt's cast. It took him fifteen minutes or so to get his casting down. Joe was glad he recommended to work out the kinks casting into a thin riffle, so as not to spook all the fish lurking in the prime lies of the pool.

"I'm feeling like I can cast this without hitting myself in the back of the head now."

"I'm ready when you are." Joe smiled back at Matt. *These Millers were methodical and disciplined.*

Matt squared his shoulders and got his hands ready near the reel. His movements, even with a sore back, were skilled and precise. His first cast was about three feet off the bank. He let out a slow "uhhhh" but resisted the urge to lift and pull up the line out of frustration. He completed the drift.

"That look like a good drift?"

"Yes, you can impart subtle lifts and drops. Just a slight rise of the wrist. But that was good. I think you were selling your skills short."

Matt was focused. He gave a nod of his head and made the next cast. The fly hit the water less than a foot off the bank. He tilted his right arm forward and quickly retrieved the slack line with his left hand. The leader jerked downward and it startled Matt and Joe. Matt steadied his left hand on the rod, pinning the line against the rod and quickly lifted the rod over his left shoulder.

"Fish on!"

Joe was fired up. It was fun to be a guide. He was hoping Ethan was having fun, too. Joe grabbed his net and moved upstream of Matt. The fish leapt from the water and landed with a flat splash. It was a good-sized brown trout and was fiercely shaking its head. Matt was definitely slow playing his fishing skills. He quickly guided the fish toward Joe who scooped it cleanly into the net. Joe's face felt warm with a smile. He turned to Matt with the net in his left hand and slapped a high five with their right hands.

"Woohoo!" Joe felt like he may be even happier than Matt. "That was impressive."

Matt let out a deep breath. "Thank you, Joe! It always feels good to land a nice fish. What is that? Maybe fourteen or fifteen inches?"

"Looks about fifteen to me. What a great way to start the day."

"Fun! Fun! Thanks, Joe!"

Over the next hour and a half, Matt worked up through the next three pools methodically. Every ten casts or so, Matt needed to stop and stretch his back. Even into his mid-fifties, Matt was athletically skilled enough not to let an injury impact his casting accuracy. But as the day went on, he was likely to stiffen and feel some soreness. Joe was anticipating an early end to the day fishing with the Millers.

Matt was able to catch two more fish in the morning and induced another good-sized trout to chase down the fly, but it did not strike. It's always the ones that get away that anglers talk about after the day. At least five times after missing the fish, Matt would exclaim, "Damn, I cannot believe I missed that fish!"

Each time, Joe could hear the voice that he remembered from the courthouse when Matt was aggravated with his son. Once the sun cleared the tree tops and the haze had burned off the water, Joe and Matt walked up about a third of a mile to meet with Ethan and Jacob. Joe caught Ethan's eyes as they came around a bend in the river. Ethan's smile started just at the edges of his mouth, but as his head lifted and his eyes adjusted to the light, his smile grew to take up nearly his entire face.

"Hey, Matt! Hey, Joe! How was the morning?"

Matt spoke up, hoping to one-up his brother, "Landed three, moved a big one. These browns love these little streamers! How's my nerd brother doing?"

Jacob was just inside the stream bank and turned his head up towards the trio.

"Got four, sucker! Ethan here's a deadshot guide! Woohoo, this is fun!"

Ethan was beaming. "Jacob is skilled, and his casting is tight."

Joe added, "Matt, too. You guys must've had a heck of a teacher!"

Matt chuckled. "Our dad casted like he made his bed. All that military training went into everything he taught us!"

"Indeed." Jacob turned back to the stream and made another cast.

"Ethan, do you want to switch to the dry dropper?" Joe inquired.

"Yeah, Joe, let's go with the foam beetles and a sunken ant dropper. You good rigging that up?"

"You bet'cha."

"I think I've only got a couple hours left before I need a rest. My back is starting to lock up," Matt said. "Are you good with that, Jacob?"

Matt had leaned toward Jacob as he lowered his voice. He seemed to be slightly embarrassed about his injury.

"Yup, that was a tough spill you took. I don't want to leave you worse than I found you!"

Ethan rigged up Jacob's rod and the two anglers took turns fishing each run and pool as they advanced upstream. They each caught five more fish, with Matt catching the largest of the day, but Jacob catching one more fish than Matt. They kept a running tally and busted each other's balls on each bad cast or hang up.

"Do you ever stop competing?" Joe couldn't help but give them both a hard time.

"Hopefully not until one of us is six feet under. More fun that way." Matt slapped Jacob on the back as they walked back to the car.

Joe took out the sandwiches, drinks, and snacks. "Lunch for the road. Courtesy of the Courthouse Diner."

"This is great. Thanks, Ethan. Thank you, Joe. What a great little stream. Right in town, too. Great weekend for us with one day on the Delaware and another on this gem."

Jacob was very appreciative. He gave Ethan a nice tip and Ethan barely could contain himself, dropping half of the bills on the ground, before snatching them up and stuffing them in his pocket.

Ethan could barely speak. He shook the men's hands, strong and confident. Joe was so proud of Ethan. Jacob walked up to Joe with an outstretched hand.

"Good to see you, Joe. You are looking good. It's good to see you looking so good. And you've got one heck of a guide as your friend. I'll be in town through tomorrow night. We are presenting on the library renovation tomorrow morning. Maybe I'll see you around."

59

An Offer

After a few minutes of packing up the gear, switching from frantic working energy to the post-excursion reflection, Ethan popped. "That was awesome! That was so lit! Full on Joe. I can't believe I did that!"

"You crushed it, dude. Watching you, I felt like you'd been guiding for years. I saw you as an expert and excellent teacher. Knowledgeable, precise, and easy to understand. Crushed it."

"Crushed it." Ethan repeated.

"Let's go tell Alan and Georgia."

Ethan gave a quick nod with the smile still wrapped around his head.

They pushed open the heavy door of the fly shop and Charlie ran to Ethan. Alan and Chuck were sitting at the counter. Joe felt like they interrupted a moment. Ethan rolled on in.

"I think I crushed it, Mr. Baker!"

"What?"

"I guided the Millers with Joe! They tipped me eighty bucks! Eighty bucks!"

Chuck turned away and petted Charlie. He was breathing deliberately and slowly.

"Tell me all about it!" Alan's eyes cleared and he became present with Ethan.

Ethan explained in great detail starting with streamers, hook sets, missed fish, brotherly competition, spots he hit along the stream, and how the day ended. Ethan bounced around the room and didn't seem to breathe. Alan asked questions at each of Ethan's breaks. Joe noticed Alan's skill of listening was fine tuned. *I can learn a lot from him.*

Chuck intently sat with Charlie. They seemed to be consoling each other. Joe wasn't sure if Chuck heard one word that Ethan said. Joe put the rods that Ethan borrowed in the back office.

In a moment of silence, Chuck sat up. "I'll check in with you later tonight, Dad."

Alan nodded and Chuck shook Joe's hand, patted Ethan on the shoulder and headed out.

Alan took the opportunity to redirect Ethan.

"I know Georgia's going to want to hear all about your day. I think she's still at the diner? Why don't you go share the news? She'll be ecstatic to hear about your day."

"Sure, sure. Thanks, Mr. Baker!"

Joe held back. As the door closed, he turned to Alan. "Sorry we interrupted your conversation with Chuck." Alan didn't take the bait.

"Not at all. I was waiting to hear from Ethan all day. What an exciting day for him and thank you. I'm sure your presence and guidance helped him. That seemed like it could be awkward for you. You put Ethan first. Very generous."

"I was just thinking back to what you said to me after we caught Ethan stealing the feathers. It was wise, and it changed my point of view dramatically. I never thanked you."

"Did Georgia tell you?"

"Yes, I didn't mean to be in your business. I'm sorry if I'm invading your privacy. You impacted me and sharing that with you has been on my mind. My mouth got in front of my brain again."

"No need to thank me and it's okay. It's not something I want to hide or avoid. I'm just trying to figure out what to do. I think Chuck is struggling more than me. Georgia, too, for that manner."

"They love you. It's hard to process."

"I'm sure. It's stage two. They caught it early enough that with some chemo and radiation I should be good. The doctor said it should go well, and I should have a good chance at a full recovery. It hasn't spread or anything. But things may be rough for a few months. I may need some help around here if you decide to stick around at all."

"I didn't know what stage it was. That sounds like good news, catching it early. You really mean that, about me helping out? I'd love to help you, but I'm not sure if I'm sticking around. I'm beginning to wonder if chasing my wife's memory around this town is good for my mental state."

"Well, think about it. Chuck is very busy and wants to make detective. Working in a fly shop isn't in the cards for him."

Joe reached out and shook Alan's hand. With glassy eyes, Alan put his left hand on top of Joe's hand. "Thanks, Joe."

Joe walked back over to the diner and Ethan was still talking non-stop, even as he devoured a piece of cherry pie. Georgia's eyes showed a combination of excitement and overload from Ethan's verbal diarrhea. She took Joe's entrance as an opportunity to break the stream of consciousness.

"Coffee and a water, Joe?"

"Yes, ma'am. Is he telling you the play-by-play of the day?"

"I feel like I was there! Sounds like he's on his way to be the best guide ever. I'm so proud of him."

Ethan blushed and looked down to chase the last bits of pie around the plate, making sure to get every bit of whipped cream.

"He was fantastic. Calm, instructive, and a natural teacher. Jacob was asking him about bugs and Ethan knew all the answers and he put them on fish. And he was fun. He was hyper focused at first and then relaxed into a great grove. He is a natural. Like Robert Redford."

"Who?" Ethan had finished cleaning his plate.

"Are we that old, Joe?"

"Yes, we are, but you should see that movie! It's a classic." Joe suggested to Ethan.

"She's already got a full-page list of movies I'm supposed to see." Ethan rolled his eyes.

"Jeez, the eye roll. I didn't think professional fishing guides would give eye rolls?" Georgia quipped.

"Teenaged ones do." Joe patted Ethan on the back. "Can I get a Reuben and fries to go?"

"Yup, and travel cup for the coffee?"

"Thank you."

"Ethan, I was thinking it may be good to take notes on your observations on fishing, and even notes from guiding today. Water temperatures, flies, rigs, approaches, water you fished, stuff like that. You really have so much knowledge already. May help you moving forward and who knows, you may want to write a book someday?"

"A book?"

"You wouldn't have to, but wouldn't it be cool to be a famous fly-fishing author?"

"You think I could do that?"

"I think you could do anything. And I'd buy that book."

"Hmm."

"It takes a lot of work, just like guiding, but you can do anything. What are you going to do tomorrow besides take those notes?"

"You're giving me homework?"

"Just suggestions. I am going to miss you tomorrow. I'll have to finish all the painting myself. Just me and Earl. So sad."

"Buy some donuts and maybe I'll still help you."

"Ha! Enjoy your day. I'll get you a donut another time. And take some notes."

60

A Full Day Before Breakfast

The alarm went off just as Joe felt he was falling asleep. Dreams, borderline nightmares, of car accidents and unfamiliar family arguments interrupted his mind each time his body settled and drifted off. *One more day of community service. How many more days in Remberg?*

His plan had been interrupted like his sleep, but he had the agency to set his own path. Fate led him here and kept him here and he found more confusion than answers. Holding the receipt in his hand, he decided to consider this as the doodle of a teenager and not as a prediction come true or disrupted. If life was about the journey, enjoying the present and treating each day as an adventure, Joe was spending far too much time in his head. Time for some coffee and a good breakfast and a commitment to learn to enjoy the day. At this point, Joe wanted a clear head. Everything seemed scrambled since she left.

Joe smiled as he opened the diner door. He loved how opening the doors in Remberg brought him back to a time of youthful hope and cheerful smiles. Well, most of them. Georgia looked up and smiled; she didn't even ask this morning. She grabbed a white mug and saucer and set it on the counter at the far end. She laid down the busy menu and placemat and a rolled napkin filled with silverware. She placed a small glass of water next to the coffee mug and wiped the condensation off her hand onto her apron.

"Good morning, Joe!"

"Good to see you, Georgia. Did Ethan talk himself to sleep or is he still bouncing off the walls?"

"He crashed hard once we got home. Well, he did take about four pages of notes…not sure what got into him there. Getting him to write down anything for homework was always a struggle. Then he crashed."

Joe chuckled softly. *The kid listened to me.*

"How's Alan doing?"

"You know, it's funny. I spent so much time pining over the man. After one conversation it's like we've been together for many years. I am worried about the…" she paused.

"Cancer?" Joe filled the silence.

"Well, obviously that, but I was thinking about the physical part of a relationship. We've kissed and hugged and stuff but that's part of it you know. I'm afraid that will mess it all up, and plus we need to focus on his health."

Joe felt uncomfortable in any sexual conversation. The strict religious upbringing his father instilled in him created a conflict between feelings of shame and his desire to be more progressive.

"Uh, not sure what to say about that. I guess if things are meant to be, that will work out and find its time. It's only been a couple days."

"Yeah, yeah, I know. It's important though and our relationship feels old and comfortable without that step, that's all. Just worries me, that's all."

"Understood." Joe wanted to be supportive but also wanted this conversation to end as soon as possible and put the lid on that part of himself.

The door opened, saving Joe from further embarrassment. Or maybe not.

Jacob Miller walked in the diner, dressed in his presentation suit. Dark gray with a blue tie.

"Joe! Good morning! You're everywhere in this town."

"I was about to say the same thing about you. Of all the gin joints…"

Jacob laughed. "Presentation is at 9:30. Trying to get my energy right."

"You're in the right place. Best home fries for miles. I see you have your lucky suit on too."

"Whatever it takes to be confident, right? I learned that from the master."

"You knew that already."

"I learned so much from you. Not blowing smoke. Hey, can you join me? I could use some advice on a few things."

Joe turned and looked awkwardly at Georgia. *Out of the frying pan.* "Sure thing."

Georgia smiled and nodded at Joe.

"I can bring over your menu and water if you want to grab the coffee."

"Thanks."

Joe picked a booth several spots away from Jody's picture and set down his coffee. Jacob slid into the seat across from Joe.

"Your friend Ethan, that young man is one heck of a kid."

Georgia smiled as she filled Jacob's coffee.

"He is certainly that."

Jacob and Joe put in their orders and handed the menus to Georgia.

"Ethan thinks very highly of you as well. He told me about how since you've been in town you've been helping him learn about how to be confident and see the value in what he has to offer. He said that you've been a friend and a mentor to him. I told him that's what you always were to me, too."

"I appreciate that, but you're being too nice to me Jacob. Are you buttering me up for something? Joe had a slightly joking tone.

"You need, at some point, to learn how to take a compliment, my friend. But yeah, I have an ask."

"Okay, so what is it?"

"Ethan told me that you talked to him about drinking and how it can burn your life down like a fire. And that happened to his mom, but that you stopped drinking so that wouldn't happen to you."

"Ethan talked more yesterday than he has since I have known him apparently." Joe shook his head and his eyes widened.

"He reminded me how much you had gone through and I just wanted to say I'm sorry."

Joe felt his chest tighten and his eyes became glassy. He looked down.

"Thanks, Jacob."

He gathered himself as Jacob lifted his full cup with two hands and took a slow sip of coffee. "Without you letting me go, I probably would still be drinking, or worse. So, thank you."

"It was one of the hardest conversations I've ever had. But I didn't let you go. I gave you a leave of absence."

"Oh, yeah. It felt like I was fired."

"Well, I want you to come back whenever you're ready."

"What?"

"Specifically, we have a couple bigger projects we just won in our Denver office. I know you wanted to head out west at some point, right? Fish the great trout streams of Colorado and Montana?"

"Well, yeah."

"How would you like to be the Denver Civic and Restoration Studio Manager?"

"Wow. I didn't think this is where you were headed?"

"We have a house rented there where I've been staying when I head out there. It's nice and was more economical than hotels. You could live there as long as you want or until you found a place. And I'd give you a twenty percent raise."

"Wow. You think I could handle it?"

"Look, Joe. I got promoted over you because I played the game better. I always knew that. I know you did, too. I can cover that part of the job for you. I can keep the business pieces moving, but I'm spread too thin and you're the best architect I know. I'll handle the bullshit you don't want any part of. This is a really good market and we have a tremendous head start. With you doing great work, we'll be set. And it gives you a new place, a new start, out in that John Denver country you've always been drawn to. And I trust you to do great design and construction work. It's perfect."

Georgia's eyes darted back and forth as she approached the table. She put the plates of omelets and home fries on the table.

"I'll be back with the toast."

"Wow." Joe stared at the food. "I guess Ethan is a good salesman for me, too."

"He definitely believes in you, too." Jacob took a bite. "Think about it."

Those words made Joe think of his conversation the night before with Alan.

"I'll think about it. When do you need to know?"

"In the next week or so? You were going on a trip, so maybe you can head out there and take a look. You can stay at the house."

"I'll think about it and get back to you in a week."

The men talked about the town and the library while they finished their breakfasts. Joe wished Jacob good luck on the presentation and then Joe headed off to the park.

61

The Judge's Bench

"Morning, Joe."

"Good morning, Mr. Hunter."

"No donuts this morning?"

"I still am feeling it from all the donuts last Friday."

"Me too."

"So am I putting the finishing touches on the pavilion today? I have to finish the second coat of the blue."

"That was the plan, thanks. Let me know when you've finished up. I also need help emptying the trash receptacles after the weekend."

"Sounds fun."

The sun already felt warm. A kingfisher floated down the stream corridor and Joe looked out along its path. His brain reset while he precisely laid out the tarps and taped out the gold edges of paint. The rhythm of painting the benches and interior rails helped the time pass. Joe listened to the birds and whistled through as many Chris Stapleton songs he could remember.

He was hoping painting would take all his time, but he still had a half an hour to go. Trash patrol would be a fitting end to his community service experience. Joe took the supplies back to the shed and put everything away. Earl stepped out of the office and handed Joe a pair of gloves and several large bags.

"There are four bags to replace the four spots along the trail. One is at the pavilion and the other three are equally spaced along the trail. Then you'll be done. Pavilion looks great, Joe. Thank you."

"Thanks. I think it looks nice, too."

Joe headed out along the trail and grabbed the first bag at the pavilion and the second was at the first bend in the trail. Joe approached the turn and saw a figure sitting on a park bench overlooking the stream. A tall man, with his legs crossed and his hands folded across his lap. He was dressed nicely.

"Judge Perkins?"

"Good day, Mr. Barden. Are you finishing up?"

"Yes, sir. I finished painting the pavilion today. I think it looks good."

"It does look good. I normally sit there and eat my lunch each Monday. I'm glad I noticed the wet paint before I sat down."

"Shoot! I forgot the signs."

"Yes, you did. It would be good to put those up after you're done."

"Will do."

"Why don't you take a seat and chat with me before my lunch break ends?"

Joe's heartbeat accelerated. He felt like he got called into the principal's office.

"Is there something you need help with?"

"Well, I wanted to thank you for working with Ethan. He's a good kid and he needed some help to find a good direction to head. I've heard you've given him some good nudges."

"He is a good kid." Joe took a deep breath, trying to breathe in some courage. "I've been told you're the 'Guardian Angel' of Remberg, that you look out for everyone. That's how Seth Stewart referred to you, at least."

The judge lifted his right leg and put it on the ground, next to his left, sitting up off of the park bench a little straighter.

"I've never heard anyone say that before. That's a nice thing, I suppose. By God's will, I try to help those in need. As the scripture says,

'Like good stewards of manifold grace of God; serve one another with whatever gift each of you has received.'"

"I don't know the scripture well, but I feel like I know good deeds when I see them. Thank you for facilitating so many good deeds around here."

Judge Perkins turned his head and his eyes met Joe's with an inquisitive look.

Joe took another deep breath, with tears welling in his eyes.

"I know you helped Ethan. I also know you helped my wife when she was a teenager. She was Jody Murphy."

The judge looked down and nodded.

"Yes, I picked up that you were married. Jody was a wonderful young lady. I was sad that she didn't come back to visit. She experienced a lot of loss here in Remberg. The pain she must have felt..."

"Is there anything you can share with me about her time here? She never spoke about growing up here or about her parents. I never pushed her to tell me. It just seemed too painful."

"I helped her parents write a will and establish an estate. They were one of my first clients when I got my law degree. I spent a lot of time in the library and I knew Lilian very well. She was always kind and help-ful. The car accident was just awful; so sudden and tragic. They were Jody's world, and their passing was more than she could bear at such a young age. I felt it was my responsibility to help her, so I did. I took care of as much as possible with the estate. I knew she wouldn't be able to do it on her own. She wanted to push the pain away."

"I feel like I don't know the whole story. I've been trying to put it all together, but I can't find anyone who knows the whole story."

"I don't know who would know the whole story besides Jody. I was a lawyer who helped her and I did my job to the best of my ability, through God's will. But I'm not a storyteller or historian, I apologize. In addition, they were my clients and some of the details are lost in my mind with time and others I swore an oath to never tell. I take that very seriously."

"I understand. Thank you for helping them. I'm trying to put together the pieces of a puzzle and I don't know what the picture looks like, so any additional information helps. Why did you help Ethan?"

"He's another child who lost their guide in life. I made a promise to Ethan's grandmother that I would look out for him and his mother. I couldn't find a way to help Kimberly, but I wasn't giving up on Ethan."

"You *are* the Guardian Angel."

"Doing my part. At the risk of being too forward, I wanted to talk to you about your part. Listening to Georgia, it seems like you're becoming part of the fabric here in a short period of time."

Georgia may think that about everyone who she talks to in the diner."

"I've known her for a long time; she knows a good man when she sees one."

Joe looked down and nodded. "She is kind."

"She also will need help with Ethan."

Joe's head cocked to the side.

"The foster system holds a child in a foster home for 15 months. Ethan has been with her for almost 12 months. It's hard to take on raising a teenage boy on your own, and I hear now she is taking on caring for Alan with cancer. I'm fearful with all the factors that she won't be able to adopt or the system may distribute him to another foster family in another town."

"Wow, you know everything. Are you asking me to be a foster parent? I just don't..."

"I'm asking you to consider it."

"I'm just finishing community service for an alcohol-related driving offense. I've never even babysat. I can't see myself being a suitable foster parent."

"I'm not trying to force anything on you, Joe. I apologize if I came across that way. Ethan has responded to you and I believe you can help him. I just wanted to ask you to consider staying in town. I feel like you have a part to play here."

"That is a kind thing to say. I don't know how to respond. I do like it here and the people have been wonderful. But I sometimes feel like I'm chasing ghosts here. It's like there are secrets I will never know. That is unnerving."

"A great French playwright, Jean Racine, once said, 'There are no secrets that time does not reveal.'"

"You are overflowing with wisdom, Judge Perkins." Joe was starting to feel pushed on.

"I don't want to test your patience or try to convince you of anything. I want you to know that you are always welcome here in Remberg. This can be a home for you."

"Thank you, judge. That means a lot." Joe put his hands on his knees and sat forward, looking for an escape from the conversation. "I need to finish up with the trash. I really appreciate your time."

"Thanks for sitting with me. God Bless."

62

Briefcase Thoughts

Trash that has accumulated over the weekend in the summer is not a pleasant smell for a Monday afternoon. The old ice cream cones in the bottom of each bag are especially aromatic. Swatting flies adds to the ambiance.

Joe wondered if packing up the trash was signaling the end to his time in Remberg. *Is the party over? Is it closing time? Time to clean up the mess and head out.* The judge and Alan had made compelling arguments to stay. Remberg brought Joe a sense of community but also connected him to a tragedy he wasn't sure he could handle. Then Jacob offered him his value back and a new beginning in Colorado. *Rocky Mountain High.*

Unresolved secrets, a fun, fishy kid, and friends versus a new town, solitude, and the chance to productively finish out a career he took his life to build. Joe wasn't sure what rocks to flip over or what path to follow. First off, he wanted to put the trash in the dumpster.

The door was open to the park office. "Joe?"

"Hey, Earl."

Earl held a clipboard and a pen, with the biggest smile Joe had seen on his typically grumpy face.

"Mr. Barden, the State of New York releases you from your community service and I appreciate the nice paint job you put on our cupola finial."

"Thanks, Earl."

A chorus of out-of-tune singers emerged from the park office. Ethan was holding a cake with a few candles. Chuck, Alan, David, and Georgia followed Ethan from the office.

"For he's a jolly good fellow, for he's a jolly good fellow, for he's a jolly good fellow, which nobody can deny!"

"Speech, speech!" David bellowed.

"There will be no speeches!"

"Blow out the candles, you old fart!" Georgia's voice carried over the merriment.

A smile crept upon Joe's face as he stepped toward Ethan and blew out the candles.

"Thank you all. You know it's not my birthday, right?"

"Well, we wanted to celebrate the day. We can celebrate your birthday whenever that may be, too!" Georgia smiled and put her arm around Joe.

"Ethan wanted to celebrate, but still wasn't ready for any donuts. I wasn't sure what kind of cake you liked, so we went with a raspberry shortcake. This is the last good week of raspberries and I just love them. So maybe this cake is more for me." Georgia ever so slightly blushed.

"This is wonderful. Raspberry is great. Thank you! I should complete community service more often. Well...maybe not."

"We liked to celebrate around here. Every day is an accomplishment and something to be cherished. Like Muhammed Ali said, 'Don't count the days; make the days count!'" Alan always found an encouraging word.

"Dad, you are just a walking inspirational quote," Chuck quipped.

"That's how I survived being the dad of three boys. Always had to find the bright side."

"Burn!" Ethan piped in.

They laughed, made fun of each other, and ate cake. In the back of his mind, Joe was wondering if Jacob did well in the presentation.

"So, I just finished cleaning up all the trash and was released from community service. Does this mean someone else has to clean up?"

Earl chimed in, "I can clean up, but you or Ethan should take this cake home."

"I vote Ethan. He lives in a house with a fridge and he's thirteen."

"Sounds good to me!"

"Alright all, some of us have to get back to work." Georgia hugged Joe and the group headed off to town.

Joe said his goodbyes and headed to Stewarts Garage. Jazz radiated from the shop, as usual. Today was what sounded like a tenor saxophone. Cindy had played the tenor saxophone in middle school and high school. When he wasn't making fun of Cindy for being in the band, as any sibling would do, Joe was always a little jealous that she had musical talent. Joe loved going to her jazz band performances, but he never told her.

"Hey, Seth!"

"Joe! Got some good news for you. The Tahoe is up on the lift. It'll be done by 5 p.m. No more handcuffs and walking days for you!"

"Thank you, Seth. Everything came in this morning, I guess?" Joe wasn't sure if that was a sign of anything and couldn't feel any excitement or disappointment that he could now leave and be back on the road.

"Is that a tenor sax?"

"Good ear. Yes, this is Dexter Gordon. The "Sophisticated Giant" they called him. He was known as a clever fellow, as well as an amazing musician."

"You are like the walking version of your library there, Mr. Stewart."

"Not just a grease monkey?"

"A Renaissance man."

"Ha. I don't know about that. So, do you want to pick it up tonight? You can keep it here tonight or for a few days if you need to. Just let me know."

"Okay. Thanks. I don't have a clue what I'm going to do. I think I'll call my sister. I'll check back in a little later and let you know, if that's okay?"

"Sure thing. No rush."

Two steps out of the shop and Joe's mind traveled back in time. Back when Joe was in high school, one of his best friends was an irreverent smart ass named Brian Dehlin. A fun and witty lacrosse player who went on to be a doctor. Joe spoke to him occasionally since college— periodic phone calls, some group texts, Christmas cards for a while. He did come to the funeral, but Joe felt like they were losing touch. Brian's father, Tim, was an accountant. He wore glasses and had a leather brief- case. When Joe started at his first architecture position, he went and bought a briefcase. He later switched to a backpack to hold his laptop, but he always thought of Brian's dad when he carried that briefcase. It was nice to click the latches and shut the lid. He felt like a professional with that suitcase. It still made him smile.

Tim Dehlin was stern and didn't smile a whole lot, but on occasion he kindly came through with pointed and useful advice. When Joe was deciding where to go to college, the pressure from his parents was immense. The strain of the financial commitment wore on his father, which made the whole house on edge. Joe just wanted to decide and be done with it, but he was overwhelmed. Tim could tell and sat him aside one day. Joe remembered the conversation like it was yesterday.

"Something deep is on your mind. I can see it in your face."

"I need to decide where to go to college. I don't know how to decide and my dad is really irritated with me."

He took off his glasses and rubbed them with his handkerchief.

"Whenever I've had to make a tough decision, I've had to write it down. I write the decision at the top, then I make two columns below, one labeled 'For' and the other labeled 'Against.' I try to write as many things as I can in each column. By the time I'm done writing, I know where my heart lies. Sometimes it only takes writing one line; some- times I fill the whole page. But I always know when I put the pencil down."

Joe had used that process for nearly every hard decision for decades. It had left his mind for a time. But now it was squarely back in. He needed to write it down and he wanted to talk to Cindy. He grabbed his phone.

"Hey, Sis."

63

Two Columns

"Hey, Bro! How are you?"

"Good. How is Branson?"

"Well, the shows were fun. It's like a combination of a beach town and old town Las Vegas. I love it, but I'm ready to go home. I'm flying home tomorrow."

"Ending the trip early?"

"Yeah, I left the trip open ended and now I want to end it. Saw the shows I wanted to see and now I want to get home. I've been thinking about your call too. I want to be able to help you."

"I could certainly drive home, too. I'm only a five-hour drive away."

"The whole point of your trip was to use the reel that Jody gave you and explore the country. You got stuck, stranded, and I was supposed to help you with the house. I'm not living up to my end of the bargain."

"Are you kidding?" Joe felt his blood pressure elevating. "Do you know how much you have helped me? I'd be drunk and on my way to the grave without your help."

"I'm not sure about that, but thanks. You looked out for me my whole life and never asked for anything in return. I want to help you how you helped me."

"No scoreboard here but thank you."

"Okay, enough back and forth. I've been thinking about what you need. Can you explain it to me in more detail? I can stop by the house in two days."

"Okay, thank you. Being here in Remberg, I am discovering some puzzle pieces around Jody's life here. But I don't know what picture I'm trying to match or even if I have all the pieces, which I probably don't."

"So what pieces am I looking for?"

"I'm not sure. But I think Jody kept files, along with all of our information in files boxes in the back room of the basement. I never went through any of that stuff. If there is any paperwork related to her parents' accident, estate, or death, or anything that was important enough for her to keep all this time is worth looking at. She had a boyfriend who passed away. His name was Cody Franklin, so anything about him. Like I said, I don't know exactly what I'm looking for."

"Well, that's some more details and something for me to focus on. So are you okay? Do you have a car again?"

"I'm good. The car will be fixed in an hour or two."

"Well, that's great. Are you going to head west?"

"I forgot to tell you. Jacob offered me a job as the Studio Lead in the Denver office."

"What? He just called you? Out of the blue?"

"So many weird things have happened. He is here in Remberg. I fished with him yesterday and he offered me a promotion today. He's overwhelmed and needs some help. I think seeing that I'm clean and sober helped convince him to make me an offer."

"Well, he was always so appreciative of you."

"Yeah, I guess. It didn't always feel that way. They have some cool projects and he thought I would do well in Denver. Devil you know, maybe? But they have a house for me to live in and I'd get a raise."

"Sounds like quite the opportunity. And you get to head out west."

"You make it sound really good."

"Okay, well I'm gonna go. I'll text you when I'm back home. I'll swing by the house on Wednesday."

"Travel safely. Thanks, Sis."

Joe grabbed the composition book and made a large cross. He wrote "Remberg" and "Denver" across the top. He started the list. Under the right column he wrote job security, career challenge, Rocky Mountains, adventure, fresh start. He took a deep breath. He chewed on the end of the pencil and then wrote in the left column: friends, fly shop, diner, Mill Creek, Catskills. He sat the list on the small table. He circled "friends" and "Rocky Mountains." Another deep breath. He circled "fresh start" and wrote "Jody mystery" under the left column. Joe underlined "friends." At the very bottom of the page, he wrote "Leave no stone unturned." He decided what to do. He wasn't sure what was right, but he wasn't going to ponder anymore.

As he put his pencil down, his phone buzzed. It was a text from Jacob Miller.

"It was great to see you. I'm headed back to Baltimore. I think we did great today. We shall see. Shoot me a text if you want to head to Denver. Whatever you decide you can stay at the house if you go there. Talk soon and take care."

Joe looked back at the list and then at the phone. Another buzz. Text from Seth Stewart.

"All done Joe! I'm having the guys load your boxes back in the trunk and I also cleaned out your coolers. They got funky! See you soon!"

Joe looked back at the list. He needed to go see Georgia. It was 4:15 and he was hoping she'd still be at the diner. He took the composition book and wrote "8 days." Joe quickly walked to the diner.

He pushed open the door nearly out of breath, turning his head quickly to scan the interior of the restaurant. She was in the back corner at a booth, with slightly more than a handful of tables occupied. Joe caught Georgia's eye. He tilted his head towards the counter and she nodded.

"You look in a hurry there, Joe. Coffee and a water?"

"Yes, please. I wanted to talk to you about something I was thinking about."

"Why do you always have an intense look and something to talk about?"

Joe's head lowered and shoulders raised, "I guess I'm intense and talkative?"

"Sorry, I wasn't trying to be snappy. That came out strong." She poured the coffee.

"I'm leaving tomorrow morning."

"What?" She stopped pouring the coffee and stared at Joe. He regretted his word choice and tone.

"Seth finished the repairs. I want to continue my fishing trip out west and…"

"You suck at saying goodbye, Joe."

Joe gripped the coffee cup and took a sip. Then a deep breath. Georgia stared at Joe. He spoke softly: "I was hoping I could ask Ethan to come with me. I'm headed to Denver, stopping to fish along the way, maybe a spot in Omaha for a steak."

"Omaha for a steak?"

"Well, it's just a long way from Wisconsin to Denver. Why else would I stop in Omaha, except for a steak?"

"To see Warren Buffet."

"He stopped taking my calls."

"Smart ass. I'm still pissed you said you're leaving."

"Georgia. Jody left me a note and I'm thinking she wanted me to go on an adventure and reconnect to my youth and to fishing. You have a new relationship and some health things to handle. I can be in Denver in eight or nine days with some fishing stops. I love fishing with Ethan and hanging out with him. It's summer. You can take care of helping Alan and I'll pay for Ethan to fly back when we get to Denver. What do you think?"

"You're staying in Denver?"

"I don't know yet."

"What's in Denver?"

"The Rocky Mountains. I can live like John Denver." He smiled. Georgia stares without blinking, no smile.

"I got offered a job there, and I always wanted to live out west. I'm thinking I may take it, but I haven't decided yet."

"Well, shit. That sounds kinda perfect for you."

"Sort of does."

"Shit. I was hoping you'd stay here."

"That was two shits."

"Cause I give them."

"I ran into a buzzsaw today."

"You're throwing me a curveball, Joe."

"Sorry. So?"

"Go ahead and ask him. It's okay with me if he wants to go. And I can pay for the plane ticket."

"Thanks, Georgia."

64

Keep Living

Joe ordered a burger and some fries. Georgia warmed up a little as she passed the plate across the counter.

"That is nice you're taking him."

"He's a good kid. It should be fun. Anything I need to know? Does he snore like a lumberjack or anything?"

"He eats a lot and often. Bring snacks. If he has too much sugar, he talks a lot. Oh, and he really hates loud noises. I don't know what happened, but he shuts down with loud noises."

"Thank you, Georgia. That's good to know. I'll make sure he checks in with you each day."

Joe sat quietly eating and running through all the things he'd need to pack. He needed to buy the fishing licenses and check to see if his gear bag was loaded up with tippet and leaders. His mind started to run off. *Where am I going to fit all the stuff for someone else? What if he just talks the whole time? What if I can't sing along to my music without irritating him? What the hell do I know about taking care of a thirteen-year-old? What was I thinking? I've never been around a kid at all. I barely know this kid.*

Joe's face flushed and he felt his hairline moisten. He put his hand on his forehead. Writing down the reasons and filling out the columns went fast. The decision came fast. He didn't give the decision any time to sink in. *That may have been fine when it was my life, but now I am bringing along a thirteen-year-old into my aimless life. Maybe I'm being dramatic. It's only eight days.*

"It's only eight days." Joe's thoughts slipped out of his mouth.

"What was that, Joe?"

"Uh…nothing, just talking to myself."

"Well, you'll have someone to talk to for the next week."

Joe looked down and took a deep breath.

"What is it, Joe?"

"I'm panicking. I've never been around a teenager for more than a couple hours except for when I was one. It seemed like a good idea a few minutes ago, but now that I am faced with calling him, I'm panicking."

"Okay, well, you can change your mind. Or you can call him and ask him. Up to you."

"I started on this trip based on the last wishes of my wife. To leave no stone unturned. To go fishing. To…find a way to keep living." He felt his breath quicken. "Before I left, I didn't know what to live for."

"You go deep real quick, Joe. I appreciate it. You're an open book. Wide open. Sometimes it's slightly uncomfortable, but you have a charm that we all adore. I do have to tell you something. Hold on one second."

Georgia ran a bowl of chicken and rice soup and a cobb salad over to a couple in a booth.

Joe's body cooled and his mind slowed. Condensed water dripped down the side of his glass. He lifted his index finger to catch the droplet.

Georgia leaned over in front of Joe and lowered her voice. "Before you came here, Ethan barely spoke to me. Chuck picked him up for shoplifting a couple times. The kid threw rocks through a greenhouse. He owes me $1,800 for repairing the plastic sheeting down at the nursery. After his time fishing with you and painting the gazebo, he hugged me. He hugged me. And he talks to me every day, all day. Since you came here, he's like a different person." Georgia wiped a forming tear from the corner of her eye to avoid any smearing of makeup. "You should go on the trip."

Another deep breath from Joe. The chart always seems to work.

"I'll call him now."

Joe looked at his phone and scrolled through and found Ethan's contact.

"What's up, Joe?"

"Hey, Ethan."

"You okay? You never call. You just text."

"Wanna go on a fishing trip out west? I asked Georgia, and she said it's up to you. Just for a little over a week." Joe's voice shook slightly.

"Where?"

"I mapped out a drive to Denver, with stops at the Au Sable River in Michigan. Then going to the Driftless region of Wisconsin. After that we'd stop in Omaha, Nebraska, for a night before driving on to Denver and the South Platte River. Lots of bucket-list places."

"Bucket list?"

"Dude. Places to fish before you kick the bucket."

"Are you sick or something?"

"No! It's an expression. Just places that are famous to fish." Joe's nostrils flared.

"Ha. I know. I'm just messing with you. I'm stoked to go. When are we leaving?"

"Tomorrow, first thing."

"I have to finish up some flies for Mr. Baker."

"How many?"

"A dozen hoppers. That's not too bad. Okay, well get to it and give me a call when you're done. We can talk about packing and all that. I need to go get the SUV"

"Sweet! Thanks, Joe! I'm so fired up!"

Joe settled up with a reserved Georgia and headed to pick up the Tahoe.

Dark clouds were moving in from the west and Joe could feel the humidity in the air. The darkening sky contrasted against the bright, white trim on the courthouse. *It is a beautiful town.*

Joe was looking forward to hearing jazz emanating from Seth's garage. He impulsively snapped his fingers. Joe had already downloaded *Monk's Dream* on his phone after repeatedly hearing Jazz played at the shop. The syncopated beats match the rhythm of his mind, which was often angular and abrupt. In some ways, jazz required a mind clearing level of attention that was similarly required for fly fishing. Joe needed to concentrate to clear his mind of the noise and relax, he was beginning to learn what could help him find those moments.

As Joe approached the garage it was strangely quiet. The door to the shop office was open a few inches. Joe stuck his head in. The lack of music caused him to hesitate before he committed to going in completely.

Joe called out, "Hey, Seth."

There were lights on, but Joe heard no movement or response. He walked in the office, but no signs of anyone in the shop. He walked to the back room with the slow steps of an actor in a horror movie.

"Seth?"

A bay door opened and startled Joe. The black Chevy Tahoe entered the bay.

"Yo, Joe! Here she is!"

"You scared the crap out of me. No music, no one around, I thought I was walking into a crime scene!"

"Oh, jeez! Harry's son was playing in a big American Legion game this afternoon, so I gave the guys the afternoon off to watch the game. Plus, I needed to fill the car up with gas and give it a go around town to make sure everything was good to go. You are set. I didn't mean to scare you. Music must've shut off while I was gone."

"Man. I automatically thought the worst. Whew."

"Well thanks for worrying! Want to give the truck a look around?"

"Sure thing."

"I got the insurance payment today, too, which covered everything, so we are good!"

"Thanks, Seth. It means a lot."

"Oh, and I packed up all your gear. I'm a little OCD, so sorry if it's packed in too tight. You'll have some room to move around in there."

Joe popped the trunk. "Wow, that is packed like Tetris. Looks great. Ethan is going on a fishing trip with me, so I'll need the space. This is perfect."

"You can still get to all your fishing stuff. I put that on top in that bin. There should be room for the stuff you have at the hotel, too."

"Thank you so much. I'm going to be headed out west for a little bit, but this place made an impact on me, I will definitely be back."

"Safe travels, have fun, and catch some big fish. I'll catch you when you head back this way. Take care, Joe."

"You too, Seth."

The men shook hands and Joe drove back towards the hotel. The steering wheel felt foreign to Joe. It was like the voice of someone he hadn't talked to in a long time—familiar but not comfortable. Time to pack up the hotel room.

65

On the Road Again

It amazed Joe how little he had needed in the last week and a half. Packing up the things in his room took about ten minutes. He had a house full of stuff he didn't miss. Well, he missed his bed and some photos of Jody, but that was about it.

He opened the computer and pulled up Google Maps. He laid out the routes between Remberg and Grayling, Michigan. From Grayling to Viroqua, Wisconsin. From Viroqua to Omaha, Nebraska, and Omaha to Denver. Two-thousand one-hundred and fifty miles.

Jacob had texted over the address and the key code to the front door of the townhouse in Denver. This was going to happen. Based on the short time frames at each location, Joe planned on getting hotel rooms. Then time wouldn't need to be spent on setting up and taking down tents, and starting campfires. This wasn't the pace of a trip he imagined when he initially planned the trip, but he didn't plan on having a companion or wrecking the car after a collision with a deer.

Joe texted Ethan, "Finish your flies yet?"

"Almost done."

"Nice job. We won't be camping, so you don't need to pack sleeping bags and stuff. But make sure you have rain gear and plan for weather that may be pretty cold as well. Remember that there is no such thing as bad weather, just poor clothing choices. I can't remember who said that, but it's true." Joe's thumbs were getting tired.

"Sounds good. Won't take me long to pack. Eight days, right?"

"Yup, we may be able to do some laundry somewhere. Especially in Denver. Bring rain gear, a wool hat, and gloves for sure."

"Gotcha. No Cap. What time are we leaving?"

"6 a.m. You can sleep in the car. We have a ten-and-a-half-hour drive."

"Okay. That's a lot."

"See you at 6!"

"Bet!"

"You're gonna have to teach me your slang or stop using it."

":-)"

In the quiet of the room, Joe looked back at the list. The underlined term of friends stuck out to him. He set his alarm for 5:30 and drifted off to sleep.

Joe's eyes opened one minute before the alarm went off. One deep breath and his mind went on the mission of making sure he took all his possessions out of the hotel room. Following Seth's skillful packing example, he added to the back of the Tahoe without taking up much more room. Joe always appreciated when people skillfully approached tasks others considered a mundane nuisance. His impatience was sometimes a deterrent to improving but seeing the beauty of efficiency always made him happy.

He made a coffee and filled the travel mug. He double checked in the bathroom and under the bed. He was leaving nothing behind. He said goodbye to his home for the last week-and-a-half with a nod and headed for the Tahoe. The first few moments of a road trip were almost always the best for Joe. All the hope of the trip flowed into opening the car door, putting the key in the ignition and starting the car. He set the first song. "Call Me Al" by Paul Simon. Joe loved the music video with Chevy Chase; it always made him smile. He was about five minutes away from Georgia's house. Joe decided he would sing his lungs out on the way over and then see how things go with his car ballads once Ethan was in the car.

Ethan was waiting at the door as Joe pulled up. Two bags, his vest and two fly rod tubes. He was an economical packer. Joe was already happy with the trip.

"Good morning, Joe!"

"Man, Ethan! I am impressed: you're at the door, your bags are outside and you packed tight."

"Thanks! Georgia helped. I can't take full credit."

"Look at you two world travelers, two rambling men!"

"Rambling men?" Ethan hadn't heard the term before.

"You're in luck, Ethan. That's the next song on my travel playlist."

"You have a playlist? For real?"

Alan drove up and parked behind Joe. "Morning, boys."

"I didn't expect to see you." Joe reached out and shook Alan's hand.

"Well, I wanted to say goodbye and I also pulled together a fly box for each of you."

"Wow, Mr. Baker. Thank you."

"You're welcome, Ethan. This is special for your trip. The first three rows are flies for the Au Sable, the next three are for the Driftless, including the famous pink squirrel. The next three are the super tiny midge flies for the South Platte. I want you two to send me pictures in return. Also, I included some chubby Chernobyls for any dry droppers you wanted to throw just in case."

"Wow, Alan. This is beyond nice." Joe's eyes widened looking at the beautiful collection of flies. "This is too much."

"You both have given me a lot this last week or so." Alan glanced at Georgia and smiled. "Be safe and send pictures!"

"Will do." Joe shook Alan's hand again.

"I have a small bag and a small cooler bag of snacks for you boys, too. Come here and give me a hug. Both of you!"

After a short group hug, Ethan and Joe climbed in the car and looked at each other. "You ready?" Joe asked.

"Let's go."

The truck shook to a start and the two companions settled into their seats. They waved at Georgia and Alan and headed towards the interstate.

"Okay, Ethan. Ten hours and fifteen minutes or so until Grayling, Michigan. We're going to stay in a cabin within view of the river. I set up a float trip through a local guide service. Have you been on a float trip before?"

"Only wading. That is dope."

"I don't know much about the river. Do you mind looking up on your phone and telling me about it as we drive? That'll keep me from singing, too."

"Sure. I don't mind if you sing. Do you sing bad?"

"Ehh. To me it sounds okay. Jody said I sounded like the guy from Hootie and the Blowfish."

"Who's that?"

"Dude. Just look up fishing information on the Au Sable River."

Ethan read about the river over the next forty-five minutes. Over the next several hours, they discussed strategies and ideas about fishing snags and log jams, using streamers or dry droppers, until it was time to stop for a bathroom break.

"I really appreciate that you don't have the bladder of a toddler. Stopping all the time really adds so much time to a trip. You're a pretty good travel companion, so far."

"So far? Were you worried?" Ethan seemed a little insulted.

"Honestly, yes. You just never know if your travel habits will jive with someone else. You didn't even mind my singing."

"Well..."

"And your jokes are funny enough." They laughed as they pulled into the gas station. "So have you ever pumped gas before?"

"Nope, I haven't driven either."

"Well, you're not driving anytime soon, but I'll teach you how to pump gas."

"You make it sound so exciting."

"Just hope I don't have to teach you how to change a tire any time soon." Joe knocked on his dashboard.

66

The Right Hand

Many hours and almost the entire snack bag later, they arrived in Grayling, Michigan. Ethan was super disappointed that they didn't have Grayling in Grayling anymore. He was happy they had brown trout and it presented Joe the opportunity to tell Ethan about the Lorax. *How does the kid not know the story of the Lorax?*

They arrived at the lodge around a quarter after five. The river meandered behind the line of dark log cabins, each adorned with bright green tin roofs and well-constructed Swedish cope corners. Joe was reminded of the small town in New Jersey where his aunt and uncle lived growing up. Joe and his mother would visit with them and paddle canoes throughout the connected lakes. Joe loved log cabins ever since those times in New Jersey. The log cabins each had a small porch with a pair of pine rocking chairs. Small chimneys stood proudly on the left side of each roof line. A bright-red door led to the entrance of each cabin.

They checked into the Hendrickson Cabin. Each cabin was named after a famous dry fly. There were two small rooms and a kitchenette. The back porch overlooked the river. The river ranges from sixty to a hundred feet wide, with low stable banks. Hemlocks, white pines, red and sugar maples lined the banks of the river. A lot of deadfall had accumulated as log jams, sometimes called sweepers. Sweepers can trap canoes and kayaks, trapping unprepared rowers in dangerous situations. The cover provided by these fallen logs creates perfect lairs for large brown trout. As they protect the fish from predatory birds, they provide easy holding water for fish to stalk prey, and they make it downright difficult to throw a fly anywhere near them. But God help you if you get a canoe stuck in one.

Ethan dropped his bags and scurried over to the river. He looked back at Joe, wide eyed. He stepped into the water in his sandals.

"It's in the 50s!" He turned over several rocks. "Lots of case caddis, small mayflies, and a couple large stoneflies! Bug factory! There's got to be some big fish in here!"

"The lodge has a little greasy spoon. Why don't you call Georgia real fast and we'll grab some grub? Maybe we'll have some time and be lucky enough to have an evening hatch."

"I think Alan made some good choices for us!"

"Matching the hatch?"

"No cap!"

"Call Georgia! Man, I sound old. But call Georgia."

"Okay. I couldn't resist turning over some rocks."

Joe smiled and helped Ethan up the stream bank.

Ethan ran into the cabin and called Georgia. Joe could hear the excited tone of the conversation forty feet from the cabin. He took the moment to take a few photos of the cabin and the river. His phone rang.

"Hey, Sis." His heart skipped. Until he saw her number light up his phone, Joe had forgotten about Cindy going to the house and looking through whatever records Jody left behind.

"Hey, Joe. Why are you in Michigan?"

"Are you tracking me?"

"Find my phone, donkey. Someone has to keep track of the wandering and sometimes accident-prone fisherman."

"Fair enough. I may need to turn that off at some point. But that point probably shouldn't be now."

"Yeah, probably not. But why are you in Michigan?"

"I'm driving to Denver. The Tahoe got fixed and I was ready to travel."

"Lonesome on the road yet?"

"Well, I brought the kid, Ethan, with me. Georgia needed some time to take care of some things and he's a good fishing buddy."

"You never even took me fishing, unless Mom and Dad made you."

"You hated to fish!"

"Yeah, but I liked to bug my brother."

"Well, maybe you can come and visit me in Denver and I'll take you fishing."

"You're staying there?"

"Maybe. I'm not sure. I'm still thinking about the job offer. Did you stop by the house yet?"

"Not yet. I'm sorry. It was just hectic getting back and all that. I'm going tomorrow. I'll text you and let you know what I find. Patience!"

"Thank you for taking care of so much. It means a lot to me."

"I know. So where are you fishing?"

"The Au Sable River, near Grayling. I'll send you some pictures tomorrow."

"Sounds fancy. Are you going to catch fancy trout there?"

"Hopefully just some big, regular ones."

"Fancy sounds better."

"Maybe for shows in Branson, but not for fish in Grayling."

"Touché. Okay, tight lines. Is that what I'm supposed to say?"

"Not to an old-timer, but sure. Thanks. I'll talk to you tomorrow."

"Goodnight, Joe. Take care of yourself and have fun."

"Thanks, Sis. Goodnight."

Ethan joined Joe out on the porch and then they headed to the main lodge, following the scent of french fries, which led to the small restaurant off the stream side of the facility. On three sides it was screened in, so the patrons sitting at the picnic tables could view the river and hear the water tumbling over the rocks and be serenaded by frogs and crickets into the evening.

The waiter approached Joe and Ethan and handed them a small paper menu.

"Evening, fellas. My name is Jeff. I'll be your server tonight. Can I get you guys something to drink? A pop or something?"

Joe looked at Ethan. Ethan looked confused. "May I please have a Sprite?"

"Sure thing." Jeff looked toward Joe.

"Can I have a decaf coffee and a water?"

"Yes, sir. You two here to fish?"

"Of course! We may go tonight, but we're on a float tomorrow." Joe had a big wide smile.

"Are you going through the Lodge?"

"Yup."

"That's fantastic. You'll have a great time! Do you mind me asking where you're from? I don't quite recognize the accents. And welcome to Grayling!"

Ethan jumped in. "I'm from New York, near the Upper Delaware River."

"Nice, so you're experienced at those Catskill streams, but it's a little bit different here, but you've got to have skills if you're from there!"

Ethan smiled and nodded. Joe spoke up.

"I'm originally from Maryland."

"Ahh, that's the southern accent!"

"Maryland is in the south?"

"Compared to Michigan, it sure is!"

"I guess so. Where are you from?"

Jeff held up his right hand, with the palm up and pointed towards the thumb with his left pointer finger. I'm from Newberry, in the Upper Peninsula, which is right about here on the map of Michigan. I'm a Yooper. So they say."

"Yooper?" Ethan was inquisitive.

"Some people say that as sort of derogatory, like you're backwards or something, but I love it up north."

"I've heard it's beautiful."

"It is. Lemme grab those drinks for you."

Ethan leaned forward. "He's pretty chatty. Very nice though."

"I was thinking the same thing." Joe chuckled.

"You know, I've never had trout before."

"Wow, that's surprising. Want to try it?"

"Yeah, they have bacon-wrapped trout. Seems like a great way to try it."

"I'm sold, too. Let's do it."

"This is fun. This is the furthest I've ever been from home."

"I forgot about that. This is quite an adventure. Now you know that your right hand can serve as a map of Michigan. I think we're about here." Joe pointed to his palm just below the wrist.

"I've never seen that before!"

"Me too. Learn something new every day."

67

Risers

"Wow, this is bussin!" Ethan gulfed down the trout, making sure he had a bite of bacon in each forkful.

"I guess that means you like it?"

"Ha, yeah. Bussin' means delicious."

"Every tribe has its own language, right?"

"What do you mean?"

"Do you think someone who isn't a fly angler would know what tight lines means or what a Walt's worm is? Every group has its own jargon, its own vocabulary. It's how you tell if someone is in your tribe."

"Never thought of it like that."

A noticeable slapping sound and splash drew their attention to the water. Jeff refilled their glasses. "Yellow drakes and white flies have been hatching. Splashy rises normally indicate emergers, or diving caddis."

"Well, we should finish up and get out there. You sound like a guide. Thanks for all the insight."

"I guide on the weekends when there is overflow. Tight lines gentlemen. I'll bring the check."

Ethan looked concerned. "I don't know if I have yellow drakes or white flies?"

"I think I have some, and I grabbed a hatch chart when I checked in. Also, they have some "hot flies" near the counter at the front desk, if we don't have anything that works."

The two settled up and they headed for the cabin. They would be lucky to have thirty minutes before the darkness overtook them. Joe regretted he didn't buy headlamps. They may need to stop and get some along the way to Wisconsin. Ethan quickly laid out his fly boxes, desperately looking for a size 16 yellow drake. "Does a sulphur work?"

"Probably. But we're in luck. I grabbed the last four size 16 Roberts yellow drakes at the front desk. Cool to have a fly shop, hotel, and restaurant all in one."

"I was panicking. Whew."

"Remember we're going to need to have great drifts and concentrate. It's not the flies that catch the fish; it's the angler and the presentation of the fly."

Ethan studied the fly.

"I haven't tied a fly like this before, with all the deer hair wrapped around the shank of the fly. I bet it floats well."

"Indeed. Get your waders on. Time is wasting."

Ethan stumbled over the threshold and clumsily fell into the door jam. He caught himself with his left hand on the rocking chair and held his right hand high with his fly rod elevated out of danger. Looking back with a silly smile, Ethan laughed through his words, "Quite the save, huh?"

"Quite the stumble, slick!"

"Hurry up!"

"If I stumble like that, I may break my hip!"

"You're not that old yet."

Joe shook his head, "No, not yet. Hey, have you ever heard of Monty Python?"

"Um…no."

"Search for the Holy Grail?"

"Like the Indiana Jones movie?"

"Um…no. We will put it on the list. Here, tie on one of the yellow drakes."

The sun had fallen beyond the tree line, framing the tops of the hemlocks in a soft reddish glow. Waist-high river grasses lined the water line, hiding the landward edges of fallen trees that reached into the river. Branches vibrated against the rhythm of the flowing water. The river flows through a broad, deep bend on their right, shallowing into a riffle in front of their cabin. Joe brushed his hand along the orange flowers of the spotted touch-me-nots as his wading boots touched the edge of the water. *I hope heaven feels like this.*

"Look, there are risers up at the tail of the pool."

Ethan's eyes narrowed and he peered at the water's surface in the failing light.

"I think we can wade over to the edge of the bar. Do you want the run or the glide?"

"I'll follow your lead, Guide."

Ethan smiled and nodded. "I'll take the run. We can cross and hug the grassline."

"You read my mind. Remember the flow along that far bank is moving fast. You'll have short drifts, great mends or put some slack in your cast. It'll drag fast. We also will only be able to see for fifteen to twenty minutes. We each have a chance to catch a couple fish. Then we need to come back. We've got to be safe crossing the channel in the dark."

"Gotcha. I was going to try out a reach cast, put in that aerial mend."

"Aren't you fancy? I have no idea how to do any of that but go for it. Oh, and you have to watch out for those sweepers."

A pod of rising fish surfaced every few seconds in the upstream run transition into the pool. Fewer fish, but potentially larger fish looked to be rising in the back end or glide area of the pool. They slowly crossed the river and maneuvered into good casting positions. Joe watched Ethan and took a few photos. Ethan's cast was effortless and smooth. It made Joe smile to watch him. He knew so much about fishing at such a young age.

Joe turned his attention to the fish in front of him. Focusing on the concentric circles formed as each rising fish took an insect from the water surface, Joe identified a half a dozen fish he could target. He planned to start with the most downstream fish, intending not to spook the upstream feeders. The texture of the fly line felt comforting in his fingers as he pulled about twenty feet of line from the reel. Two false casts propelled the line through the guides and he rolled the line out about three feet short of the fish's lie. The fly sat up on the water surface and Joe was happy he could clearly see the fly. It drifted drag-free for approximately fifteen feet, a very long drift with variable current seams. The second cast landed the fly softly five feet above the target. Joe began the countdown, "Three, two..."

"Woohoo!" Ethan hollered as his rod bowed against the pull of a trout.

Joe looked back to his fly. He couldn't find it on the water. He panicked as he couldn't find the fly. Instinct took over and he raised the rod. He immediately felt the pull. "Double!"

"Woohoo!" Ethan cheered on Joe.

The two anglers were able to keep their fish out of the downed trees in the water and bring them to net. The darkness was setting in and Ethan's adrenaline was pumping. "Should we try for another?"

"I think we should end on a high note. That was awesome. We have a big day and lots of casts to make tomorrow. Plus, I need to hear all about your fish."

"Ok. Fair enough."

68

The Float

They replayed their "double" at least a half a dozen times before they dozed off. Ethan was animated, jumping around the room, almost as if he was the trout dancing on the line, trying to shake the hook. A long drive, a meal full of trout and bacon, and catching a beautiful brown trout on a dry fly was a full day. On a dry fly! Joe faded off to sleep thinking he hadn't had a day like that in a long time.

They awoke to the default ringtone alarm on Joe's phone. It was funny to Joe, even in a waking moment, that Ethan's phone alarm was set for twenty minutes earlier, but somehow Joe only woke to his own phone's alarm. "You ready, Sport?"

Ethan shot up. "What? Huh?" He rubbed the sleep from his eyes and smiled. "How cool was that double!"

"Maybe we'll have another today? We should grab some food. I at least need coffee."

"Can I have coffee?"

"Did Georgia let you have coffee?"

"Not diner coffee."

"Well, let's not pump you full of caffeine for the first time and then put you on a small boat for eight hours. Let me just say that sometimes coffee can trigger your stomach in ways that are not conducive to traveling far from a toilet."

"Gotcha. I'm definitely not looking to poop myself."

"Agreed, although it would be a funny story. But I'd rather tell Georgia fishing stories."

"Me too."

Coffee, juices, and blueberry muffins were sitting in a basket outside their cabin. "Joe! Look! We got breakfast delivered!"

"How convenient!"

They scarfed down the muffins and Joe met the baseline for his coffee intake. They were meeting the guide at the lodge entrance before heading to the boat launch.

The first thing that Joe noticed was the boat. A beautiful wooden drift boat, painted dark blue above the water line. Bright white cursive lettering denoted the boat as the Irish Rover. It was clean and crisp. It was as much a work of art as it was a boat. He wouldn't dare compare it to a canoe, but it was long, lean and looked brand new. The trailer was weathered but well maintained, hooked up to an equally weathered and well-maintained gray Toyota 4Runner. Ethan couldn't stop smiling.

Don McGlinty stepped around the front of the truck. He was a thin, fit man, slightly shorter than Joe and slightly taller than Ethan. Don clicked his fingers on the edge of the truck, with the nervous tick of a former smoker.

"You Joe and Ethan?"

"That's us! Are you Don?"

"In the flesh. Nice to meet you both. Did you bring waders?"

"We thought if we got out, we could wet wade? I do have them in the truck if need be."

"You probably are good. But the water is still in the fifties; it's a shock to some folks."

"I was just wet wading on the Delaware River, which was at 58, so I should be good." Ethan sounded like a seasoned fly fisherman, causing Don to give a double take.

"You're thirteen?"

"Yessir. I led my first guiding trip last week in New York." Ethan bragged and smiled.

"Wow, today is going to be fun. I've got two pros with me."

"I wouldn't go that far." Joe tried to lower expectations. "We've never fished in Michigan before, and we don't have a lot of experience fishing around all these sweepers and jams."

"Well, it's my job to help you. What were you looking to focus on today?"

Joe looked at Ethan and shrugged. Ethan jumped in.

"I would like to work on my streamer game. I haven't thrown streamers a lot. But if there are chances for dry flies or a dry dropper, that is the most fun for me. I'm just excited to see the river."

"Hmm."

Don looked up and seemed to be thinking through how to meet Ethan's expectations.

"The dry dropper will be easy to do and should produce some good fish today. Water levels are low and it's very clear, so streamers may not be as successful, but there are a few pools we could try to cover with streamers. The streamer bite is better at night this time of year, but I'll see what we can do."

"I don't want to push it and just spook fish all day, so no worries either way."

Joe noted that Ethan sounded like he was suddenly older. His confidence was growing.

"We appreciate it. Like Ethan said, no pressure if it's not a good fit. Let's just have fun. And for me, please jump in and let me know if you see anything I should correct with my casting or any technique. I'm just back into fishing after a few decades on the shelf."

"Were you injured?"

"No, no, nothing like that. I was married and busy working. I just lost track of fishing. But I've found it again."

"That's great. It's a sport you can participate in for a long time. You've got lots of time to fish ahead of you. Your wife doesn't like fishing?"

Joe looked down. "We didn't really try to fish together; we did a lot of hiking together."

Don looked at Ethan, who slightly shook his head side to side. He got the message.

"Hiking is great, quality outdoor time. Are you guys ready to hit the river? We don't want to miss any fishing time today. Oh, by the way, do you like turkey or corned beef?"

"Turkey." Ethan put his hands together nervously.

"Corned beef for me," Joe said with a nod.

"Let's go." Don smiled and shook both of their hands. "Today is going to be a fun day. We're going to catch lots of fish."

Joe and Ethan followed Don to the boat launch and parked under the shade of a large maple tree. Don expertly backed the boat onto the ramp and slid the boat into the water. His 4Runner was packed so that each box and cooler could be loaded onto the boat efficiently and without moving a box twice. He had done this a few times before.

"Alright, who's taking the front seat?"

Ethan and Joe looked at each other. Don spoke into the silence.

"Let me make a suggestion. This upper reach has a few more shallow riffles than the lower section. Having Joe in the front would even out the weight and help us not drag the bottom. Then in the afternoon, Ethan can get the front seat. Cool?"

"Makes sense to me." Ethan made it a plan.

"Okay, let's start with the dry droppers. We'll use a large caddis and a yellow Frenchie. The yellow drakes are still coming off."

"We caught a double last night on the yellow drakes. It was awesome." Ethan was bubbly.

"That is a fun hatch! You guys are pros!"

They got into the boat and Don pushed off. They were on the way.

"First rule is fish near the boat ramp, because no one ever fishes it. Joe, do you see that sweeper around 2 o'clock?"

"Yup."

"Okay, try to cast so the dropper hits the boulder right above and you can drift in close to the tree. You're going to lose lots of flies. Occupational hazard, so don't worry about it and I'm prepared for it.

Ethan, Joe will be fishing the front of the boat. Your flies should never be ahead of me, okay? We don't want to cross and tangle lines."

"Gotcha."

"See that boulder that's shaped like a booty?"

Ethan laughed and blushed. "I think so."

"You know it. Same thing, Ethan. Try to bounce the dropper off the booty and let the drift swing close to the rocks below. Joe, cast about 15 feet upstream of the rock in that seam."

In unison, the pair drew the line and casted. Joe's cast was off target and his nymph landed about fifteen feet upstream of the rock and the caddis dry fly landed just to the left of the nymph. Ethan's cast was a few feet downstream of the rock.

"That'll fish. Ethan. Just let it drift. One of the cool things about being in the boat is you can get longer drifts and we're moving at the same speed, or close to it, as the fly."

Joe felt the adrenaline kick in. Maybe it was the coffee. But the morning fog was burning off the stream as his mind began to focus on the flies. Suddenly the dry fly plunged below the surface. He lifted the rod.

"Hey now!" Don saw the hit the same time Joe did. "Great set! Fish on!"

"Fish on!"

"I'll net it if you can just direct it to me. Ethan, you're good with your drift, so just watch if Joe's fish runs and pull up your line quickly."

Joe kept pressure on the fish and after several acrobatic jumps that warranted a few loud "Woohoos!" from Ethan and Don, Joe brought it to the net. The bright yellow belly of the fish glowed off the water and the white tipped edges of the pelvic and anal fins looked like icing on a lemon cake. Don lifted the net so Ethan and Joe could clearly see the fish. It was stunning.

Ethan leaned over.

"Wow, you've got to get a picture of that one."

"No doubt! Ethan, are you good with photos or do you want me to?"

"I got it."

Joe lifted the fish from the water. It wiggled and he nearly dropped it.

"Easy there, buddy." Joe spoke softly to the fish.

The side of the trout had dozens of brown dots and a few red circles with stunning white and light-blue halos. Joe smiled, as much as he could, as he tried not to drop the fish and get it back in the water in a few seconds. The fish slid back in the water and with a few flicks of the tail, the spots of the fish faded into the dark water and disappeared.

The remainder of the morning, Ethan and Joe traded off catching trout, some on dries and some on the nymph dropper. They didn't see another angler, only kingfishers, blue and green herons and a lone mink. Don directed the boat to a point bar and set up lunch. They looked out into the lush forest and wetlands and snacked on their sandwiches, apples, and water. Ethan was turning his head from side to side, taking it in and repeatedly saying, "This is so cool."

The opening in the forest canopy at the wide point bar opened up cell service and Joe's phone buzzed. Joe had almost forgotten he was even carrying his phone other than taking photos of the fish Ethan caught. He looked down at the phone. Text message from Alan Baker.

"Joe, I need you to call me as soon as you can. Alan."

Joe's eyes narrowed and closed.

69

Interruptions

"Don, I need to make a phone call. I know we are about to get back in the boat. Are there any spots close by where you can wade fish with Ethan? I don't think this will take long, but I don't want to take away from his time on the river."

Don paused and made eye contact with Joe, then nodded.

"Sure, there's a good run just around the bend. Ethan, have you finished your lunch?"

Ethan felt the awkward emptiness in the space.

"Everything okay, Joe?"

"More than likely, but I need to make a phone call."

Ethan looked concerned. Joe knew he had a poor poker face. He learned from Jody that it wasn't worth trying to hide too much of his reactions. It just made him so uncomfortable that it leaked out in his language and mood.

"Better off being open and honest." Jody would say.

Ethan and Don disappeared around the bend in knee-deep water.

"Hey, Alan. Everything okay?"

"It will end up that way, but right now it's not great. We had to rush Georgia to the hospital. Looks like she needs an emergency appendectomy, but it may have burst. She's getting tests run now."

"Well, shit."

"No kidding. I wanted to tell Ethan, and Georgia told me not to bug him on the trip, but that didn't seem fair to me. She wants him to stay on the trip with you, but..."

"He should probably head back."

"She didn't want that. But I wanted Ethan to know. She will probably have surgery tonight. Maybe a couple of days in the hospital to recover."

"Okay. I can talk to him."

"I did check flights from Grand Rapids to Binghamton. There is one that leaves at 6:30 p.m. tonight and gets in around 11 p.m. Chuck said he could pick him up. Let me know and I can order the ticket."

"He's never flown before, right?"

"I don't know, but probably not. That's a small airport. They normally set kids up with someone to direct them to connecting flights."

"Well, shit."

"Yes. Fishing been any good?"

"It's been really fun. The kid is a helluva fly fisher."

"That he is."

"I'll talk to him and get back to you. Take care of yourself and tell Georgia I'm sending positive vibes, thoughts, and prayers."

"Will do, Joe. Talk soon."

The sound of the river filled Joe's mind again. "Well, shit."

He looked to the river bend. Over the rushing water, voices carried, "Fish on!"

Joe's eyes glassed over and he walked slowly into the stream. A large brown trout jumped clear out of the water, tail wagging across the surface before crashing with a loud clap against the water.

"Woohoo!" Ethan bellowed with his rod held upright over his head. Don scooped the fish into the net.

"Fish of the day so far!"

"Did you see that, Joe?"

"You're killing them, E.!" Joe was impressed with the kid.

"Woooo!" Ethan pumped both his left hand in the air.

Joe took a picture and patted Ethan on the back. "You are a ninja, man."

"Thanks, Joe. How was your phone call?"

"Not great. I'm just going to tell you everything straight up. Georgia is in the hospital. Her appendix may have burst, and she needs emergency surgery."

"What?" The blood drained from Ethan's face.

"She didn't want you to cut the trip short, but Alan and I think it would be good for you to fly back tonight. Chuck can pick you up if you decide to go."

"It's up to me?"

"Sort of."

"Am I allowed to be in the hospital?"

"I think so. It would be nice for you to be there for Georgia. It's the right thing to do. We can go fishing again. We can even do another trip. But she needs you."

Joe could see the wheels spinning in Ethan's mind. It was a lot to put on a thirteen-year-old. Ethan exhaled. "Okay."

Ethan and Joe looked at Don.

"When is the flight?" Don asked. "Even if we row straight to the car, it's about two hours."

Joe looked at his phone. "It's in a little over six hours."

"Think she'd mind if we fished on the way out?" Ethan meekly smiled.

Joe chuckled, "I don't think she'd mind. But we can't lollygag. We still need to get your stuff from the lodge and drive two hours to Grand Rapids."

Don added, "I'll just row out and you guys can keep the drifts, and if we catch any, we catch them. But I'll get you to your car in two and a half hours or less."

"Deal."

Ethan took the front position and smiled. He seemed to disconnect from the change of plans and any stress in his future. Throughout the rest of the float, Ethan caught a handful of trout, all of a good size. Joe caught a couple but was off his game. He missed several hook sets and had Don shouting, "Set!" instead of the cheering call out of, "Hey now!"

Joe was staring off into the trees, losing track of his flies and definitely his focus. He caught a glimpse of several deer and what he thought might have been a black bear cub. Even when his mind was spiraling through scenarios and emotional uncertainties, the peace of the river and the forest kept Joe calm. Watching Ethan cast and catch fish was entertaining but also depressing. He was going to miss Ethan. Joe decided he would carry on to Denver and complete his trip, but the thought of traveling by himself wasn't as freeing as it felt ten days ago. Loneliness was starting to set in and he was still on a small boat with two other people.

Arriving at the boat ramp in relative silence, Don spoke up, "Remember the rule."

Ethan had been sitting watching the river, taking it in, but at Don's encouragement he popped up and casted to the push of a large log about forty feet from the take out. As soon as the fly landed, the water boiled and the fly was drawn downward. The biggest brown trout of the day engulfed a foam beetle and startled Ethan as fumbled to regain control of the fish. The trout pulled downward and upstream, dragging the front of the boat bankward. Ethan tilted the rod to the left, parallel to the water, attempting to turn the head of the giant trout away from a large log jam.

"You've got it, Ethan. Keep it outta there but let him tire. You can't horse it out of there."

Don's voice was calm and steady, like a T-ball coach. Ethan's left leg slipped and he caught himself. He recentered his weight over his feet and widened his stance. "You're doing great, Ethan!"

"He's tiring. I think you can lift him, guide him to the net, and get his head up." Don's voice was calm and unwavering.

Ethan was quietly talking to himself. Joe couldn't quite make out what he was saying, as he took a video of the battle. The large fish came up to the surface right next to the boat and then sped upstream and disappeared back into the water.

"The boat scared him. We'll get him back. You've got him. Keep the pressure on."

Ethan's breathing was heavy. He brought his left hand to his right arm to help support his tiring arm. Suddenly the line snapped back and the rod straightened.

"What? What happened?"

"Ah, damn. Sorry, Ethan. You didn't do anything wrong. You fooled him and saw him, but just didn't net him. I'd call that an LDR, a long-distance release. That beast was at least twenty inches."

Ethan sat in the chair, deflated.

"Tough one, E. It happens to all of us."

"Yeah, that sucks, but what a great day. Way better than what Georgia is going through. I'm bummed, but now it's time to see my foster mom. That's why it's called fishing and not catching right. That's what my grandfather would say."

Joe nodded. "That's true, very true. Let's get you back to see Georgia. You are awesome, Ethan."

They helped hook the boat up to the trailer and pack away the gear. It was a great day on the river with Don despite the abrupt change in plans. They got back in the Tahoe and headed to the cabin. Joe looked over to Ethan.

"Thank you. You're a heck of an angler and a good fishing buddy. That was the best two fishing days I've ever had."

Ethan hid his eyes. "Me too."

Ethan packed quickly and quietly. The radio was low, almost imperceptible and the two sat silently on the drive to Grand Rapids. After the night before when Ethan was exuberant and descriptive in every fishing moment, the silence was amplified. Joe couldn't find words. He was scared for Georgia. He was sad to leave Ethan. He was scared of his future. It would be Joe and John Denver songs in less than a half an hour. *Country roads take me home. But where is that?*

70

—

Keep Mending

Joe helped Ethan into the small airport and they walked to the check in counter. Alan had called ahead and ordered the ticket.

"Are you Ethan Bennett?" A tall, thin gate agent spoke in a crisp tone. "Hi, I'm Mark. We received a call for your ticket a couple hours ago. Do you have any identification?"

"He has a birth certificate, insurance card, and a fishing license. Does that work?"

"Let me see the birth certificate, thank you."

Ethan looked at Joe and then the gate agent repeatedly. He struggled with where to put his hands. Joe patted him on the shoulder and smiled.

"Easy peezy."

"All good. Are you checking any luggage?"

Ethan slid his large duffle bag holding his fly rods and his smaller bag with his clothes onto the small scale next to the counter.

"I'll ship you your waders and fishing vest. You will have them in less than a week."

"No rush. I'll probably be busy." Ethan smiled.

"You may have a backlog of flies to tie." Joe grinned.

"I want to try to clean up the house for Georgia." Ethan scratched his ear and looked down. "Then I can tie some flies."

"Fair enough. You have Chuck's cell, right? He said he'll be at the airport when you get off."

"Yup. I'll be good. Easy peezy."

The gate agent interrupted, "Okay, Ethan. This is Bridget. She will help you through security and direct you to your gate. Mr. Barden, there will be a gate agent waiting for Ethan in Detroit to escort him to the connecting flight to Binghamton. We will make sure he is safe and in the right place at the right time."

"Thank you, Mark and Bridget. You good, Mr. Bennett?"

Ethan pulled on his ear lobe and tears streamed down his cheeks. Joe bit his lip and hugged him.

"You're a good man. I'll see you. We need to catch that one."

"Yes, we do. I'll see you. No cap."

Bridget smiled brightly and tilted her head toward Ethan.

"Hi, Ethan. We have less than fifteen minutes to board. We need to go if that's okay."

Ethan nodded. Joe squeezed his shoulder as he headed down the hallway to the security checkpoint. Joe wasn't sure if he needed to stand and wave as he goes, like in the movies, but he didn't want to look like a sap or get all weepy. A two-hour drive back to the lodge with weepy swollen eyes wasn't Joe's idea of fun. Time to roll down the windows and sing at the top of his lungs and take another step forward. John Denver leading the way to Colorado.

Joe sat in the car and watched the condensation form a droplet that slid along the side of Ethan's abandoned soft drink. *Dr. Pepper? Who likes Dr. Pepper?* Joe wiped his eyes and pressed play on the phone, turning up the volume.

His phone buzzed with a text from Ethan: "Taking off. I'll see you. Keep mending."

Joe didn't have it in him to sing. He just let the music sink in. Occasionally he'd lapse into a daydream until he'd mumble "Fish on" to himself.

The gravel crunched under the tires as he pulled into the lodge. The phone rang. Cindy.

"Hey, Sis."

"Hey, Bro."

"You okay? You seem subdued. Like me."

"I'm at your house, Joe. I went through four boxes of records Jody had filed away. Did you know she put stones in each of the boxes? What's that about?"

"She always had a fan on, but she didn't like when paper blew around. We collected rocks from everywhere we hiked…they were everywhere around the house. So she put them to use."

"Well, it sure as shit made the boxes heavier than they needed to be."

"Okay. What's your edge about?"

Cindy took a deep breath. It felt like a thirty second pause.

"Joe, I feel like I shouldn't have done this, like I'm invading Jody's privacy."

"I asked you to look for me, Cindy, and Jody's gone. She doesn't care about her privacy." Joe's heartbeat quickened. "What did you find?"

"Something I feel like I shouldn't have found. And I don't even know what to make of it."

"Spit it out. It's been a long day."

"I'm going to scan it and text it to you. We can talk it through together."

"I wish you would just tell me."

"I don't know how to explain it. This is hard to talk about, okay."

"Jesus, Cindy."

"Open your text message before I hang up on you. I found this document in a sealed envelope with Jody Murphy handwritten on the outside."

Joe opened the file attached to the text. It was hard to read on his phone. He read it slowly.

CONFIDENTIAL

Circuit Court of New York

Summary of Proceeding for Termination of Parental Rights

Cabinet for Health and Family Services

Birth Mother: Jody Murphy, age 18

Adoptive parents of Minor (female): Walter Bennett, Father, age 36, Shirley Bennett, Mother, age 37

Cindy spoke the entire time that Joe was reading, but he didn't hear a word.

"What?"

"Are you okay, Joe?"

"Jody had a baby."

"That's what I've been talking about."

"I may need to lay down."

"Are you sitting? Take a deep breath. They lived in Remberg. They had a daughter. Did you run into any Bennetts in Remberg?"

"Yes, Cindy. I just put one on a plane." Joe's voice left him.

"Joe, Joe, are you okay?

"No. I need to go. I'll call you later."

Joe wanted a drink for the first time in weeks. He walked like a zombie to his cabin. He left the door ajar and laid flat on the bed.

Jody had a baby. She had a fucking baby and never told me. A baby. My wife had a baby and didn't tell me. Kimberly Bennett was her daughter. Ethan is her grandson. What the fuck? And she kept it under the stones. Leave no stone unturned. Some bullshit. After all we went through.

His tears were turning to anger. He clenched his fists and stood up, stepping to the door. A mirror by the front door caught his eye. The sight of his swollen red face slowed his pace and he closed the door and sat on the porch. He heard Georgia's voice in his head. *"Maybe she felt responsible."* Joe's anger softened. *It wasn't about me. It was never about me. She was a kid dealing with unimaginable grief. I can't relate to that. But Ethan...*

The timeline laid out in Joe's mind. Her boyfriend came back injured from the minor leagues and she got pregnant. He left and committed suicide. She discovered she was pregnant around her graduation. She told her parents and they quickly died in a car accident. *I wonder if she told them that night?* *"Maybe she distracted them or she felt responsible."* *Repeated in his mind.*

Jody couldn't get past it and then it became too late. She was sick and her daughter had died of an overdose just months before. Did she know? She could've found out.

She felt responsible. And she couldn't share it. The tears overwhelmed Joe again. *If only she would have shared it with me. What in the hell do I do now?*

Joe reached for the fly rod propped up against the porch. *Go. Spend time on the river. Get out of your head!*

Concentrating on taking one breath at a time was all Joe could do. Autopilot clicked on and he slid one foot into the stocking of the wader and then into the boot. The next foot went into the wader and he stood to wiggle the stocking foot into the boot. He gripped the laces tightly and knotted the boots. He looked at his phone. 8:15 p.m. Based on last night, twilight would last until close to 9 p.m.

Joe grabbed the yellow drake and took another breath. *Settle. Settle.* His heart rate was slowing down and his hands steadied. He remembered his way along the trail from the night before and made his way to the stream, gliding his hands against the jewelweed at the water's edge. The orange flowers popped against his hands, reminding him of their "touch me not" common name.

Being outside, hearing the water flow past the boulders and trees, Joe could breathe freely. His mind settled. Joe crossed the stream, pulling out and extending his wading staff. Without Ethan there to help him, a fall could be painful, if not dangerous. He pushed downstream, toward the position Ethan fished from the night before. Every step around the corner opened up a greater view of the next reach of the river. He smiled. *I never know what's around the corner. What do I know?* He waded into position and pulled some fly line from the reel, preparing to cast. *I do know I miss her.*

Joe managed to catch two brown trout. He whispered, "Fish on." He took a picture of each fish and thought to send them to Ethan when he got back to the cabin. *Now I miss him.*

71

More Boxes

Joe sat on the bed looking out the window, holding a wood-framed photo of Jody. The sun felt warm on his face even as the amber and maroon leaves began to fall outside. It felt odd to be in a new house in a new place. He looked down at the photo and tears came to his eyes. *Am I doing the right thing, babe? I need you with me.* The door slammed downstairs rousing Joe from his trance.

Cindy yelled from the front of the house, "Joe, where did you want these books to go? And hurry this box is heavy!"

"Just put it down if it's too heavy! Sitting room downstairs will be the library. Just inside to the left."

"That was the last box in my car. I wanted to finish before our busy day."

"You know, unpacking boxes is way worse than packing them."

"Joe, you didn't even pack any of the boxes. I handled all of that."

"I know, I know, thank you, thank you. Jeez, Cindy, I was speaking in general, not specifically."

"I just want you to recognize that you have a cool sister."

"I better recognize, huh!"

"You are a dork! Come on, stop unpacking, and get dressed. We have a wedding to get to!"

"I'm not wearing a tie. Fly shop managers don't wear ties."

"Weird to say?"

"Well, I'm also a contractual employee of the Department of Public Works. I'm becoming a Renaissance man."

"Learning that from Seth, huh?"

"He's got me covered by a long shot."

72

Mended Hearts

Two large stacks of paper sat in front of Joe. He felt the pen in his hand and squeezed it tightly. He could hear Jody's voice in the wind and in the sound of the river:

Head back to the water and find a way to mend your heart.

With glassy eyes, Cindy squeezed his shoulder. He wiped the tears from his eyes and reached for a tissue. Judge Perkins pushed the box toward Joe.

"You ready, Joe? It's a big day."

"I bet you've had lots of big days as the Guardian Angel of Remberg."

The judge laughed and nodded.

"Today is a long time coming in a few different ways."

Cindy, Ethan, Georgia, Alan, Chuck, Amanda, and David laughed with them under the blue and gold pavilion.

Joe lifted the pen and signed the paper.

"It's official."

He stood and Ethan hugged him, and he looked at the judge, who handed him another tissue.

"I've officially adopted a professional fishing guide! Now Alan and Georgia have to make *their* commitment official!"

Alan and Georgia approached the table and signed their marriage license.

"Okay, Judge. Now you need to do your job."

The group gathered to witness the marriage of Alan and Georgia. Pictures of Kimberly and Jody sat on the bench, surrounded by a collection of river stones.

"You may now kiss the bride." Judge Perkins smiled as Alan and Georgia embraced and kissed.

Ethan couldn't help himself. "Woohoo! Fish On!"

As a fluvial geomorphologist and fly angler, Scott Lowe sees the magic, mystery, and power in flowing water. As author of his blog, *Fly Fish Mend*, and his first book, *The Mend*, Scott connects the healing elements of nature with the sense of community and the attention required in fly fishing. Whenever he's not at soccer games, band concerts, plays, dance competitions, and basketball games for his children, Scott ties average flies and attempts to fool trout with the in Maryland and Pennsylvania.

Acknowledgements

This book started with an inspiration that became an idea that built and became a story in my mind. Any faltering along the way and I would not have created this world and told this story. On many days I wanted to falter! There were so many people who provided support, encouragement, and advice that kept me moving.

Without the guidance, platform, and accountability of the Writing in Community program provided by Seth Godin and Kristin Hatcher, I would not have developed the discipline to keep up the practice of writing. Drip by drip. Thank you!

Throughout my time in Writing in Community, I was lucky enough to connect with many brilliant writers who showed up to support me nearly every day. Kristi Casey, Abbey Spiro, and Stacey Mayo are thoughtful and creative, and were with me on my entire journey. Support from Russell John, Mark Brement, and Karen Collins came at critical times and with tremendous positivity.

The wonderful artwork of my cover and the sketch inside the book were created by Emily Dolbin. Emily is a children's book author (https://www.emilydolbin.com) and talented artist who I am lucky to have as a friend.

Angela Davids (https://www.angeladavids.com/) was incredibly helpful as my patient copy editor who helped me correct my tendencies for bad comma usage and over capitalization. Thank you!

Thank you to Murray Friedman and Tom Gamper for letting me pick their brains on running a fly shop and working as an architect, respectfully. Brian Bernstein and Mark Cheskey are my fly fishing sherpas, and their many lessons permeate this book. Brian also served as a beta reader, and his feedback was incredibly helpful. Time on the water with Dominick Swentosky and Bill Dell helped me to frame the guided experiences in the story. Sam Parrotto has helped me more than I can ever explain with just about everything. Thank you, Sam.

Without my family, I would be lost. Thank you to my mom and dad for always supporting my writing. My mother-in-law, Linda Shannon, helped inspire the book through her commitment to her family and showing me that items packed in simple boxes can hold the deepest meanings. My sister-in-law, Bridget Wiedeman, volunteered to be a beta reader and helped me immensely to further shape the story. My children are integral to my life and to the completion of the book. Cameron and Colin helped me to understand the mindset and language of a teenage boy. Lucy encouraged and supported me with ideas on plot and characters. Kayla has been a consistent help with graphics and artistic support of my blogs. As our voracious reader, Samiah was very helpful with plot points, title selection, and character development.

My beautiful wife and partner-in-life, Chrissy, was patient and supportive of the late nights writing and discussing the dilemmas of my characters. Thank you, Chrissy.

To all my friends, keep mending…

www.ingramcontent.com/pod-product-compliance
Lightning Source LLC
Chambersburg PA
CBHW070657010826
48975CB00014B/2019